D1810182

'BOX OFFICE' BROWNING

By the same author

The Winning Side
Pokerface

In the Cliff Hardy Series
The Dying Trade
White Meat
The Marvellous Boy
The Empty Beach
Heroin Annie
Make Me Rich
The Big Drop
Deal Me Out

'BOX OFFICE' BROWNING

From tapes among the papers
of Richard 'Box Office' Browning,

transcribed and edited by
PETER CORRIS

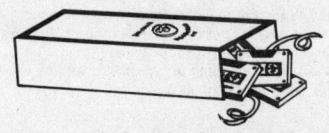

VIKING

Pelican Books
Penguin Books Australia Ltd,
487 Maroondah Highway, P.O. Box 257
Ringwood, Victoria 3134, Australia
Penguin Books Ltd,
Harmondsworth, Middlesex, England
Penguin Books,
40 West 23rd Street, New York, N.Y. 10010, U.S.A.
Penguin Books Canada Limited,
2801 John Street, Markham, Ontario, Canada L3R 1B4
Penguin Books (N.Z.) Ltd,
182-190 Wairau Road, Auckland 10, New Zealand

First published 1987 by Viking

Copyright © Peter Corris, 1987

All Rights Reserved. Without limiting the rights under copyright reserved
above, no part of this publication may be reproduced, stored in or introduced
into a retrieval system, or transmitted, in any form or by any means
(electronic, mechanical, photocopying, recording or otherwise), without
the prior written permission of both the copyright owner and the above
publisher of this book.

Typeset in 11½ on 13 Paladium by Midland Typesetters, Maryborough, Vic., 3465
Made and printed by the Australian Print Group, Maryborough, Vic., 3465

CIP

Corris, Peter, 1942-
Box office Browning.

ISBN 0 670 81696 5.

I. Title.

A823'.3

FOR
Drs Paul Beaumont, John Burgess,
John Elder & Graeme Pittar,
with thanks.

CONTENTS

INTRODUCTION

The death in August 1984 of Richard Browning did not go completely unnoticed. The *Pasadena Standard* for the 20th day of the month carried this short report:

Pasadena, Friday. Police have no further clues in the case of the mysterious death of Richard Browning. Browning, whose body was found on his avocado ranch by Edwin O. Bradley yesterday, was in bed with a gun beside him. A considerable quantity of money, liquor and drugs was also found in the room. Bradley, who was delivering an order of liquor phoned in by Browning two hours before, deposed that he saw 'a young, blonde woman jump into a car and drive off at speed' just before he reached the house.

Richard Browning is believed to have been born in Australia. He enjoyed modest and erratic success as a film actor from the 1920s until the 1970s but has lived in obscurity since that time. Efforts are being made to contact two of his former wives who are believed to be still living. At a low point in his career Browning was given the ironical sobriquet 'Box Office'.

An autopsy revealed that Browning had suffered a gun-shot wound in the chest which *might* have been self-inflicted. The wound could have been sufficient to kill him but the quantities of liquor and drugs found in his system could equally have been the cause of his death. No trace was found of the blonde woman. Only one of Browning's wives, of whom there were certainly four and possibly five, was located. Mrs Pauline Potts of East Palo Alto, who had a brief film career as Pauline Kiss, expressed indifference when she was told of Browning's death. Her prediction, 'I bet he don't own the ranch', proved to be accurate. Browning appeared to have no assets beyond some expensive clothes and a De Lorean car. (The drugs and money were confiscated by the police and subsequently disappeared.) The owner of the avocado ranch described him as a 'free-loading, blackmailing, squatting son of a bitch'.

The Pasadena authorities contacted Browning's agent, N. Robert Silkstein Jr., who suggested that they sell the De Lorean to pay for the burial expenses, and burn the clothes. However, the clothes along with several crates of liquor were delivered to Silkstein in Los Angeles. Silkstein drank the liquor and stored the clothes in the basement of his office building along, as he said, 'with some other crap that that bum had left with me over the years'. I investigated this material in 1984 when I was in Los Angeles researching a book on Australians in Hollywood.

The great bulk of the Browning papers consists of unpaid accounts, letters threatening to sue, subpoenas and the like, but, in addition to his erratically kept scrapbooks, which were of immense value to my research, I found ninety-seven cassette tapes, stored in a box which had formerly contained Old Grandad bourbon whiskey. On these tapes Browning had recorded his memoirs. The box had evidently been kept at the farm and was delivered to Silkstein along with the liquor. The cassettes were erratically labelled and numbered. Browning evidently broke off recording sessions and resumed them at whim and on whatever tape was to hand. Hundreds of hours have been spent on attempting to put the record in chronological order. This work is as yet incomplete but it has been established that the words transcribed from the tapes and published here represent the first chapters of Richard 'Box Office' Browning's long journal.

Browning's voice is occasionally indistinct on the tapes, either from age or the effects of liquor or drugs or all three, so in several instances his meaning has to be guessed at. I have attempted in punctuating the text to reproduce Browning's style of delivery. A few footnotes have been added to clarify matters which Browning took for granted or to add information of interest.

As to the authenticity of Browning's record, it is difficult to judge. Although an old man when he began recording, his memory appears to have been particularly good, especially when he had photographs, letters, news clippings and other supportive documents. Sometimes, to his annoyance, his memory fails him. Broadly speaking, his accounts of the major public events of his time agree with the accepted historical record. However, in his version of his own involvement in these events, and his dealings with his contemporaries, there may be a large element of invention.

His motivation, at first, was money. N. Robert Silkstein recalled Browning 'coming in here, smashed as usual, and saying that he was writing a best-seller. This was some time in the 70s; he'd been after a bit in *Jaws* – didn't get it of course – and he needed dough. I never saw a word on paper and who'd give a shit, anyway?' For once, Silkstein's commercial instinct failed him; Richard Browning's biggest part was his life – active involvement in two world wars, survival of Prohibition and the Depression and participation in half a century of movie-making. Alone in his Pasadena farmhouse, obsessively telling his story, he gave a great performance for the tape recorder and there was no agent around to take his ten per cent.

P.C.
Sydney, 1986

1

It was Les Darcy[1] who gave me the idea to go into pictures. I was walking along by the Cooks River one day, it must've been in 1916, and here's Les standing on the bank, sopping wet and wrapping himself in an overcoat that must have cost twenty quid.

'Hello, Dick,' Les said. 'How's tricks?'

We wouldn't have met since our school days, almost eight years back, and I'd grown – to six foot two and twelve stone in fact – but Les had recognised me and spoken up like the uncomplicated fellow he was. I'd seen him of course, pounding chaps to jelly in the boxing ring.

'Not bad, Les,' I said. 'What're you doing?'

'Making a filum,' says Les. The water was dripping from his trouser bottoms all over his boots, good boots they were, too. His hair was lying flat on his Irish skull and he was slowly turning blue around the mouth. It was July, you see, in Sydney, Australia, and no time for swimming, especially in the Cooks River which is dirty, cold and has treacherous currents. Now Les Dorsey, which was how they used to pronounce the name, was not the smartest kid at the Oakhampton Public School, but he wasn't the dumbest either. Knowing Les, I knew the next question to ask.

'How's the money, Les?'

'Not bad. Better than for fightin'. 'Course, it's not as much fun.'

Les started to shiver and a bloke ran up with a blanket and wrapped it around him. 'We're going to have to do it again, Mr Darcy,' this bloke says. I ran my eye along the bank a bit and saw a few people standing around; a big, burly fellow was carrying a bull horn, another had a sheaf of papers in his hand and when the group broke up I could see a camera on long tripod legs standing on the river bank.

Les pulled the blanket around him. 'Dash it,' he said. That was Les. You or I would've said something stronger but Les was a good Catholic boy and that was about as strong as his language went. What can you expect of someone who thinks it's fun to climb into a ring at Rush-cutters Bay stadium to go twenty rounds with the top middleweights in the world?

Les jogged on the spot. 'You should have a go at this game, Dick. You've got the looks and it's not dangerous, not really.'

'What're you doing now?'

'I have to jump into the river, swim out a bit and save a girl who's supposed to be drowning. Piece of cake, but they can't get the dashed camera angle right, or something.'

'Girl,' says I. 'What girl?'

But Les was jogging and looked ready to do some sprinting. I'd seen him swim back in our school days and I knew he could plough across the Cooks River and back for an hour or so without turning a hair. I also knew that he'd be more interested in how many times he could swim across and back than in any girl. I was different; I left Les jogging up and down and went closer to the water.

Out in the middle of the river there was a sort of raft and standing on the raft was one of the most beautiful girls I have ever seen from that day to this, and, believe

2

me, I've seen a few in the spots where they congregate. She was a little blonde, not more than five foot, and her clothes were wet and clinging to her and the sight was more than you usually saw in those days unless you were paying through the nose for it. *Wasted on Les*, was my first thought, and *Just the job for me*, was my second.

I watched while a man and a woman who were also on the raft made hand signals towards the bank. A short character in knickerbockers and shirt sleeves plucked the tripod legs out of the mud and moved the camera closer to the water and the big chap, whose muttonchop whiskers and full rig with watch chain I could now see, raised the bull horn to his mouth. Les stripped off his clothes and made his very considerable muscles ripple. I waved and moved away. I've never been an envious man and I was glad to see old Les enjoying himself and making money. Pity I hadn't thought to touch him for a sovereign though. Les sprinted to the water with his boots on.

I sighed and started to climb the bank, slipping a bit in the mud. At the top the first thing I saw was a brand new six-cylinder Buick, gleaming like a sunrise and with a pair of boxing gloves resting on the bonnet. Enough said. Les's car. He must have had more money than all the kids from Oakhampton Public School, and their parents, had ever spent in all their lives. Don't take that for jealousy or spite; I had absolutely no stomach for the way Les earned his money and he probably knew it. It was hard to tell with that shrewd little Mick whether he was kidding or not when he said the picture game would be right for me because I had the looks and it wasn't dangerous. He might've remembered my trick at school of delaying the fisticuffs until a teacher arrived and then looking innocent. That wasn't Les's style, he'd punch first and take the thrashing afterwards. It never seemed smart to me, but here we were, eight years on, and he had the Buick and I was on my uppers.

3

I was back in George Street, heading for the centre of the city, before the thought hit me that I could've asked the film chaps for a job. I suppose it was the sight of the blonde on the raft that drove practical matters from my head – she wasn't the first woman who'd cost me money and she wasn't the last by a long chalk. I had a room at the Hotel Metropole, but don't let that fool you; I had the price of one drink in my pocket and not a penny more.

So I ignored my aching feet and the wear and tear on the shoe leather, let the trams go past and walked. There were a few cars in the street, none as flash as Les's Buick, but most of the traffic was horse-drawn. The street smelled of horses and dust and those are the two smells I associate with Australia in those days.

I turned off at Hay Street to take part of the walk through Chinatown. I don't know why, but I've always liked Orientals. I liked them up around Maitland where they fossicked around the old diggings and sold things door to door and I liked them in the East later where they were as thick as flies. Why, one of my wives was part Chinese which shows that I've never been anti-coloured. As I pushed my way along Dixon Street, threading through the market stalls and the shoppers and the merchants in their white shirts done up at the neck with no tie and their wide, black trousers, I whiffed what I later discovered were jasmine and incense but were then just known to me as China smells.

With the old nostrils flaring and the eyes on the look-out for women with mysterious slanting eyes and narrow bodies wrapped tight in silk, I felt good about being in the city and bad about the thought of going home which would be my fate unless something turned up soon. Outside the hotel I brushed the dust off my clothes and shined my shoes with my handkerchief before striding across the lobby to collect my key at the desk. This was getting to be more of an ordeal day by day as my stay lengthened and my funds ran out. I was finding it harder and harder

4

to stay away from the hotel (hanging around would have been a sure sign that I was an idler). Why else d'you think I'd have taken on a hike to the Cooks River?

The chandeliers seemed particularly bright in the late afternoon gloom and the carpet seemed particularly thick and restful under my tired feet, but all I could think of was that these were luxuries I couldn't afford. I grinned cheerfully at the desk attendant's quizzical look, took my key and went up the steps in a sprightly manner that caused my knees to tremble when I got out of sight of the lobby.

I drew a long, hot bath in the bathroom at the end of the hall, and whistled 'I love a lassie' while I scrubbed. Then I lay in the soapy water reviewing my situation. My expensive college education hadn't prepared me for this tight spot and I couldn't believe that my lack of breeding made any difference. Now you may wonder what a one-time pupil of a glorified shed like the Oakhampton Public School was doing lying in a bathtub in the Metropole under the gold-plated taps, skiting about his college education. Well, it was no credit to me. My Pa, William Browning, was descended from a convict (a fact that the family later kept very dark) and my mother was a bog Irishwoman named Colleen Kelly. Their six children, of whom I am the youngest, were evidence of their lack of sense and one of the causes of their poverty. Pa share-farmed at Oakhampton as a neighbour of Ned Dorsey's when the run of luck that lasted until his death (and maybe beyond) started. First, he found a massive gold nugget on the farm and was canny enough to take Mother's advice about getting a miner's licence before he announced the find. He multiplied some of the money on the Muswellbrook Cup and invested some more in a company that made a piece of mining equipment – a water pump or a safety lamp or something. The company started paying dividends from the day Pa laid his money down and pretty soon 'Wild Bill' Browning was filthy rich.

Which was why I came to spend five years at Dudleigh Grammar while my older brother Tom remained illiterate until he drank himself to death at forty. Well, it was more than two years since I'd left Dudleigh, somewhat under a cloud because of a cricket match. I won't go into the details. Tennis and cricket were my sports at Dudleigh and I'd done well at both, but the honour of the school and all that sort of thing never meant as much to me as money in the pocket. It's easy to throw a tennis match; who hasn't double faulted at the wrong time or missed a vital smash? But it's a bit harder at cricket to get away with. Anyway, I'd bet on the other team, got three of my own side run out and hit up a catch to the bowler that his grandmother couldn't have dropped.

I suppose I was a bit obvious about it and the school found it could get along without me, the fees 'Wild Bill' was happily shelling out and the donation he'd promised if I matriculated. I intercepted the last of Pa's fee cheques, did a bit of artwork on it and got by on the proceeds for a while. Then it was a pound here and a pound there, some lucky punting and a soft job with a wine and spirit importer selling the better stuff to the better people. I took a commission or two a little early to cover some betting losses and that job went west. Finally I touched Pa for money by mail, got a bit but also the message that there'd be no more until I showed up in Newcastle (where the Brownings now lived in style) and gave an account of myself. That was how things stood as the bathwater got cold around me.

I've learned a lot of useful things in my long, useless life and one of them is this – never take away a paper you pick up in a hotel lobby. Read it, sure, do the crossword, but put it back where you found it. After my bath I spruced up a bit and went downstairs intending to spend my remaining cash in the bar. A paper was lying on a chair; I picked it up, glanced at it, and tucked it under my arm.

'Sir. Mr Browning!'

One of the whey-faced desk attendants was beckoning to me and I went across.

'When were you intending to settle your bill, sir?'

'Why?'

'You've stayed beyond the period covered by your deposit.' He looked at the paper under my arm. He'd seen it all before – guest without the price of the daily rag in his pants – he could probably read my mind. 'Considerably beyond.'

No 'sir' this time, you see. I tried to act huffed, said 'Tomorrow' sharply and turned on my heel. He had the last word though.

'First thing.'

I had a bottle of stout because I thought I might need the sustenance with lean times coming up. I took the drink and the paper over to a table as far from the lobby as I could get. I took a drink. It was an occasion: in front of me I had the last drink I could pay for and a paper I'd got for free. It was time to smoke my last cigar. The cigars were a perk of the wine-selling job. Quite rightly, the boss had thought it looked well for his salesmen to be seen smoking the best and he made us a generous allowance of Havanas. A keen smoker from ten years of age, this was apples to me.

I puffed, swallowed and opened the paper. There it was on page 3. I can see it today:

FRANCIS LONGFORD FILMS 'THE BOUNTY'

The item went on to say that sequences for the Crick and James production of *The Mutiny of the Bounty* were being filmed at Watson's Bay. Leading screen players,

7

George Cross, John Storm and William Power had been engaged etc. etc.

I drew in smoke and tried to remember what I'd heard about the Bounty mutiny at school. It wasn't much: rebellion against lawful authority, seamen cast away on a savage island, mutineers hung from the yardarm, Captain Bligh's heroic open boat voyage to somewhere. It sounded like a rattling good yarn in which there had to be a spot for a stalwart chap like me – preferably as one of the loyal officers standing to attention while they strung up the mutineers.

Watson's Bay was only a ferry ride away and I could raise the price of a ticket by selling a shirt, but I had the problem of the hotel bill. The bar was filling up and I finished my drink and cigar and stood up to go because I didn't want to be caught in a drinking school and not be able to shout my round. I'd folded the paper after reading the film bit and the sight of it lying there beside the smouldering cigar butt gave me an idea.

I strode across the lobby like a man on his way to see the Governor and I positively raced up the stairs. Packing my bags barely took a minute. I tore up a bedsheet to make a knotted rope. My window gave out onto a dark laneway, much too high to jump but it was an easy trick to lower the bags down. After that I waited until the coast was clear and scooted to the bathroom. I piled the crumpled paper in the bath with some of the torn sheet and set fire to it. An open window gave a bit of draft and some sprinkled water produced smoke as well as fire. I ran down the hall shouting 'Fire!' at every door. I bellowed 'Fire! Fire!' up the stairs and saved 'Help! Fire!' for yelling down the stairs.

Before I could catch my breath the place was full of women shrieking and men swearing. They were running around clutching clothes and hats; one woman even held a dog in her arms which was against hotel rules. Some people give no thought to others. The desk attendants bounded up the stairs; the doorman left his post and I walked out of the Hotel Metropole and around the corner where I collected my bags. I recall that I was giving my impression, highly regarded in sporting circles, of Peter Dawson[2] singing 'The Road to Mandalay' as I strolled off towards Circular Quay.

2

If you've heard of Sydney at all, you've probably been told that it has a wonderful climate and is warm all the year round. This is eyewash, as we would have said in Sydney in 1916, or horseshit as we say in Pasadena. Sydney gets cold in July and that's the way it was that night on the Quay. You see, the idea of going to Watson's Bay had got hold of me and I didn't give any thought to where to spend the night. I wished pretty soon that I'd thought to find a boiler room somewhere or at least a pie stall. I hadn't even had the foresight to take one of the hotel blankets with me.

I froze as I waited through the night for the shops to open so that I could sell a shirt. My companions on the Quay didn't have shirts and would have stripped mine from my back given the chance. So I kept moving, whistled Scottish airs and looked as if I could handle myself at any time of the day or night, and they kept clear. But it was a long, cold night and I was glad when the shops opened soon after seven o'clock. Trouble was, the pubs opened too, and the smells of food and drink tormented me.

I laid out my best cambric shirt in front of the little Jew tailor. He picked it up (I have to admit his hands were cleaner than mine), and carried it over to the light.

'One shilling and sixpence', he says.

I exploded. 'It's worth a pound at least.'

He shrugged. 'To me, Abraham Rosenbloom at your service, it's worth one and six, maybe less.'

I took the money and headed for the nearest pub where I had a rum against the cold and a roast beef sandwich for my growling stomach which had had nothing but a bottle of stout in it for twenty hours. That left me the price of a one-way ticket and threepence to spare.

The harridan of a ticket seller looked at my bags: I had a heavy, strapped-up leather bag and a light canvas to swing on my shoulder. She looked so long that I began to wonder if the police had put about a description of the man who'd raised the alarm at the Metropole, but her eyes only flicked over my face.

'You're going the wrong way, son.'

'And how is that, madam?'

'Should be off to the war.'

'Watson's Bay,' I said firmly.

I went directly to the washroom and did the best I could with soap, cold water and my cut-throat while the ferry ploughed through the water. I've always been a good sailor and grateful for it because a lot of my voyages have been made at a cut below first class as you'll see. I scraped the whiskers off; the moustache needed a trim but I thought I was likely to lose half of it if I tried. I went up to the enclosed deck and looked out at the white capped waves riding in to shore. I don't know why it is, but a big dose of nature like this always makes me thoughtful: this time I thought about the war and Richard Browning, or rather, about Richard Browning and the war.

Maybe it was my Irish heritage but more likely it was reluctance to engage in physical conflict – in any case, I just couldn't feel that the war had anything to do with me. I was twenty years old and, like a young fool, I

11

couldn't imagine living beyond thirty; little was I to know that I'd see eighty and more. I didn't want to spend any of it shooting at Turks and Germans who'd done me no harm and who might shoot back and cut the time left down to nothing at all. Some said that it would be over by Christmas; if it wasn't and the conscription demanded by hot heads (old chaps mostly I'll be bound) went through, I'd be caught. Meanwhile I wanted none of it, and if I *had* to join the army, I'd try to delay it until it was time to throw my slouch hat in the air and cheer in the peace.

Once past Rose Bay the water got calmer; the sun was going up into a clearing sky and the breeze had lost its edge. I went out on to the deck and looked enviously at the mansions of the rich. That was the place for me, driving home to slip into the blazer and flannels and carry the drinks out on to the terrace.

The ferry made a few stops which, as far as I was concerned, were of interest only for the quality of the women getting on and off. Nothing to report. There were only three or four passengers left aboard when the wooden jetty at Watson's Bay came into view.

Watson's Bay was not a pretty spot at that time. (I've heard that it's now crammed at weekends with people eating fish and chips and swilling down Australian wine which is horrible to contemplate, especially the wine.) There were a few smart houses on the hills overlooking the bay, but that elevation was mostly commanded by the Catholic church and associated buildings. There was an unpaved road and a lot of bush. I suppose there were less smart houses lower down and among the trees but I never got to see them. The bay was home to a down-at-heel fishing fleet; there were fishermen's shacks along the beach, slipways and a few crumbling jetties. The ferry bumped against the one solid jetty and I went ashore lugging my heavy bag and vaguely disappointed that the film people weren't on the beach with the cameras set up.

I was looking about, hoping I wouldn't have too far to walk when I heard sounds of disputation behind me. A woman was struggling with one of the ferry hands, a brawny type who had hold of her by the arm while his other hand was trying to get a grip elsewhere.

'Let go!' she yelled. 'I want to see the captain.'

'You'll see him all right. And the police.' He tugged her loose from the rail and started to half-carry her towards the back of the ferry.

None of my business you might think, and you'd be right, but she was an uncommonly good looking woman with a great mass of dark red hair and a stylish costume that showed off her figure. I got a flash of silk-covered ankle as the deckhand lifted her. That sort of thing is a green light to Browning and I was back at the rail hollering to set the lady free before I knew what I was doing.

Despite sleeping out and a cold water shave I retained the clothes of a fashionable salesman and the bearing of a Dudleigh man, and the sailor showed the natural deference of the lower orders by releasing the woman.

'What's the trouble?' I barked.

'No bloody ticket, that's the trouble. It's back to the Quay for her.' He looked at me more closely and perhaps saw for the first time that I was young, or perhaps I sounded less assured than I thought, for he made a grab at her and snarled. 'An' what's it to you?'

'An oversight, surely,' I said. 'Madam, you can buy a ticket at the office here.'

The man attempted to seize his quarry again but she dodged. 'She ain't got no money.'

I looked down and the bold, handsome face nodded sadly up at me. Again without thinking, my hand went to my pocket. 'I'll take care of it. Let her go. Come along, Madam.'

I had the coins out and would have thrown them but if I'd missed and they'd gone in the water my noble gesture would have been for nothing. Noble gestures are not for

13

wasting. I bent, very dignified, and placed the money on the rail. Money out of my pocket and a woman's hand in exchange, it's the story of my life. I helped her from the ferry while the sailor scooped the money. When he was satisfied he slung a bag made of black velvet stretched over a bamboo frame up on to the jetty. Glass tinkled and broke inside the bag and he laughed.

'Brute.'

'Whore.'

There didn't seem to be much to add to that so I shepherded her along the boards towards the land. She came willingly enough as women do if you handle them right. I took the opportunity to look her over thoroughly and my estimate of her value went up. She was quite tall and well-made, age about thirty. That was all right with me; my first woman, the mother of the chap I'd laid the bet with at Dudleigh, was a good ten years older than that and I can remember the sweetness of her flesh even now. Over the years I've had women younger than me and a good deal older (not lately of course) and I couldn't say that I have a preference either way.

'Thank you, sir.' Those brown eyes were nicely painted up and while I wouldn't say that the sailor had got her profession exactly right, she wasn't from the Salvation Army either.

'Dick,' says I, 'Dick Browning. And you are...?'

She thought for a minute. 'Suzanne Select.'

I swept off my hat. 'Miss Select, I'm pleased to make your acquaintance. I didn't see you on the boat and can't think how I could have missed you.'

'Gallant, sir. You weren't supposed to see me. You'd have been badly out of place if you had.'

'Ah.' We smiled at each other; I found that I was still holding her hand and she wasn't wrenching it away. We got to the end of the jetty and I helped her down. The strap of her bag was cutting deep into the fabric of her glove and I took it with my free hand. I nearly overbalanced at the unexpected weight. We seemed to be two of a kind, Miss Select and I – carrying everything we owned with us.

I grunted. 'How did you expect to get off the boat?'

'I thought there'd be more people. I didn't even know where Watson's Bay was. I only arrived from New Zealand a few days ago. Then I heard about the film.'

I took another look at her and damn me if I couldn't see a tint or two in her skin and a few kinks in her hair that indicated Maori blood. If New Zealand hadn't come up I doubt if I'd have noticed.

'We seem to be on the same course,' I said. 'Are you hoping for a part in the film?'

'Yes. Where are they, d'you think?'

I looked up the hill and to east and west. There wasn't much to see – a grubby beach, and more trees than houses further up as I've said, which is the wrong way round for me. Then I noticed that one of the buildings wasn't a house at all but a hotel. I'd mixed a bit in theatrical circles while peddling grog and, in my experience, when an actor wasn't acting he was drinking or more likely doing both at once. I pointed to the sandstone pile.

'Let's ask at the pub.'

It was after nine and getting warm; the grey clouds of the day before had given way to clear skies the way it happens in Sydney and the bay was sheltered from the breezes. I was beginning to sweat with the weight of the bags and the steepness of the climb when we reached the steps of the hotel. It was a big place, thrown up any old how and much added to over the years. I sat on the steps and mopped my face with my kerchief. Miss Select had beads of sweat on her upper lip but otherwise looked as if she'd just stepped out of the powder room. Her eyes were bright, her lips were red and she was already in my debt. I gave her hand a squeeze.

'Around the back like workers, d'you think? Or in the front?'

15

For an answer she picked up her velvet bag and climbed the steps.

The hotel was a plain sort of place with a good but well-used carpet, and fittings that could have done with a dust cloth. I caught sight of a saloon bar door half-open and inviting but it was a bit early. We went across to the desk where the attendant looked up with the sort of smile I hadn't had from hotel desk attendants lately.

'Sir? Madam?' He was a little bantam of a fellow with his hair parted in the middle and slicked down. His collar was very white and his dark suit was scrupulously brushed. I was suddenly aware of my own need for pressing and brushing.

'We are looking for Mr Longford's film company,' Suzanne said.

'Are you players?' He seemed ready to leap the desk and do anything we asked. I couldn't pass up that kind of reception: I inclined my head and looked determined.

His voice became breathy. 'Timothy Goodluck, at your service. Miss Lyell and Mr Longford are in the courtyard. Please leave your bags here and follow me.' He banged a bell and a kid came scuttling in from the east; Goodluck indicated that he was to take care of the bags and then he came around the desk and set off through an archway towards the back of the hotel. He was moving in such sprightly fashion that I could see the new leather on the soles of his buttoned boots. I shrugged, gave Suzanne one of my wide grins, the kind that used to enrage the masters at Dudleigh, and we followed Mr Goodluck down a hallway that became rather more grand, with mirrored walls and some marble facings, as it progressed.

Suzanne took a look in the mirror and adjusted her jacket and lace blouse on the move. I own I slapped away some dust and made sure my tie was properly centred – there's nothing like the company of a smart woman to keep a man up to the mark himself. Goodluck led us through a sitting room to a set of French windows which were full of light flooding in from a flag-stoned courtyard. A couple of tables were set up out in the sun and twenty or more people were milling about. We stepped out into a buzz of voices and a metallic clicking that turned out to be a cameraman cranking his equipment. His swearing contributed considerably to the noise. Goodluck smiled at some of the people, a motley bunch, some in street clothes, some dressed like sailors and others wearing grey dusters, like clerks in a dry goods store.

Everyone ignored Goodluck but he pressed on until we fetched up at a table where a dark-haired woman, wearing what looked like riding costume and smoking a cigarette in a red holder, was sitting. She was scribbling on some papers with a pencil stub while trying to listen to a woman who was talking into her left ear. She also argued the toss with a man who was trying to correct what she was writing as she wrote it.

'Miss Lyell,' Goodluck babbled, 'I've brought along two more players, Miss Lyell.'

She looked up for an instant. She was pretty, with big eyes and a cleft chin. 'Good. See Francis. I'm busy.'

3

A woman who'd spoken to me like that would've got something sharp in return, but Goodluck just turned away and pointed across to the far wall. He was still beaming as if he was happy to have had his head snapped off.

'Mr Longford's over there.' He sniffed. 'In his shirt sleeves. What shall I put on the bags?'

'Browning and Select,' says I, giving him a wink and a pat on the shoulder. 'I'll see you later, Mr Goodluck.' He nodded and went off; if he'd known that that wink was all I'd had for him he'd have stepped less sprightly.

Suzanne and I walked across to where Longford was leaning against a wall talking to the chief camera operator, the man who'd been swearing before and still didn't look too happy. Mind you, it was hard to read his expression because he wore huge, spreading moustachios; it's a wonder they didn't get caught in the sprockets. Raymond Longford[3] was Mr Square-Jaw-and-Steady-Eyes himself. I heard later that he'd fought in the Boer War (more fool him, that was a duckable war if ever there was one), and had been a sailor and bushman. He looked all of these parts – tall and strongly built, ready to cross-cut saw a giant redwood or furl a topsail, if you know what I mean.

18

I waited for a pause in the cameraman's stream of complaint and then stepped in with, 'Richard Browning and Miss Suzanne Select, Mr Longford. Miss Lyell sent us over to you.'

Longford lifted his craggy jaw and looked at us. 'Lottie did?'

'Yes.'

'Why?'

He was either very distracted or not very bright; either way in a condition to be taken advantage of. 'For roles in the film,' I said firmly.

'Oh.' He glanced across to where Lottie Lyell was still scribbling and dealing with three people at once. 'Well then, excuse me, Fred.' The moustachios backed away and Longford, like a sensible chap, examined Suzanne closely.

'Say fish,' he said abruptly.

'Fuhsh,' says Suzanne.

'I thought so,' he crowed. 'New Zealander, Maori too, eh?'

'A buht.'

'Fine. Excellent. Authenticity. Miss...?'

'Select,' sticks in yours truly quickly, seeing which way the wind was blowing.

'Miss Select. I'm keen to use Polynesians in the film. We've done so in New Zealand and Norfolk Island but, unfortunately, those people are not available for these sequences. I'm sure your services will be of value.' He reached out and touched her head. 'Excuse me, truly wonderful head of hair you have.'

'Good,' says I, not wanting to be left out.

Longford looked me up and down and frowned. 'I don't think...'

'If I work, he works,' Suzanne said. It seemed like a noble gesture at the time and I squeezed her hand – it should have been her throat. Longford twigged as well he might; he was in a peculiar partnership himself. He sighed and pulled at his finely chiselled nose. 'I'm sure we can find something for you to do, Mr...'

'Browning.'

'See the wardrobe mistress, through there.' He pointed to a gate at the end of the courtyard. 'She'll direct you to the rehearsal area and make sure you see the paymaster after that.'

'We will,' I said.

He nodded and walked over to the table where he waited to get Lottie Lyell's attention.

'Thank you,' I said to Suzanne.

She winked. 'We're square.'

The rest of that day I don't care to remember. It didn't start off too badly although it was a little like being checked over before a yearling sale. I was signed on to the payroll after a record was made of my particulars: Richard Kelly Browning, born Oakhampton, January 1895; height six feet two inches; weight twelve stone; hair, dark; eyes, brown; teeth, full set, intact etc. After that the nightmare began; they shaved off my moustache and stained me a nasty brown colour. I spent most of the next eight hours up to my chest in cold water, around two headlands from Watson's Bay and opposite a clean little beach, pulling on ropes and heaving at boats, doing the same thing over and over. I began to see what Les had meant about it not being much fun, although I'd still have preferred it to twenty threes with Jimmy Clabby.

I caught a glimpse of Suzanne at the meal break although they kept the male and female workers well apart. Despite her Maori blood she'd needed a little staining too and they seemed to have wrapped her in a sheet of bark. Still, she flashed me a smile with her own full set intact that looked whiter than ever against the darkened skin. I went back into the water thinking that, with half an ounce of luck, I'd be well rewarded for my noble and manly conduct some time before midnight.

Towards the end of the day they started giving out tots

of rum each time we came out of the water and I was first in line every time. My hands were torn and sore – I needed the anaesthetic. I got a final stiff drink as the shadows lengthened on the beach and we were instructed to return our costumes and assemble in the courtyard for our pay. I ought to have mentioned my fellow workers but, truth to tell, I can't recall much about them. They were extras, like thousands I've seen since on all four continents, and they tend to blend into one insignificant mass. (It's different with the stars of course, Doug and Mary, that swine Flynn, good old David Niven – they stay very fresh in the mind.)

Dressed again, but feeling a bit naked without my upper lip hair, I wandered into the courtyard hoping that another rum might be available before the handing out of the shekels. Damn me if Suzanne wasn't there already chatting away to Lottie Lyell like a long lost sister. She saw me and beckoned me over.

'Here he is, Miss Lyell. Isn't he handsome? Especially without the moustache.'

That was pretty high-handed I thought, but she'd washed the stain off and was looking near to her best. I don't know whether she'd had any rum – probably had.

'Hmm,' says Lyell. 'Yes, he'll do.'

The upshot was a session of still photography, God knows what for – very exhausting, but more money for both of us.

As I recall, I ended up with nearly three pounds in my hand and Suzanne must have had more because she had been in close-up scenes and had had to do some acting. (I've never seen the film so I can't say whether her scenes survived to the final print. As she was an amateur they probably didn't.) It wasn't a bad result for a couple who'd fetched up penniless on the beach that morning and we celebrated in the saloon bar of the hotel with a drink or two before ferry time. I tipped the hotel kid (avoiding Goodluck, never could stand men who parted their hair in the middle) to carry the bags down to the jetty. My hands were only fit for holding a glass or, perhaps, for cupping gently around an obliging woman's warm breast.

Such thoughts were very much on my mind as I stood with Suzanne watching the approaching ferry churn up the water. Our luck had been right in because this was the only day of outdoors filming Longford and Lyell had scheduled. *The Mutiny of the Bounty* was all but finished but for some studio scenes in which there was no place for amateur blow-ins. Gently, as much for the sake of my tender palms as for gallantry, I put my hand on Suzanne's arm. The flesh yielded nicely under the silk sleeve.

'Well,' says I, 'what about a night on the town? We could get a room in a hotel and go out and kick up our heels. What d'you say, Miss Select?'

She turned up her face and parted her dark brown lips slowly. 'The Metropole, Mr Browning?'

'Er, what about the Adams? Fine house, the Adams.'

4

Earlier that year, the wowsers had got their way and the pubs closed at 6 pm. [4] Part of the reason for this was to keep the soldiery sober and so increase the chances of their being killed by the Hun rather than by one of their comrades. But it was also the old, old story of the people who didn't know how to have a good time trying to stop those that did. On the surface it might have seemed to be working; the streets were quieter and the dimmed lights in the hotels probably convinced the wowsers that the menfolk were at home saying their prayers.

Of course it wasn't like that at all; the early closing merely brought into existence sly grog shops and various dodges to ensure that a sporting gentleman could have his pleasure as before – although he might occasionally have to swill down what was in his cup quicker than he might like and might also spend the odd night in the lock-up. I'd done both over the past few months.

The trick was to book into a sporting establishment like the Adams Hotel, drop a little oil into the right palm and learn where the high life was going on. There might be a card game in the hotel or a party where, for a modest charge, all your requirements could be met. Also popular were private theatrical amusements with food and refresh-

23

ments provided. It was with something such in mind that I booked into the Adams with Suzanne as Mr and Mrs Robespierre. You have to understand that I looked a deal older than twenty – the height helped and two years of living by your wits gives you a certain bearing. Besides, I was probably a bit tipsy from the rum and whiskies I'd absorbed and, if there were any funny looks from the underlings at the Adams, I didn't notice.

I was dead keen to get down to it as soon as we had the door closed behind us but I had to practically force Suzanne to the bed: she was mumbling on about a bath. I got her stripped down; I can still remember those big, soft breasts with the pale brown, spreading nipples . . . but oddly enough I can't remember much else. There was a lot of tumbling and fumbling about with ties and laces and, what with my youth and the liquor I had on board and one thing and another, it was all over before it began. I can't honestly carve a notch on my pistol for Miss Suzanne Select although she behaved as if I could, ooh'ing and ah'ing and groaning about stallions and unicorns and such.

I fancy I had a bit of a sleep and then she was there, standing over me with her bosom pushed up under a blue satin bodice and a light feathery wrap around her creamy shoulders. I could have made a much better job of things there and then but she wasn't having any.

'Come on, my bucko,' says she, 'let's see what sort of time you can have in this town with a pound in your pocket.'

I practically *did* have a pound in my pocket, of rampant malehood, but she was eager to be off and I had to struggle from the bed and stagger down the hall to perform an uncomfortable and perfunctory toilet. Then I followed that tall, swaying illusion down the stairs towards a night of pleasure.

I can't honestly say that I remember much of it. A few words and coin passed between Suzanne and the night

doorman and then it was out to the street and into a
motor cab. For a newcomer to Sydney she found her way
around very quickly. We went to Adolphe's for a meal
and then to the Beefsteak Club where there was dancing
and wine – not that there hadn't been a good deal of that
with the food. I seem to remember music and feathers,
but perhaps I was just humming to myself while I held
Suzanne's wrap. I was pretty stewed on top of what I'd
already drunk after a hard day's work. I was only twenty
after all.

In the cab on the way back to the hotel we giggled and
Suzanne took the hat with the ostrich feather in it from
my head and replaced it on her own. I belched mightily
as I recall and told her I loved her.

'Yes, darling,' she said.

'Prettiest woman in Sydney.'

'Only in Sydney?'

'. . . world.'

'Yes, darling. Mind my stockings. Oh, we're there.
Thank you, cabbie for a very smooth ride. Pay the man,
Thomas.'

'Richard, Tom's m' brother.'

'I look forward to meeting him . . . Come on, darling
. . . up the steps and try to stand up straight . . . I'll get
the key . . . you hang on here. Watch out for the pot
plants.'

I held on to a polished brass bar that seemed to be pitch-
ing like a ship's rail in a blow and watched Suzanne sweep
across the lobby to the desk. I was trying to bring my
real nose into contact with a nose in a mirror when she
got back and helped me up the stairs. God, she was
strong . . . I remember looking forward to undoing that
bodice and getting a faceful of those . . .

When I woke up she was gone, of course. Also gone to Auckland or Paris or God knows where, were my watch and cigar case not to mention two shirts with studs – everything in fact that was portable and of value. I'd been paying for everything, waiters and what have you, but what little money I had left was gone too.

So there I was, a bare thirty-six hours after my flit from the Metropole, and in much the same circumstances. All I had to show for the time was a clean-shaven upper lip, getting stubbly now, and a headache that was threatening to blind me. I probably hadn't even got my pecker wet. I crawled down the hall to the bathroom and cleaned up – at least I hadn't done anything disgraceful in the regurgitative line. Back in the room I felt better; Suzanne's perfume hung irritatingly in the air but I consoled myself with the thought that I probably hadn't picked up a dose of clap. Breakfast, that was the thing. Probably hadn't drunk all that much. Probably succumbed to fatigue after all that rope hauling.

I strolled out into the hallway and glimpsed nemesis. One of the hotel flunkeys was stationed at the end of the passage. He fiddled with a vase of flowers and didn't acknowledge my salute as I passed, so I knew the word was out. I was watched into the dining room and while I ate. They served me courteously enough; I might have been a well-heeled young eccentric, but they were ready for the worst. I ate hearty – eggs and bacon and lashings of toast and coffee – they made quite good coffee in the Adams, probably the only place in Australia that did. I admit I dawdled; only a fool advances into trouble and there was always the chance of a gas explosion or the Germans shelling the city from the harbour.

But nothing like that happened; I slurped down the last cup of coffee and went up to the desk. All that gilt and glass and brocade I'd been too drunk to notice before impressed me now. I hadn't even had a snort in the Marble Bar.

There were two coves behind the desk: one looked like the regular thing – pasty face, hair plastered down and fingernails buffed. The other had foodstains on his waistcoat and tobacco stains on his moustache. I fear I fingered the place where my moustache should have been.

'Sir?' the attendant said.

'Can't pay the bill,' says I. 'The woman I was with has flitted with the cash. I've been robbed!'

'Indeed?' Pasty-face took a step back and the other chap moved forward.

'Richard Browning?'

I nodded. My mouth was suddenly very dry.

'I am Sergeant Carlisle, New South Wales police. I am arresting you on two charges of misappropriation, one of wilful damage and one of disturbing the peace.'

'Can I get my bags?'

Carlisle smiled and tugged at his yellowed moustache. 'Are they heavy?'

'Moderately.'

'Get them by all means. You can carry them the mile or so to Darlinghurst lock-up.'

'Those bags stay here,' the attendant said firmly, 'to be held against the debt. That's the law.'

'That's hotel law,' the Sergeant said. 'If it was real law we'd have to run one of the bags over to the Metropole, wouldn't we, Mr Browning?'

I managed a weak smile; it never hurts to respond to the jokes of those who have you by the balls. Carlisle looked me up and down. He was a stocky chap, around five foot eight but about my weight. He gave a fierce grin.

'I don't think we'll need the cuffs,' he said.

I'd been in lock-ups before as I've said, but as a representative of Robespierre's Wine and Spirits Ltd, and even as a senior at Dudleigh, I'd had enough money on me to pay the fine in the morning and walk away. This was different. They charged me at the lock-up, barely gave me time to use the bucket in the cell, and then trotted me off to the Magistrate in Bent Street. I mean trotted literally; I was herded into a closed carriage with benches along the sides together with a dozen or so common fellows. Whip up the horse and it was Sydney through bars after that.

I had the option of getting a solicitor of course, but that would have meant a communication with 'Wild Bill' and if there was one way I didn't want to approach that worthy it was as a penniless wastrel who started fires in hotel baths. So I sat pat through the whole dumb show, pleading guilty as charged. In fact I just let the law take its course and allowed my case to merge in with whatever else was going on – in this instance various minor matters, mainly to do with excessive intake of liquor. (This is always the safest course, providing you're not had up with a mob of arsonists or sex offenders. Judges seem to have a highly developed concern for the virtue of their womenfolk and the sanctity of their property.)

Although my clothes were smart enough I was on my second day in the one shirt and after the mauling they'd had in the waters of Watson's Bay my hands didn't exactly look like those of a gentleman. I glanced around the court-room to see if one of those ferrety reporters was present – the sort of chaps who make it hard for a man to remain incognito. Half of them are in the pay of money-lenders and the like, always standing by to nobble people. But there were none around and my case went through pretty satisfactorily, if you call two months hard labour satis-factory. I did; one of the old drunks in the wagon had told me to get ready for six months.

The same wagon trundled us off down the dusty road to the state prison at Long Bay. The place had only been opened the year before and none of my fellow convicts had been there.

'Christ, I wish we was goin' to Parramatta,' one of them, an old inebriate with black gums, lamented. 'I don't like the sound of this place.'

'What're you talking about, you old fool?' The speaker was a mud-bespattered, bedraggled creature I'd taken for just another drunk who'd learned his trade in Victoria's time; now that he'd spoken I realised that he was much younger, not much older than myself. 'Parramatta's a hell hole.'

'But I've been there thirty times,' the old-timer whined. 'It's like home.'

The young chap laughed and I could see youth in his face under the mud and whiskers. 'Time for a change then, Grandfather,' he says. 'Maybe this Long Bay'll be like a holiday home.' He looked around the bucking, rumbling wagon at the dead, dispirited faces and finally turned his gaze on me. 'I can tell you one thing about it.'

I leaned forward, drawn by his intense grey-eyed stare and the light, British-accented voice. 'And what's that, mate?' I said.

He chuckled. 'There's a women's reformatory next door, so I'm told.'

The others were snoring or belching or coughing the dust out of their throats, but he had my attention. 'Is that so?'

'Such is my information, Mr . . .?'

'Richard Browning.' We reached across from one bench to the other and shook hands. 'And you are . . .?'

'Jeremy Farnol, at your service.'

'At His Majesty's service,' the old-timer croaked. A cloud of dust caught him in mid-cackle and he sank back against the wall of the wagon, wheezing and choking. Farnol pulled his coat collar up and lapsed into silence. I looked out at the white dusty road and thought about

Miss Suzanne Select. She was no doubt waltzing around Sydney with her film earnings safe in her purse, along with the residue of mine. I permitted myself a small fantasy: I was a deck hand on a Sydney harbour ferry and I'd caught Miss Select travelling without a ticket. Her petticoats billowed up like sails as I tossed her over the side into the deep green water.

5

Long Bay gaol probably isn't fit for a human being now, but in 1916 it wasn't fit for a dog. Behind the high walls were a couple of buildings sited on a hill so that winds blew in from all quarters. As the old lags had told me, the compound was new which meant that the place was like the Tennessee dust bowl when it was dry, and a sea of gluey mud when it rained. And it was cold! Prisons are either ovens or deep freezers in my experience: I recall one in Mexico where I sweated myself down to about a hundred and fifty pounds and one in Scotland where it was so cold I left the skin from the tips of my fingers on the window bars. I've yet to spend a summer and a winter in the same prison, thank God, which is not to say it couldn't still happen.

We were tumbled out of the cart into a courtyard surrounded by a high wall. The cold wind swirled around inside the wall. The dust drifted in the air and gave the old fellow who'd expressed the wish to go to Parramatta a coughing fit that dropped him to the ground. The prison guard kicked him several times; he staggered up, still coughing.

Ah hah, thinks I. This is the time to keep the eyes down and the balls covered. I shuffled along like the oldest and most wretched member of the group and I noticed that Farnol was doing the same.

They herded us into a shed, made us strip and issued us with shirt, trousers and jacket made out of a material as hard as tin. The boots had the weight and solidity of tree roots. I had my first, but by no means my last, experience of being fingerprinted, and then it was off to the cells. This was in the mid-afternoon and I thought it might be a settling-in period for newcomers. Not so. We were locked in the cells around this time every day for the whole of my time there and it was one of the worst features of the experience. I used to pull myself up to the window and gaze out at an afternoon going to waste, a time when I could have been relaxing with a drink or spinning a yarn to a pretty girl.

We were four to a cell and I landed in with Farnol, the old Parramatta lag, Henry Barton, who claimed that he hadn't been sober since he'd returned from the Sudan War in 1885 except for periods of imprisonment and not always then, and a fourth man whose name I forget. He died of syphilis of the brain on my second night which accounts for my lapse of memory. My recall of names has always been exceptionally good, especially for those who mistreat me. For example, the principal guard in our cell block was Gregory Flinders – that's a name which has remained crystal clear in my mind for more than sixty years.

Barton and the syphilitic went to sleep on the two lower bunks which left Farnol and me standing by the door. And this wasn't one of the cells you see in the Western movies, with bars from floor to roof on two sides. Come to think of it, I've *never* seen a cell like that except on a movie set. This was a concrete box, eight feet by eight, about seven feet high, with a solid door in which there was a hatch that could be slid up from outside to allow food and drink to pass into the cell, and the piss bucket to pass out.

'Well, Browning,' Farnol says, 'what brings you here?'

'You were in court.' My spirits were low and I didn't feel like chatting.

'I was asleep. Come on, tell us the tale; we've got a lot of time to pass.'

Like most people I'll talk about myself until the audience drops off. I told Farnol the whole story going back as far as Dudleigh Grammar. I'll allow I embroidered a little, such as by suggesting that it was my romp with Mrs Carew (my fellow wagerer's mother, you'll recall) rather than the run-outs and the skied catch that expelled me from Dudleigh. Farnol swallowed it all down with his eyes gleaming and he chuckled often. *Splendid chap*, thinks I.

'Excellent, excellent,' Farnol chortled when I'd finished. 'What a cad you are. I hope I can remember it all.'

'Eh?'

'I'm a writer, old chap, or trying to be one. It runs in the family, writing.[5] A few of us have had a go at it and I'm the latest. There's great material in your story.'

I felt a bit glum about that but there was an obvious rejoinder. 'Well, Farnol, you've heard me out. What're you in for, eh?'

He chuckled, shook his head and vaulted up on to a top bunk. I heard him rustle around for a while and then his breath came in deep, steady gusts. Henry Barton snored and I own I felt like weeping as I stood there with my back to an iron-bound door one foot thick at least.

It was Farnol who explained to me why Flinders was giving us such a hard time. This was after his third up-setting of the slops bucket so that the contents poured back into the cell. At least ten times he'd delayed our getting to the mess hall so that we had to eat our meal, typically a disgusting mess of boiled lamb and rice, stone cold. At first I couldn't believe what Farnol told me.

'He thinks that of *me*?'

'Of us both, probably.'

'There was none of that at Dudleigh,' I said.

'Not much at Rugby either,' he said. 'Plenty at Winchester though.'

It puzzled me why the English named their schools after games and guns and thank God I didn't make this point to Farnol. He already treated me like a colonial ignoramus and I'd learned to keep my mouth closed and eyes and ears open. I was a good mimic as I've said – my Peter Dawson impression, remember? – and I picked up a pretty good English gentleman act from Farnol and others which I turned into money many times. (I've often wondered whether Farnol got any books published. I'm not much of a reader, especially of novels. I've started a few but I don't recall ever finishing one.)

Anyway, once I'd found out about Flinders, who was a fat, fair individual by the way, with a nauseating kiss curl plastered to the centre of his forehead, I took good care never to be alone with him. The daily routine, as far as I can remember it, was: awake at 6 am, mess hall at 6.20 am, cell cleaning until 7.10 am, exercise until 8 am and work from then until midday. There was a half-hour meal break before two more hours of work after which we were locked in the cells, fed at 6 pm and lights out at 8 pm. This schedule allowed prisoners little time to make themselves available to men like Flinders but it was managed – around meal breaks, on sick parade and at the twice weekly bath muster.

Flinders could not have been more wrong about Farnol and me. If anything, Farnol was a randier cove than myself and, apart from note-keeping, he gave little thought to anything save the fair sex.

For this preoccupation there were good reasons: the work was hard – we built sections of the prison and the walls, cleared scrub on the hillsides, stacked bricks and timber. The food was bland – boiled meat, rice, potatoes, bread, sweet tea and fresh fruit once a week. It was boring but filling and nourishing enough. I missed my grog and good cigars – the tobacco ration was of poor quality twist that I could hardly smoke. I used to barter it for extra soap and fruit and luxuries like biscuits. On this regime, anyone given to dissipation but blessed with generally sound health, like Farnol and me, saw it improved and we suffered from our natural urges accordingly. I'd lie in my bunk and listen to Farnol sighing and thrashing around and eventually giving himself relief and try to concentrate on thoughts of aromatic Havanas, French brandy and the thrill of having an outsider go first past the post with some of my money on its back.

Occasionally, of course, Flinders cornered me in the wash house and the conversation would go something like this:

He: *You have very white skin, Browning.*
Me: *Not when I've had a bit of sun on it, Mr Flinders. Gets rough and red I can tell you. Could you please step aside, sir?*
He: *I could make this place a lot more pleasant for you, Browning.*
Me: *Oh, it's not so bad, sir, considering the type of people you have to deal with.*
He: *What d'you mean by that? Is that insolence?*
Me: *No, sir. Do you mind, sir? I'll be late for prayers.*

After a few such encounters my nerves were shredding and I had to have further consultation with Farnol.

'You should have a moustache, old chap,' he said.

'I had one but I had to shave it off to work in the film. What's that got to do with it anyway?'

Farnol went on to explain that I should grow my moustache back because Flinders and his kind didn't like

35

facial hair. (Things changed a hundred per cent in that regard over the next fifty years.) But I needed a quicker solution than that and Farnol could see the point; his food was cold too and we were both trying to avoid using the bucket at night to cut down on the amount that might be slopped on the floor any morning.

'An Eton chap told me about something he did once,' Farnol said. 'Desperate measure, but it worked.'

'Tell me, I'll try anything. Otherwise I'll kill that bastard and get myself topped.'

Farnol told me. The next bath day I was slow in washing and made sure that Flinders noticed it. When the last of the other inmates had left he was there, truncheon in hand and with his pink face flushed.

'I know what you want, Mr Flinders,' says I.

'Yes?'

'The harassment will stop?' The word puzzled him and he looked uncertain. I was fighting the nausea that was rising remorselessly in my guts. 'I mean the business with the bucket and the food . . .'

'Yes. Yes.'

I turned around, unbuckled my belt and let my trousers fall. I could smell him getting closer and I had to grit my teeth as I felt his hand reach for the band of my drawers. At least he was direct; there was none of the amorous fumbling that Farnol had warned me about. He pulled my drawers down and immediately let out a high-pitched scream.

'What is *that*!'

'Nothing.'

'Have you got them anywhere else?'

'Not where it matters, not for a long time. Come on, Mr Flinders . . .'

But when I turned around he had gone. I had given myself an 'Eton arsehole' – made from a combination of soap, hair, blood, iodine and whatever other substances were to hand. The effect was of a large, raised, multicoloured wet sore placed near the anus.

Flinders ceased his attentions and Farnol and I were able
to get on with the standard prison activities of malinger-
ing to avoid work, bartering to secure the finer things
of life and planning for the future. Apart from seeing himself as a great author, Farnol had another object in view
which was to obtain access to the Women's Reformatory.
He had made a close study of our sister institution when
outside on work detail, questioning prisoners and guards
and plotting the schedules of deliveries and other
visitations.

It occupied his nimble mind, kept him cheerful and
passed the time, but there seemed little prospect of
success.

'It can be done,' he would say. 'It must be possible.'

'If you can fly or tunnel, certainly.'

'Or if I were a woman.'

'Flinders could help you there.'

After a period of hard study, Farnol informed me that
he had a plan.

'I'll need your help, Browning,' he said.

'Ah,' I said cautiously.

'Did I or did I not save you from the clutches of
Flinders?'

Put like that, what could I do? I agreed to help him
although the plan seemed more and more bizarre as it
unfolded. Farnol had a subtle mind and he early
associated the idea of posing as a woman with the notion
of playing the clergyman. He rejected it as too obvious
a stratagem (I use his words) but eventually he hit on the
variation. There were a number of Jews incarcerated
along with the rest of us – gentiles, Asiatics, Aboriginals,
etc. – and on Saturday a rabbi visited to minister to their

spiritual needs. Pick-pockets, pimps and forgers mainly, their needs in that regard were probably minimal but Rabbi Jacobsen appeared on their Sabbath without fail.

'I've got a costume,' Farnol said, 'black coat, white shirt, horsehair beard. It's cost me dear in tobacco and letter writing I can tell you.'

'You're mad.'

'Not at all. I've spoken to our Israelites and I am informed that the rabbi visits a number of women of their faith after his work here. One of these women in particular is said to be fond of male company.'

'Even suppose you got out and got in, as it were, how would you get back?'

'That need not concern you. What I need is a diversion to be created so that the passage of two rabbis is not noticed.'

'Impossible.'

'Not so. The Hebrews will delay Jacobsen until after the guards have changed shift. Some abstruse point of Old Testament interpretation, no doubt. The second shift must be so occupied as to be unconcerned by his late appearance. You have the necessary qualifications, Browning.'

'How so?'

'A fire, a small one.'

Saturday was a work day in the prison but there was a certain laxness in the arrangements that Farnol planned to take advantage of. The Jewish religious service interfered with the head count and heavy lunches, an anxiety to leave early, and interest in public sporting events all contributed to a lowering of vigilance. Farnol would be able to absent himself from the work detail and lunch, and a fire in the cell block would cover his absence and return as well as providing a distraction to the new guard.

I wasn't happy about it though. If the plan went wrong I would be associated with a rebellious escapade or, at worst, an escape attempt. My task was to be at the head of the prisoners being returned to their cells and to have the fire underway before the lock-up was completed. It was risky but I agreed. Farnol was a forceful character and considerably older than me; well, a few years older at least.

The selected Saturday arrived. Farnol slipped away before muster and I toiled through the morning imagining him, behind a copper in the laundry, scrubbing himself to get rid of the prison odour and glueing on his false beard. After a shortened afternoon work session we downed tools and I worked my way to the head of the line, shoving unceremoniously (and uncharacteristically) to get to the front. The guard touched me on the shoulder just as I was about to step through the door as the second man in line.

'Fall out, Browning.'

I stared at him and shuffled forward.

'Fall out, I say. You're to see the Superintendent.'

My bowels loosened as Nature apparently intends them to do when danger looms, and I was escorted down a series of light-starved passages and up a chilly staircase or two.

I imagined the interview: *You are evidently the brains behind a mass escape attempt, Browning. What have you to say?*

The guard knocked on the Super's oak-panelled door and we went in. I'd only seen him at a distance, haranguing us at assemblies and, heavily flanked by guards, inspecting walls and certain special facilities like the solitary confinement cells. Up close he was unimpressive; a little, roundish chap, thin on top and short of chin. He waved the guard back and beckoned me to stand closer to his desk. He'd been half-standing and now he dropped down into his big chair. He was smiling. *Can't be solitary or the cat*, I thought.

'Representations have been made, Browning, on your behalf.' He turned over a piece of paper on his desk. 'From a firm of solicitors in . . . Newcastle. Ah, Dunstan and Houghton.'

My heart sank. I glanced out the window; it was a novelty to look out of an unbarred window. As it happened I had a clear view of the visitors' entrance by the main gate and I saw Farnol, in fusty black, crisp white and frothy horsehair, being marched towards the cells.

The Superintendent scribbled. 'You are to be released today on licence.' He looked at the solicitor's letter again, paused and got up into the half-squat again and stuck out his hand.

'You know what my advice to you is, Browning?'

I gripped his smooth, oily-feeling hand in mine which was roughened by hard work. 'Tell me, sir.'

'Join the army, young man. Join the army.'

6

I was surprised by the cool reception I got from my fellow inmates after I was marched back to my cell. Barton turned his back on me and a couple of the others growled like animals.

'I say, Barton,' I said, 'I'm getting out.'

'Judas.'

'What's that? August? No, now. Today.'

'You sold him out, didn't you? You smarmy scab. If I was younger I'd split you up the middle. You better be getting out, you wouldn't last long in here.'

I saw it then. They thought I'd informed on Farnol. 'But look,' I gabbled, 'I didn't . . . I mean, they came and got me before I . . .'

'Good plan,' Barton said, still with his head turned. 'Worked. When did you say you were getting out? You better hope it's before evening muster.'

I sat shivering in the cell. I'd have sworn I could hear the scraping of metal on stone as makeshift knives were sharpened. I stirred myself to gather my few things together – they'd allowed us to use our own shaving tackle and I had a book on card-playing techniques that I used to carry around with me. Farnol's meagre possessions were on his bunk and I idly turned over the pages of a tattered copy of the *Strand*.

'Don't rob him as well,' Barton snapped.

'As if I would!' But I dropped the magazine. 'Where is he, anyway?'

'Solitary, where else?'

'Did you mean that? I'm in danger here?'

He chuckled and turned. His eyes were bright in his drink-blotched face. 'And outside too. The word'll get around, believe you me.'

'You mean . . . in Sydney?'

'And elsewhere.'

This was terrible. I didn't fancy the idea of looking over my shoulder every step I took along Pitt Street, or being afraid to take off my pants in Kate Leigh's[6] in case some low-life wanted to make a reputation. Barton was watching me with a smile splitting his ravaged face. *He's ragging me, surely*, I thought.

'Er, Barton . . . how about Newcastle?'

His shout of laughter brought on a one minute coughing fit. When he recovered he stuffed shag in his foul clay pipe and tried to hold the match steady over the bowl. 'Worst place of all for someone like you.' He drew his hand sharply across his throat. 'Toughs everywhere, razor men.'

'Jesus!'

'Only thing for you, boyo, and I tell you this because I suppose you can't help being a coward and a weakling, is to go bush.'

Now, contrary to what you may have heard, not all Australians like the bush or feel at home in it. I detest it myself – nasty grey drab stuff, full of snakes and nothing to drink. My idea of the countryside is the Bois de Boulogne or Central Park without the muggers. But what choice did I have? Alive in the bush would be better than dead in the city, just.

I put a brave face on it, did some scoffing for Barton's benefit and to cheer myself up. It was only after they'd conducted me from the cell that I thought I should have left some sort of note for Farnol. I resolved to write to him when I reached safety (I never did, write, that is).

The release procedure was pretty simple – a strip wash (although I'd already had one that day), down some stairs to an airless basement where I signed a paper and received two pamphlets – one on the evils of drink and another arguing the case for conscription in Australia. The latter was a piece of freelance propagandising by the store-master who winked at me as he handed over my clothes and a letter bearing the solicitor's name stamp. Inside was the magnificent sum of five pounds. There was a note in the envelope, not written by 'Wild Bill' of course; I was never sure that he *could* write, but from Dunstan or Houghton advising me to proceed to Newcastle at once. I tore it up.

Newcastle lay to the north. I walked out of Long Bay prison and turned my thoughts south. I had a vague ac-quaintance with the Illawarra district to the south of Sydney, having spent some of the last summer there in the company of a publican's widow at Coalcliff. The name sounds unsalubrious enough and indeed the miners of the south coast are rough fellows, as miners are everywhere. But mines, after all, are underground, and the hotel at Coalcliff is poised on a headland overlooking a fine beach and a splendid sea. I had visited the hotel on my wine and spirit selling duties, fallen in with the bereaved Kitty Neilson, who was gamely struggling to carry on, and so found myself a soft billet.

I'd managed to convince old Robespierre that the south coast was promising and needed a locally based man to explore it. (All twaddle, of course; the miners thought beer was the only drink worth swallowing and the farmers thought the same. The only other inhabitants of con-sequence were God-fearing folk who seemed to fear liquor about equally with God. There was, I'll admit, a priest or two with a nose for port but that was a limited market.)

43

Nevertheless, I bunked in with the consolable Mrs Neilson, toured the district a bit in her fine buggy, and learned the lie of the land. I'd had to depart rather smartly, it must be said – a combination of a summons from Robespierre, who measured success only in order forms, and pressure from Kitty who'd taken to making remarks like 'I know I don't look my age and you are such a mature-looking man, Richard.'

It wouldn't be so bad. I could hop a train to Nowra and pick up a job on one of the dairy farms. Grow a beard, use a different name, and lie low for a while until any threat from Long Bay died down. Humping my two bags, I set off towards the nearest tram stop. I'm an optimist first and last – I might be able to get into Wollongong and see a fight or two, have a bet. Then there was Kitty just up the line . . . no, that was *too* optimistic.

Miss Select had overlooked two halfpence in the bottom of my bag; I used this to get me to the Central Railway terminus where I bought a ticket to Nowra with a flourish of the fiver. Then heigh ho for the bar to wait, behind a newspaper and in a cloud of smoke, for the train.

Train journeys were not too bad in those days. The seats were comfortable and intact, and the floors were clean – not like the things we travel in nowadays. The train stopped too often to let on the second class riff-raff (I was travelling first) and so the trip was damnably slow. But with a paper and a good cigar and a flask of brandy from the bar, the time could be made to pass more or less pleasantly.

It was winter of course, and so we smokers closed up the carriage and let the fug build. What with the gas lamps alight and the foot warmers steaming, the carriage became hot and close. I finished the paper and dropped off to sleep. When I woke most of the travellers had got off and I found myself sitting opposite an elderly gent with a red face and fierce, bristling moustaches. He was staring at me oddly; I tried to avoid his eyes but they had a mad magnetism.

'I'm too old,' he spluttered.

'I beg your pardon.'

'I'm too old for the war. God, how I envy you. On leave are you? Glad to climb into the old mufti for a bit, eh?' He reached down for a walking stick, lifted it and shook it so hard it disturbed some of the fug. 'Christ, if only I could get a crack at the Hun. What's your unit?'

I looked at the waving stick and decided discretion was the better part of valour. I mumbled something and he inclined his head at me. He seemed to be about to ask me to repeat myself but thought better of it. 'Good, good. Fine troops. Couldn't help seeing the pamphlet fall from your pocket, you see.'

I looked at the seat and saw the conscription pamphlet lying beside me. The cover had a crude drawing of a furry creature with dripping teeth, wearing a spiked helmet.

'Oh, yes,' I said lamely, stuffing the pamphlet back.

'Slackers!' the madman boomed, producing spittle as he spoke. 'I'd brain them all!' Swish, swish went the stick. I felt suddenly panicked and a cramp gripped my right calf as sometimes happens when I get the wind up. I groaned and reached to massage the leg.

'I say, old chap, a wound?'

I mumbled something affirmative, collected my bags and hobbled out of the carriage. I heard him slam the stick on the spot where I'd been sitting and spit out the word 'Hun'. The seat would be awash. I stood in a draught at the end of the carriage and, for want of something better to do, I pulled out the pamphlet and squinted to read it in the faint, flickering gas light.

'What do you want?' the pamphlet called. (Well, I could answer that easily enough – warm bed, soft woman and good drink.) 'You want a strong Empire, a White Australia and FREEDOM from military despotism.' (I could go along with most of that.) 'You want the crushing of Germany and the liberation of Roumania and Serbia.' (Not so sure about that – Germans made damn good beer and I couldn't say I knew anything about the other two places at all.) It went on hammering away at those who said industry would collapse or the country be flooded with niggers, and praising Haig and Robertson as brilliant strategists who only needed a few million more men to make their plans succeed. I felt chilled and not by the cold south coast wind. The referendum on the conscription question was coming up in October; I wasn't old enough to vote but by God I'd be old enough in January to be sent to the trenches if the bloody thing passed.

7

Nowra was a small place, centre of a rich dairy district and much frequented by city swells in the summer months. There was a single span bridge over a handsome river and a glorious white beach where the women paraded in light summer dresses shaded by their parasols. In winter the township was muddy and could be cold, depending on the wind. The night I arrived was mild but threatening to rain. Straight to the Commercial Hotel I went, depleting the fiver still further, but determined to have one soft night before I began my period of rural seclusion.

I got a room at the back of the hotel and as far away as I could from the church in the main street. The last thing I wanted was to be woken by Sunday morning bells. If all went well I could probably judge my liquor intake so that I'd sleep through till midday. I was too late for dinner but they gave me some bread and soup in a small room beside the kitchen. Good enough to line the stomach before a few brandies, thought I, and I ordered a bottle of claret to help the bread down. I'd hardly tucked the napkin in when the maid set another place at the little table and a big, red-faced fellow plonked himself down beside me. I nodded to him and started on the soup.

Without so much as a by your leave, he picked up the bottle and read the label.

'Think I'll have the same,' he said. 'Could be a long night.'

I pricked up my ears at that. I was tired but talk of a long night will always get at least a hearing from Browning. 'It's one of the better domestics,' I said, not too warmly.

He grunted and gave the order to the maid when she brought his dinner. He ate noisily and I would have been put off my food, being a bit sensitive that way, if I hadn't been so hungry and this my first meal in freedom. As a wine drinker I wasn't in his class; the level of his bottle stayed inches below that of mine. He also finished eating first, sighed and wiped his face with the napkin.

'Mind if I smoke?'

'No,' I said, still chewing bread and thinking about taking the rest of the wine up to my room. Perhaps I *was* too tired for a long night of whatever sort.

'Have one.' He put a cigar beside my plate and helped himself to another glass of wine – mine. 'You look like a sporting cove. Down for the fight?'

'Fight?'

'Shhh, man, it's a hush-hush affair.'

'Why?'

He waved his cigar. 'Wowsers are down on the game, reckon it's keeping fit fellows out of the war. Damn the war. Anyway, ask me a chap'd be safer in France than in the ring with Moffat.'

I lit the cigar and looked enquiringly at him. 'Don't know Moffat? Well, local reputation, I suppose. He's from around here, bowled them all over he has, all weights. They say he beat Hughie Dwyer[7] – unofficial, of course.'

I nodded. 'Not too many have done that.'

'No. Well, Dwyer worked around here at one time,

might be something in it.'

'And this Moffat is fighting here, tonight?'

'Mmmm, some blackfellow. Said to have a punch.'

We finished off the claret and fell to talking about fights the way men will, and the upshot was he invited me to attend the fight with him. I mentioned something about brandy and we managed to squeeze in a tot or two before we took off.

My companion was a Mr Ryan who had a large dairy farm near the town of Berry, a little to the north of Nowra, and extensive interests in the area besides – fruit canning, commercial fishing and the like. I learned this in the bar over the brandies before we got into his Buick which appeared to be only marginally older than Les Darcy's.

'And you are . . .?' Ryan said as he started the car.

I gave him the name I'd used to register at the hotel. 'Hughes, sir. William Hughes.'

We drove out along a rutted road to a rambling building with high chimneys which was surrounded by a high post and rail fence.

'Abandoned brick factory,' Ryan explained. 'Ideal spot, good solid floor, fit a lot of people in and easy to post a few watches around the fence.'

The word had certainly got around; there were plenty of miners present as well as farm labourers and wharf workers as well as a fair number of the better class of people. Some of the rougher types inspected the Buick suspiciously but Ryan was given the thumbs up by a lantern-carrying fellow who was stationed on the track that led from the fence to the factory. There were a few other cars pulled up in a row, all pointing back down the track. Ryan manoeuvred his car into a similar position.

'Everyone looks nervous,' I said, feeling it.

'Troubled times, Hughes. This could be interpreted as

49

riotous assembly under these blasted wartime regulations.' He gave a tobacco and brandy-laden snort. 'They might call the troops out.'

The line of men, huddled down into their coats against a light drizzle, waited at a wide, iron-barred door. Ryan puffed his cigar, checked his half-hunter and nodded with satisfaction when the door swung open.

'On time,' he said. 'Good organisation. Should mean the coppers've been seen to.'

'Good,' I said. I had no wish to be behind bars so soon after my release.

We paid two shillings at the door, received a cardboard disc in return and trooped into a large room lit by hurricane lamps. A ring had been set up in the centre and there were a couple of rows of chairs around it for the disc holders; the others, who had paid less, stood.

Ryan and I had a swig from the flask; we both had cigars going and there were pipe and cigarette men among the crowd so that the room soon became thick with smoke.

'Right atmosphere for a stoush,' Ryan said. 'Reminds me of the old bare knuckle days. Real fights, then.'

I nodded. I'd been bored to tears by tales of the bare knuckle days by 'Wild Bill' and others. Glove fights were real enough for me; too real, sometimes.

The noise mounted with the smoke. A few shouts and scuffles from the hoi polloi indicated that Ryan and I weren't the only well-oiled ones. After a bit, Moffat and his opponent pushed through the throng accompanied by their handlers. A tall, thin man with a drooping moustache and sleek, oiled-down hair followed them into the ring. He was wearing a white shirt and a black waist-coat which he revealed by taking off his jacket. This also revealed a pistol strapped under his armpit.

'Referee,' Ryan said.

Moffat was a fair, fattish man in his thirties. His legs looked spindly under the loose trunks and the flesh bobbed about on his upper body as he moved. The Aboriginal was thin and hard with a wide, flashing smile and a bounciness to everything he did. He hung on to the ropes and bounced, bounced again while the referee was inspecting the gloves and kept bouncing as the announcements were made. Moffat, by contrast, was perfectly still.

'Can't say I think much of Moffat,' I said.

Ryan shot me a sideways glance. 'We'll see.'

'Any chance of a schlenter?'

Ryan shook his head vigorously. 'That's why he's got the gun. You wouldn't care for a small wager, Mr Hughes?'

The thought of a few more pounds in my pocket was attractive; the longer I could put off the evil day on which I had to go to work the better. 'Perhaps,' I said. 'Let's watch a round or two first.'

The room was full to bursting; there were a few dark faces dotted among the crowd but most were loud, swearing, sweating, spitting white men. I'd heard that there were a couple of women at the Burns-Johnson fight at Rushcutters Bay seven years before (I'd love to have gone but I was too young); all I can say is they would have been sadly out of place in the Nowra brick factory that night. Would've fainted most likely; what with the smoke and the brandy I felt a little dizzy myself.

Moffat seemed to be completely over the hill while the black was just reaching his prime. The fat man was blotched with blood and panting hard after two rounds.

'A pound on Moffat,' Ryan proposed.

I looked at the other corner; the black was sitting comfortably on his stool and giving his cornerman nothing to do. He'd hardly raised a sweat and was unmarked. 'Make it five,' I said.

'Done.'

I was comforted by the other wagers I heard being made; the odds on Moffat I calculated were three to one

51

on. There's nothing I like better than beating the odds.

The pattern of the fight stayed the same for another three rounds and changed abruptly in the sixth. The Aboriginal seemed to become a little arm-weary from throwing so much leather. Moffat hit him in the bread basket and dropped him – the first knockdown of the fight. It occurred to me that I hadn't seen Moffat stagger once under the peppering he'd had. The darkies in the crowd shuffled their feet and went quiet, so did all the men who'd bet against their race. The black got up and saw out the round.

Ryan lit another cigar. 'This round,' he said.

He was right. Moffat moved no faster but he hadn't lost an ounce of strength. He was suddenly like a solid old tree, resisting winds and flood. After the middle of the round he brushed aside a long left and moved in close.

Ugh! The black's grunt could be heard above the noise as Moffat's right sank into his hard belly. He bent and swayed, still game, but Moffat battered him down with short punches. He hit the floor hard enough for me to feel it shake three rows back and lay still. The referee counted him out and raised Moffat's hand.

'Good man,' Ryan said as we pushed through the crowd to the car.

'Yes.' Ryan drove fast along the dark track; I contemplated jumping out but there was that dark, threatening bush all around and a broken leg would make me a sitting duck if any Long Bay avengers were around. 'I can't pay you the five, Mr Ryan. Not after I settle up at the hotel.'

Ryan took one hand off the steering wheel and clapped my shoulder. 'That's all right, my boy,' he boomed. 'You can work it off.'

So events more or less took the course I'd planned although I hadn't anticipated working for a couple of months for no wages nor some of the other pressures that were brought to bear. In a sense I was lucky to be working for Ryan because, as a passionate Irish nationalist, he had no use for the war or conscription. It was infernally boring to have him quote Archbishop Mannix[8] at me all the time. 'What difference could ten or twenty thousand Australians more make in an army of fifteen million?' Ryan would say and I'd nod as I milked the hundredth cow of the morning or tore another inch from my hide rooting out blackberries.

There were a fair number of Fenians around the Berry district and they protected their workers from the assaults of conscriptionists and Hun-haters. (Of course, I had more than a suspicion that the Fenians would have welcomed a German victory over England, which was going a bit too far, and it was certainly in their interests to keep their labourers on the farm with their backs bent. Ideals usually have a practical foundation, in my experience.)

The work was hard, the hours were long, the pay was non-existent, but there were compensations. There was the abundant good food, the occasional booze-up with Ryan, and there was what we'd now call a significant fringe benefit in the package. I mean Katie. By Christ, I had to go carefully there. Katie Ryan was eighteen, built like a music-hall dancer with long legs, a tiny waist and a super-structure that made you blink to make sure you weren't dreaming. She had green eyes and a mass of red hair that somehow, I don't know why and I never struck this in any other woman, helped you to think of her naked. The result of that of course was acute embarrassment, strained britches and funny walks.

You might think it odd that a man would import a young bull like me to work on a farm where his comely daughter was the only young female for miles around. It wasn't really; farm labour was in short supply for one thing and Ryan was so pickled in booze and obsessed by farming that I think he'd forgotten all about the baser passions. He only had one child after all, which was very rare for a Mick. But what a child!

She used to hang around me while I was working and I was never sure whether it was the labour that was making me sweat or something else. On the crucial day, a few weeks after my arrival, I was digging a hole for a fence post a furlong or more from the farmhouse. Katie came sauntering along through the grass; she was barefoot, holding her shoes and stockings in her hand. She sat on a tussock of grass and watched me.

'William,' she said.

'Miss?'

'How is it that you have the manners of a gentleman and the hands of a labourer? Papa says it was the first thing he noticed about you and what made him think that you might be a good worker.'

That was interesting; it sounded as if the old bastard might have set me up. The thought induced a slight change in my attitude towards his daughter. 'Well, Miss,' says I, 'I've done a lot of things. Been a sailor for one, that's hard work for the hands, but worth it, to go round the Horn . . .'

Her eyes gleamed as she looked at me. I've always had a talent for constructive lying which basically consists in not elaborating too much. I let the words tail off and gave her one of my hard, manly looks. I'd grown my moustache back and must have looked quite the gentleman pioneer in white shirt open to the waist and new moleskins which Ryan had given me. 'I'd give a lot to see the green water reflected in your eyes,' I said.

I'll swear she shivered. 'I was thinking of a picnic on the beach. Would you like that?'

I'd hardly thought of anything else but getting her into a barn or a bed since I'd clapped eyes on her. A beach would do fine, but how?

54

'How?'

'Mama and Papa are going into Wollongong tomorrow to visit a friend in hospital. I'm supposed to be having piano lesson at midday but I happen to know that the teacher is sick and won't be here.'

Scheming minx, thinks I, but the mechanics of seduction have never interested me all that much so I was happy for her to do that part of the work. I straightened up, took off my hat and mopped my brow. It was late September and a very warm day already.

'When are they going?'

'Early.'

'What of the others?' I meant the house servants and the two other farmhands.

She shrugged. 'What of them? I can deal with Cook and Bessie.'

I sank the bar into the hard ground. 'Tomorrow it is, then.'

It must have been nearly the last day in September and it dawned warm and bright the way days do on the south coast of New South Wales. Dry too, not like this damn California damp. Katie and I set out for the beach in a trap and we bowled along the hilly roads to the sea in fine style. I almost thought that she might have done this sort of thing before from the way she took roads that skirted the fronts of farmhouses and hung back at crossroads to be sure the coast was clear.

The beach was long and white with high dunes at the back, topped with thick stands of waving grass. We tramped along parallel to the Pacific for a bit until we found a dune with a gently sloping, deeply grooved back. Here we settled – blanket, basket, bottle of wine, umbrella and broad-brimmed hat, and pulses racing.

She sidled across closer to me on the blanket and put her hand on my arm. 'William,' says she, 'I want it!'

'Ah.'

'I don't want to marry a south coast farmer and hear

about cows all the days of my life. I want to be like . . . like Lola Montez.'

'Dead, I think.'

'You know what I *mean*! I want to feel passion and despair. I want to live!'

I suppose the honourable thing to do would have been to tell her not to be silly, and to point out the admirable features of the farmers' sons around Berry. I'm sure I could have come up with some if I'd put my mind to it. But I'm afraid that, after three or four months' deprivation, the sight of that red, open mouth and those enormous knockers was too much for me. I eased her back on to the blanket and proceeded to work on her with tongue and hands. But she was inquisitive and eventually I satisfied her curiosity. She was a virgin and I hurt her.

When I'd finished I rolled gently off and rested above her, half raised up on my elbow.

'Well, Miss,' I said, 'you're more like Lola Montez now than you were.'

She gazed up at me with what I took to be adoration. I gave her a light kiss on the lips.

'Is it better the second time?' she said.

8

The next few days are as fresh in my mind as yesterday, maybe fresher. If you've ever conducted an illicit liaison, or better still two illicit liaisons, you'll know what I mean: notes hidden under rocks, brushed hands and violent couplings in the time available. I don't know much about Lola Montez, they say she was a sprightly type with a fancy to do it in riding boots, well, although Katie Ryan wasn't quite like that, she had no objection to trying something new. Although she was a novice and I'd been hanging around whore houses since I was sixteen, we worked out a new wrinkle or two. (I've long been of the opinion that imaginative free love tops the bill, with commercial sex second and the conjugal act a distant third.)

We had to be careful because, although Ryan may have been deaf and blind in these matters, his good lady certainly was not. Looking back, it's possible that she may have had a fancy for me herself but matters never came to that. (I wouldn't have minded, she was a well-fleshed Irishwoman with the eyes she'd passed on to her daughter.) Katie and I cavorted whenever we got the chance, usually late at night, which meant that I went about my daytime duties in an exhausted daze. Ryan got less and less value from me and he may have been as glad as I was that our arrangement was drawing to a close. I hadn't told Katie a word about it of course. I meant to be off one fair morning, perhaps leaving her a note. (I never did write the note.)

That's not how it turned out. Ryan and I calculated that my bondage would end on 21 October and I agreed to stay on for an extra few weeks, to complete some fencing he was preparing to accommodate spring lambs. A week or two more of Katie was all right with me and, tanned and moustachioed as I was and with a bit of extra beef on me, I felt that it might be safe to drift back to Sydney. There hadn't been a whiff of any Long Bay trouble during my sojourn at Berry, and if Dunstan and Houghton had nowhere to send their letters that was their bad luck – I was damn sure there wouldn't be any more fivers enclosed.

Things went on agreeably with Katie and me going at it like fury and me trying to keep a little energy for the daytime now that Ryan was actually paying me wages. We were nearly rumbled one night by Mrs R. who went looking for her darling girl and stumbled into a bucket we'd positioned to forestall just such an event. She swallowed a story about Katie hearing a lamb bleating fit to rend the heart, or appeared to, but I fancy she eyed me all the harder after that. It was a close call and Katie and I went even more carefully.

A week or so into my time on wages and the conscription referendum came off. People came into the Nowra school and other public halls and there was nothing else talked about or written about in the papers. Ryan had been opposed to the plebiscite because he was sure it would pass.

'It'll come in, mark my words,' he said, as we worked on the fence for the lamb paddock.

I grinned at him. 'Australian women won't send their sons off,' I pointed to the animals, 'like lambs to the slaughter.'

58

'Will they not? My wife is in favour, for one.'

'That's all right for her, with all respect, Mr Ryan. She doesn't have a son.'

'There's plenty do that will vote yes.'

His conviction was beginning to alarm me. 'The unions are against it, I hear.'

Ryan spat on the dry earth. 'Unions!' He wasn't a democratic man.

That night I lay in the barn with Katie and a shiver ran through me as I thought of the mud of France. A one-legged veteran had spoken of it in the pub.

'Are you cold, poor lamb?'

I jerked away at the word. 'No, I'm not cold. What d'you think of all this conscription business, Katie?'

She kissed my ear. 'I'm sure I don't understand a word of it.'

I stared at her; her bodice was open and that usually took care of all the staring that needed to be done, but this time I was looking at her round, guileless face, and it was as if I was seeing it for the first time in its true shape. 'Do you mean to say that you don't know what the conscription debate is all about?'

'Not an earthly,' she said. 'Well, it's about going into the army, isn't it? I think you should, William. You'd look divine in uniform.'

After that, I found I could face the prospect of parting with Katie quite manfully. The conscription issue began to obsess me. I found myself thinking about it as I went about my work as previously I'd thought of Katie. One thing I was sure about in regard to my future – I wanted to have one, not to die in a ditch like a dog fighting for the temporary possession of some god-forsaken Frog village.

As always, when under stress, whether afraid or not, I turned to alcohol for comfort. I took to walking into Berry to spend part of my evenings in the pub. (I was incapable with Katie one night after a drinking session which just shows you how deep my need for comfort was.) Conscription was the main subject of conversation, together with casualty lists and talk of white feathers. It was hard to get a chat going about boxing or horses or any more cheerful topic. One old boozer in particular, a white-bearded soak named St James something or something St James, I never did find out which, professed expertise in matters military.

'Take heed, young Hughes,' he belched at me one night. 'The conscripts are in for a terrible time.'

'How d'you mean?'

'Cannon fodder they'll be, nothing more. The volunteers will become officers, rapid promotions there'll be and the conscripts will be lambs to the . . .'

'Slaughter,' says I. 'Why d'you say that?'

He rubbed his scarlet, drink-swollen nose with a none-too-clean forefinger. 'I've served in Her Majesty's forces. Served Queen Victoria, sir! Seen it often. Mark me, wise men will volunteer before this draft begins.'

'You think "yes" will win, then?'

'Nothing surer. British bulldogs breed their pups to fight. Another?'

Despite myself, I continued to talk to this Jeremiah right up to the day before the result of the referendum would be known. He put the wind up me completely with stories of the shattered limbs of shock troops while staff officers swanned about behind the lines trying to keep mud off their boots. By this time I had finished working for Ryan and was staying a night or two in the pub while I pondered my next move. Another reason for my continued presence was Katie: she had a yen to make love in a bed and was working on a plan to get to my room late at night. I confess I wanted to see that copper mane spread on a pillow.

On the day before the result of the vote was to be known I was drunk by mid-morning in the company of

St James. He breathed rum and beer over me and fear into my soul.

'Catch the train to Wollongong and join up,' he said. 'I shouldn't wonder if you weren't commissioned by Christmas. Tomorrow will be too late, lad.'

Befuddled and fearful, I collected my belongings and boarded the train. I still wasn't sure whether to go through with it or not when I reached Wollongong and I thought the matter over in several hotels until a sensible course of action became clear. I would join up, contrive to stay in Australia, gain a commission and see out the war in a safe billet. No medals for Browning, but no missing limbs either. (It was a mad plan, of course, owing more to rum than grey matter.)

I marched off to the recruiting centre in Crown Street and joined a line leading to a fat sergeant who sat behind a desk smoking a pipe. Drunken fool that I was, I attempted a salute. He sneered at me and pulled across a form.

'Name?'

'William Hughes.' God knows what made me say it.

'Any proof of that?'

I produced a reference letter Ryan had given me.

'Age?'

'Twenty-two, no, three.'

'You look it, some don't. Can you ride, shoot, lift a hundredweight and swim?'

'Yes, but . . .'

'See the M.O.' He pushed the form at me, pointed down a corridor and used the stem of his pipe to wave me away and beckon the next man forward.

The men outside the Medical Officer's room were less nervous than me and more sober. When my turn came I was inspected from toenails to scalp. Six feet two and a half inches I measured and I tipped the scales at twelve stone seven pounds.

'Just right for Carpentier,' the M.O. said. I smiled at him uneasily and was about to mention my private school education when he prised my jaws apart and looked at my teeth. He banged my chest (forty-two inches) and stuck his finger up my arse.

'Fine young man,' he said. 'Your urine would be fifty per cent alcohol but a good route march'd take care of that.' He slammed a stamp on my form. 'See the sergeant.'

The sergeant put the form into a folder and spoke around his pipe without looking at me. 'Report at 1600 hours to Captain Thorndike at the railway station. Failure to report will constitute a breach of military discipline punishable by imprisonment. Dismiss!'

'But, sergeant . . .'

'Next.'

The man behind dug me in the ribs with his elbow and I stumbled off to pick up my bags which, I later discovered, were lighter by a pair of boots – pilferer's paradise, the army was. There was nothing for it then but to seek comfort in the tried and tested way. I did this for a few hours while I mulled over the idea of not turning up for Captain Thorndike. But there's something about the army, and it was operating on me already although I'd only been on the books for a few hours, that stamps out disobedience before it takes root. Two glasses and I was thinking rebelliously, four and I was ready to turn up at 1555 hours – perhaps drink is anti-rebellion too, if taken in sufficient quantity.

I consoled myself with the thought that I'd at least avoided being conscripted and had lined myself up with the volunteers. Six glasses and I was standing in line wearing my lieutenant's insignia, being fitted for a swagger stick and ready to push the lower orders around. I bought a flask and wobbled off to the railway station. Here I met a few other chaps in a similar condition, spiritually and alcoholically. I always seemed to fall in with the lowest company in these situations, through no fault of my own. We held an impromptu party while we waited for Captain Thorndike.

My spirits fell when I saw him, even looking through the pink, boozy haze. His nickname, as I later learned, was 'Spit', short for spit and polish. Men spat when he passed, but only *after* he'd passed. He was under the middle height but compensated by holding himself very upright and tilting his head even further. He had a neat moustache and wore a uniform which even my glazed eye could see put those in the recruiting office to shame.

'Men,' he roared, two feet from my face, 'fall in!'

None of us had the remotest idea what he meant but Spit showed us with little swishes of his stick.

'Touch me with that and I'll break it across your bloody head,' one of my drinking mates said.

'And I'll shove the pieces up your bloody arse,' Thorndike replied.

The speaker fell in.

We stood, a motley dozen or so, in a ragged line while Thorndike told us we were travelling to the Liverpool army camp for basic training.

'Haven't got a ticket,' one of the better-oiled among us said.

'A wag, eh?' Thorndike said, and, believe it or not, 'Wag' stuck as this man's nickname until a mortar shell hit him in the head in France. 'You don't need tickets; you don't need anything except a pair of ears and a pair of feet. You're in the army now.'

Night fell; we waited for hours, boarded the train and chuffed off towards Sydney. It was a long, slow journey and we had an interminable wait at Redfern station, outside Sydney, until we could trans-train for Liverpool. Thorndike had gone off to travel first class leaving the rest of us on the hard, slatted seats which we softened with generous doses of rum. Every man among us seemed to have provided the same medicine. Eventually the rum ran out and we slept in fits and starts. It was just past dawn when we pulled into Liverpool. I felt dreadful, as if I'd been eating mud all night and sleeping out in the rain.

We assembled on the platform and a trolley came past loaded with the early editions of the newspapers. I held my tilting head in my hands and strained to read a front page. Suddenly, everything started to spin and I heard someone say: 'He's fainting. Catch him!' The print on the page grew to enormous size in my brain: CONSCRIPTION LOST! NO – 1,160,033; YES – 1,087,557.[9]

9

Liverpool was the first of several army camps I spent time in. I won't say that one was better than another – they are all terrible in different ways. We marched to the camp from the railway. It seemed like ten miles but was probably five. I was fit after the farm work but drained by the drinking of the day before and the disappointment of the morning. Also I *had* fainted or very nearly and slogging along a dusty road carrying two bags under a climbing sun was not what the doctor ordered.

I felt very poorly when we arrived and looked forward to breakfast, a sit down and a smoke. No such luck; we'd missed breakfast which was at 7am and I suppose, looking back, it was lucky they didn't put us straight on parade and make us double around the ground with our bags at the port. But they decided to make us look like soldiers first, so we were detailed to receive our kit from the QM. We lined up at a long shed and waited. Two hours later the QM arrived smelling of beer. I had a raging thirst and would have done anything for an ale. As it was I waited in the hot sun to be issued with a slouch hat, singlet, shirt, woollen vest, jacket, socks and boots that would have befitted a trip to the south pole. *This must be the hundredweight mentioned by the sergeant*, I thought.

The next few hours are a painful, khaki blur of metal bunks, rough blankets, wooden floors and tin plates combined with a dry, carbolic smell that rises in my nostrils to this day whenever I see an army uniform. I remember only one thing about it and that is that I acquired the cigarette habit. We were shuffled about, made to stand and wait, given some water but nothing else and I'd run out of cigars. Seeing my miserable state one of my comrades took pity on me and rolled me a smoke.

'Here you go, mate,' he said as he handed it to me. 'You look like you need something and there's bugger-all else around.'

'Thanks.' He lit the cigarette and I drew on it. It wasn't too bad. He stuck out a big, freckled hand.

'Jack Henderson's the name.'

We shook. 'William Hughes.'

'Yeah. Good on you, Bill.'

I smoked the cigarette down to a tiny stub and I got papers and tobacco of my own at the first opportunity. I've smoked cigarettes every day of my life since (except when illness, poverty or physical constraint have stopped me). I must have smoked several million of the things, coughed a few million times and felt like death on five thousand mornings. If Jack Henderson were here now I'd cut his throat.

They did parade us in the afternoon and a sergeant screamed at us while a corporal snapped at our heels like a sheep dog. I was coming out of my haze and wishing I wasn't. The dust from the parade ground blinded and choked me, the boots ripped my feet to shreds. I was sorry for every lie I'd ever told, and every mean deed, and I'd have sworn off women and drink for life to be allowed to go back to Long Bay.

Somehow I got through to 5pm when they herded us into a hot, airless hall and fed us on dry bread and stew with black tea. I shovelled the stuff in ravenously, not tasting it. Henderson, sitting beside me, ate slowly and deliberately. When I'd gulped down enough to stop my stomach rumbling I became conscious of his watching me.

'You look like a man getting more than he bargained for, Bill.'

'That's right.'

'Let me guess – you thought the referendum would bring in conscription and you joined up at the last minute so as to be a volunteer.'

'How did you know?'

'Doesn't take much to work out. There's a few around in the same boat, generally flash chaps like you, if you don't mind me saying so.'

I was depressed at the thought that my misfortune didn't even have the merit of being unique. 'Not much I can do about it if I do mind, is there?'

'Don't take it like that. We've got to have a talk.'

The tea bucket passed down the table and Henderson grabbed my cup and ladled it, as well as his own, half full. Then he bent down under the table for a minute; when he brought the cups up the level of the dark brown liquid had risen. I took a swig and felt the rum burn down my throat into my stomach.

'Ooh, that's good. Thanks, Henderson.'

'Call me Jack.'

'What brought you into the army today?'

'To get away from my missus and the pay. Also, I've got a mind to see a bit of the world, haven't you?'

'Yes,' I'd answered instinctively and I realised it was true. I *did* want to travel but I didn't want to see the world through a hail of shot and shell.

'That's the ticket. This is the way to do it for free. But look, have you noticed anything about this mob we've landed in?'

I hadn't; my eyes had either been closed, full of dust or concentrated on the ground in front of my aching feet.

I was dimly aware that the torture had been in the company of twenty or so others, but I'd scarcely looked at them. I shook my head and sipped gratefully at the rum-laced tea. I was starting to feel better and I accepted another cigarette from Henderson.

'They're all little blokes, or medium at best. You 'n me are the two biggest men in the squad and we're much of a muchness.'

I glanced at him; our shoulders were on a level but he was a little broader and thicker through than me. 'You're right,' I said, 'but what . . .?'

'It always happens, the two biggest men have to fight it out to see who's top dog. I've been through it a dozen times on the job, on the wallaby, everywhere.'

'Ah, yes.'

'Now, seems to me there's no point in our beating each other's brains out for the amusement of the shorties. What d'you reckon.'

I looked at his hard knuckles and the cords of muscle in his wrists. I nodded.

'Let's throw in together, divide up what's going.'

'What *will* be going?'

'Lots of things – there'll be two-up and cards to run, there'll be a black market of some sort, various lurks. Are you on?'

I nodded, vigorously this time. 'You bet, Jack.'

That was the way things went and it did help to mitigate the misery. Jack had been perfectly correct; others (especially the NCOs who, I suppose, were trying to run a divide and rule policy) did try to force us into conflict but they gave up when they saw we weren't having any. It suited me; I shuddered to think what Jack could have done to me with the pile driver punches those sloping shoulders and tree trunk arms could have delivered.

'Spit' Thorndike was in command of the section of three twenty-man platoons that lived, worked and sweated side by side. Each platoon had a sergeant and a corporal and the arrangement was that one of the recruits would be promoted to Lance Corporal after three months' training. Jack winked when he conveyed this news, which he'd picked up from Thorndike's orderly, to me.

'Guess who the lance jack's going to be in this outfit?'

I sighed. 'You, Jack, who else?'

'Not me, you.'

'Christ, why?'

'You're doing very well in all this training, didn't you know that?'

In fact I didn't; I was so tired at the end of the day that I fell into my bunk and slept dreamlessly. But I was a naturally good rifle shot and was built big and strong enough to take all the marching. I had good eyes so I could clean webbing and polish boots to everyone's satisfaction and my ears were keen enough to hear the commands that were shouted at me. There didn't seem to be much more to it.

'You've got it, Bill,' Henderson said, rolling a smoke. 'I don't know what it is, haven't got it myself, but you look like a leader of men.'

'Me? I can hardly . . .'

'Look like, I said. That's what counts. 'Course, you've got me to back you up.'

I rolled a smoke too and he looked at me shrewdly as he lit us up. 'I look and sound like a bloody bushie, which I am,' he said. 'You look and sound like a gentleman.'

'Which I'm not.'

We both laughed.

'Well, I'll go along with it, Jack. I suppose it's in line with what we've been doing up to now.'

'That's right. Got a few bob out of it, haven't you?'

Indeed I had. The camp had been virtually empty before we arrived and although more recruits came in the weeks that followed our group had the advantage of seniority, and Henderson had the authority within it. We ran the two-up school and took the house percentage, also the occasional big card game and controlled the trade in cigarettes which a lot of the men (myself included) preferred to the rubbing tobacco which was the only stuff available in the camp canteen. I'd spent a good deal of the proceeds on liquor and lost some on cards (even having the house percentage on your side can't compensate you for being an unlucky gambler), but I had some money saved.

Henderson and I talked business for a few minutes and then I asked him casually why the promotions were coming through in three months.

'Because that's when we're going to be sent overseas.'

My bowels suddenly loosened and I felt a twinge of cramp in my leg. I tried to look unconcerned about anything other than my cigarette ash. 'Sent where, d'you think?'

Jack shrugged. 'Search me – do you follow the war news?'

I didn't; the casualty lists depressed me nearly as much as the accounts of the glorious Aussie victories. I shook my head.

'Nor do I,' Jack said. 'I reckon most of what they print in the papers'd be lies. Egypt or France, I suppose.'

Sand and mud, I thought. *Wogs and Frogs, what a choice.*

'That'd probably mean London first,' I said. 'That'd be worth seeing.'

'Wouldn't it though. They say those London sheilahs are beauties.'

'You're a married man, Jack.'

'Not in London I wouldn't be.'

The weather got hotter and the training got more and more monotonous. Parade ground drill is the most boring thing I know, apart from burping babies. We marched, dug trenches, fought mock battles and marched some more. Ever since the Casula riot there'd been pretty strict controls on liquor in the camp and rigid military discipline generally. We got leave passes to go into Liverpool and Sydney but these visits lacked spice. Somehow the lectures we'd been given about VD in Europe and the Middle East took hold and made me cautious about sex. I stayed away from the street girls and didn't even visit Kate Leigh's. What I needed was a nice co-operative wife – someone else's – and army life made that hard to come by. I even missed Katie Ryan.

'Wag' Andersen provided a few laughs, such as when he glued together the pages of the minister's Bible and hymnal, and got a circus elephant to spend a night on the parade ground with the inevitable results. I enjoyed the shooting competitions because I excelled at it and got more 'possibles' than any other man in camp. Night sentry duty, latrine duty, and aquatic training were a misery which I only got through with the help of cigarettes and the booze Henderson brought in from the town.

The worst thing about it was the feeling of being fattened for the slaughter. Here we were, the prime of young Australian manhood, good eyes, good teeth, sound in wind and limb, being prepared to be turned into hamburger. I'd look along the ranks sometimes, or glance around the tent at night and I'd be reminded of that line of Shakespeare's from *Macbeth* about chaps getting into their graves like beds. [10] I'd shiver and take a tot of brandy. I suffered a little too when the others spoke of their families and sweethearts. I felt like an orphan and often took a drink on that account too.

I had a scare one day near the end of the training period. Among a new intake of recruits was a face I recognised. He was a big man, pock-marked and shaggy. After the camp barber had got to him with the clippers I knew who he was. With his hair cut much the way they cut it in Long Bay I recognised him as Lewis, a prisoner from the same cell block as my own. There weren't more than a few hundred men in the camp and it was impossible for me to go sneaking around to avoid him. He saw me at close quarters a few times and I saw a look pass across his brutalised face that indicated that his memory was trying to place me. I took Henderson aside one day and outlined the problem to him. Of course I lied about the details, claiming that I'd run foul of Lewis on the race-track – that he was a bookie's enforcer whom I'd outsmarted.

Henderson eyed Lewis from a distance. The ex-convict was stacking empty petrol drums, picking them up and carrying them around like milk bottles.

'I see your point, Bill. Wouldn't fancy a go in with him myself.'

'What should I do?'

'Simple enough, mate. Show 'im how good you can shoot.'

The promotions came through within a few days and I had the opportunity to put Jack's plan into operation. I had a word to the Corporal in Lewis' squad and planted the idea that his green as grass recruits should see some real army shooting.

Behold Browning on the rifle range, belly down, rifle up and the target at four hundred yards. Lewis was lined up with his comrades, a particularly unsavoury lot I thought them. They were scraping the bottom of the barrel by then.

'Lance Corporal Hughes will now demonstrate the accuracy of the Lee Enfield .303 rifle for us against a moving target.'

The target was a man-sized figure suspended from a line run between two trees at a height of about twenty feet. The figure was pulled for fifty yards along the line, bobbing and bouncing as it went. I hit it eight times.

'Lance Corporal Hughes will now shoot at a target at nine hundred yards distance.'

I scored a possible.

I don't know whether or not Lewis ever twigged to my identity but I certainly had no trouble from him and, like many of the others, he was dead before long anyway.

I would almost have enjoyed my period as a Lance Corporal in the camp had it not been for the looming departure overseas. Strutting about with a stripe on my sleeve, ordering others around and slacking myself was soup and nuts to me. I had Jack's authority to back me up too and, being basically an easy-going type, I didn't give offence to anyone really – no-one who mattered, anyway.

This near-idyll came to an end when Thorndike called a meeting of the NCOs. We assembled in a room next to the officers' mess; I could see white linen tablecloths and the light glinting on polished silver cutlery. The sight revived my former idea of winning a commission and getting an administrative job in some spot where the only lead was in the pencils. I resolved to pay close attention to Thorndike.

He was starched and polished like a shop dummy and held himself about as stiff. 'Men,' he said, 'we are to have the singular honour of joining the Third Division to fight the enemy in France.'

Believe it or not, the idiots sent up a rousing cheer which I hastened to join, hoping that my surprise hadn't been noticed.

'Embarkation is set for the 10th of the month, that is five days hence. You will be responsible for conveying this news to the men and organising an orderly departure from the camp. Further instructions will be issued between now and the 10th. Dismiss!'

They cheered again and off we trotted. I announced the tidings to the men in my unit after the afternoon parade and there was more cheering. Henderson was happy at the prospect of London and, I suspect, of shooting at his fellow man. One of the men had a camera and nothing would do but that we should line up outside the tents, fold our arms, look like heroes and be photographed.

'I want crossed rifles in the front row,' the photographer said. 'You blokes squat down and hold 'em. That's right. Pull yer sleeve around, Bill. I wanna see the stripe.'

We obliged him.

That night I noticed 'Wag' Andersen poring over a bundle of newspapers with a sheet of paper before him and a pencil travelling between the paper and his mouth. I asked him what he was doing.

'Do you know what job I did as a civilian, Bill?'

'No.'

'I was an accountant. Mad for figures, I am.' He rustled the newspapers. 'I've been doing a bit of work on these casualty lists they publish. Terrible aren't they?'

I gulped. 'Yes.'

'Found something interesting; breaking them down, y'see. Do you know what rank has the highest casualties?'

I shook my head.

'Lieutenant.'

'Ah.'

'Closely followed by Lance Corporal.'

10

Perhaps the meaning of the casualty lists had finally got through to people, perhaps it was the failure of the conscription referendum or maybe they were just sick of the war, but our send-off from the Woolloomooloo docks was less than tumultuous. There was no band that I recall and, although there were wives and sweethearts dealing out the tearful embraces, there was by no means enough of them to go around. When the ship pulled out a hell of a lot of chaps like me stood at the rail without any face to wave to, let alone a pretty one.

The troopship *Wisden* was a well enough founded vessel and the voyage wasn't too onerous, not comfortable mind you, there is no comfort in the army. We had been issued with the remainder of the gear for serving soldiers – greatcoats, tin hats, medicines and the like, and the stowing and packing and arranging of all this stuff so that it could be carried was an art to master. As well, I recall falling out of hammocks, parade and drill in small batches on the cramped deck and sea-sickness. I was spared this mercifully, but some of the men suffered terribly from it and one even died. He was buried at sea off the southern tip of Madagascar – the first of our number to die heroically for his country. As the canvas-wrapped body slid into the water I made a solemn vow that I would survive this madness at any cost.

The ship put in at Cape Town but we were allowed only brief shore leave and then in small, tightly controlled parties. It was my first landfall outside Australia and it was exotic enough, with blacks and Indians clustering about offering to sell things, including their sisters, and carry things, including ourselves. It was a noisy place but not cheerful; perhaps the pink-cheeked policemen strolling about with batons and pistols on their hips had something to do with that.

Back on board for the run to London, gambling fever took hold of the ship. I hardly saw Jack Henderson; he was too busy running two up and card games. I covered for his absence on parades, let him skip duties to catch up on sleep and generally earned my 25 per cent cut of his winnings. The men would bet on anything – when it would rain, how fast the ship was travelling, how many times round the deck made a mile. Jack backed me heavily in a shooting contest we held somewhere off the west coast of Africa. We shot at bottles bubbling along in the wake; I was in top form and Jack cleaned up. When we docked at Southhampton I had over five hundred pounds in my possession. God knows how much Jack had.

Within ten days he was broke. We were quartered in 'A' camp on the Salisbury Plain and leave passes to London were readily handed out while the authorities decided what to do with us. (The war was going badly; it was near the end of a bad winter in France with everything at a stalemate. 'Wag', who read all the papers and took what he called 'an intelligent interest in how and when I'm going to get my brains blown out', claimed that the top brass didn't know how to use the fresh troops.) Jack went to London and found his 'beauty' all right: she was a Cockney named Rose, a little slip of a thing in clown makeup and a hobble skirt and she took him for every penny.

As for myself, I was still cautious about the pox and decided to wait and work on my plan to become an officer. Officers, I felt sure, would have access to clean women. I went into London and drank with Jack and ate in the posh hotels (paying the bills myself once his money had run out) and gawking at the sights – the Tower, St Paul's, etc. It impressed me mightily but all places are the same when you're among the lower ranks and on foot. The only way to see a town is from an automobile with a chauffeur and while wearing tailored clothes.

At the camp they decided that we were inadequately trained by which they meant that we weren't trained in the English style. English officers were set over us to whip us into proper shape to be blown apart, but they didn't have much luck. I toadied to Captain Ambrose this and Major Algernon that in the hope of getting a leg up but when I saw how complete their contempt for colonials was, I lapsed into the slack, insubordinate ways of all the others.

Thorndike and the other Australian officers suffered similar slights so, all in all, we were a pretty discontented bunch when we got our orders to depart for France.

'At least the winter's over,' I said to Jack.

'Means a thaw,' he grunted. 'More mud.'

I was still trying to be cheerful. 'Wonderful wine over there.'

Jack spat. 'Wine! Haven't had a decent beer since leaving Australia.' Jack was never the same after his encounter with Rose.

Across the channel we went, more trains and marches until we joined up with the Third Division in the Somme Valley.

So much has been written about the war in France and I don't want to add to it. I was there for a year, excluding periods of leave: since then, at whatever I've done – mostly drinking, gambling, being bored to tears on film sets – memories of that year have only been just below the surface. Imagine being terrified for months, not smiling for weeks and not sleeping for days at a time and you'll have some idea of what it was like.

And I was a sniper naturally, so I didn't have the worst of it. You can be sure that I didn't see more than a few Germans in the whole time. The sniping post was sand-bagged and covered over; we shot using periscopes which we raised to see if there was any activity in the opposing trenches. Mostly I shot at German loopholes; it resembled clay pigeon shooting in that it was silly and loopholes weren't Germans as clay discs aren't pigeons.

'Going over the top' was out of vogue by this time but there were still raiding parties being sent out and men idiotic enough to volunteer for them. Jack Henderson went on many raids, not for the honour and glory but for the booty. Back he came, covered in blood but without a scratch on him, with his pockets filled with watches and rings, German money and other knick-knacks. He did a lucrative trade in Fritz rifles, bayonets and hats. Occasionally I gave Jack covering fire when he made a daytime sortie into no-man's land for a prize, and I was rewarded with tradeable Hun items. Still cautious on my London leaves, I spent little of the money I collected in France and carried a fair sum around with me in a money belt.

Our numbers were whittled down fast; by the end of 1917 only Henderson, myself and half a dozen others remained of our original intake. 'Wag' Andersen died of wounds he received while trying to pull a comrade off the wire; Thorndike was wounded and repatriated. Some men transferred to other units; I tried desperately to find a safer billet; I considered the signals, even the ambulance corps, but there were no safe spots. The sniping hole was as good as any although I suffered mightily from the cold in the winter of '17-'18.

By then few of us thought that the war would ever end; it seemed likely that the Germans would gain and lose inches of ground as we would and the game would go on for all eternity. Men lost their reason when the air around us was filled with whistling death and the ground beneath our feet shook. I wonder I retained mine. By far the craziest were the glory seekers who charged machine gun nests, next maddest were the patriots and after them the Christians. I saw a young Tasmanian infantryman pray to God to protect him only to have the prayer interrupted by a bullet through his throat. His mate, from the same town and church, took up the prayer.

Before an attack men would scribble frantically in their diaries or letterbooks. Once a man, who looked too old to be anywhere but at home by his fire, thrust a letter into my hands before he went on a raid. None of the party returned and the letter had no address so I kept it for years as a reminder of what a powerful force religion is in keeping the masses in order. I can quote from it from memory: 'I am ready in body and mind and spirit to die in this most just cause. This Christian cause. I am purified by my love for Jesus Christ who will surely protect and save me now and forever . . .' Then there was some blather about his mother.

I remember nothing of interest from the time except one incident in June of 1918. The unit . . . [At this point on the tape there is a sound of a bottle on the edge of a glass and Browning's voice becomes indistinct. It is probable that he was trying unsuccessfully to recall the number of his Brigade and taking a drink to help the process. No identifiable number comes through. Ed.] . . . near Cambrai, south of Valenciennes, taking part in a big British offensive along with some Canadians and Kiwis. The British laid down a heavy barrage and set off some mines that had been planted earlier. As always, I hung back playing an inspirational role as an organiser, message carrier and generally strutting around with a black patch over one eye. I had the nickname of 'Blackbeard' and as a sniper I was viewed as something of a star, like a quarterback, a valuable player and also one to be protected.

After the barrage had cut the wire and the British and Canadians had charged the trenches we followed, mopping up around the edges. Moving cautiously forward I came upon a shellhole about the size and depth of a California swimming pool. It was piled with corpses, mostly Canadians but some Germans and one or two British. Things were getting a bit hot in front so I stopped for a protected breather.

'I say . . .' I spun around with my rifle up but the voice came from a Canadian sergeant lying half under another man. He wriggled free and put both hands to his head and groaned. He was a small, slim man with a blackened face but I could see a finely shaped nose and a delicate-looking mouth.

'Are you hit?' I said.

'Don't think so.' He looked around the hole and closed his eyes.

'What?'

'That's everyone, the whole group.'

'What happened?'

'Shell.'

'Theirs or ours?'

He tried to grin but the movement caused him a spasm of pain and he held his head again. 'That's the stupidest question I've ever heard. It's like asking a man whether the bullet in his brain is a .45 or a .38.' He bunched his fist against his jaw. 'I'm forgetting my manners. This bloody war. Maybe you were making a joke. Were you?'

'I don't know,' I said. 'I don't feel much like joking.'

'D'you know you're the first Aussie I've ever met? I

think that's right. Hope you're not the bloody last. My name is Ray Chandler.[11] What's yours?'

'William Hughes.'

'Call me a medic will you, Hughes? There's a good chap.'

I scrambled out of the hole with no more intention of calling a medic than of painting a target on my chest, but I saw one treating a man with an eye injury close by and I told him about the Canadian in the shell hole. Many years later I met Chandler again in Hollywood; I didn't remind him of our first meeting. By then he spoke like an American, not an Englishman, but he was still a snooty son of a bitch.

Towards the end of that move forward towards a line of German trenches I did something that almost got me killed. There was an English major in charge of the movement and, for once, he was a cautious and sensible type. Several times I saw him hold men back, wait for a development up forward to clear the way and then move, with scouts out. He was my kind of officer and he had trouble controlling a hot-headed subaltern who was forever wanting to charge machine gun posts and clear trenches by means of the bayonet. He wanted to press men into this kind of service and you can bet I stayed well clear of him. It was near the end of the push, but with still some resistance to be overcome, that I saw a wounded German prop himself up on his elbow and take a bead on the admirable major. Against every instinct I stepped from behind the man I was carefully using as shelter and shot the German in the head. He gave a satisfactory squawk before he keeled over and the major and a few others saw what I'd done, even though I ducked back pretty quick behind the broadest body I could find.

We gained a fair bit of ground that day and stopped at a German trench which had been stoutly defended if the number of Fritz corpses lying around was any indication. It was a good trench, well-built and sandbagged, and yielded a little in the way of loot – the usual souvenirs but also things like pieces of sausage and the prize I picked up – a half bottle of schnapps. I stuffed it away out of sight, got myself settled in the former German sniping post and prepared for a quiet, well-oiled night. Truth was, I was a bit unnerved by the point-blank shooting earlier, not the sort of thing I'd been used to at all. I think I'd begun to get the shakes but the schnapps worked wonders on that.

Late in the night a messenger came up that Major Anthony wanted to see me. I cursed at having to leave the snug hole but I went, crouched low, following the messenger. Anthony had installed himself at the end of the trench and, like all the officers, he'd got things set up pretty comfortably – stretcher bed, food box, shaded lamp etc. I hopped down into the hole and he actually got to his feet and stuck out his hand.

'I'm Evelyn Anthony,' he said. (It might have been Glynnis or Joyce; some such name anyway.)

'William Hughes.' I shook his hand.

'I witnessed your action today, Corporal,' (I'd had a promotion you see, more for survival than anything else) 'and I'd like to thank you.'

'My pleasure, sir,' says I. Just the reminder of it would have brought on the shakes if I hadn't had the schnapps inside me.

'I'm also told that you jumped up out of a shell hole to get a medic for a wounded Canadian.'

Jumped out to get away from the bastard, thinks I, but I just nodded manfully.

Anthony motioned me to sit down on a box that he probably kept his champagne in. He got out his cigarettes, offered me one and lit us up. The night was quiet and still, peaceful after the hectic events of the day. There'd be flares later and shelling but for now we could have been sitting in Centennial Park.

'Stiff work tomorrow, Hughes. We're going to clean

out this section. The Jerries have honeycombed the terrain ahead – trenches, foxholes, machine gun nests, wire, the lot. There'll be a spot of hand-to-hand, I shouldn't wonder.'

Jesus, how am I going to get out of this?

'I'm mentioning you in my despatch, wouldn't be at all surprised if there's a gong in it for you.'

'Thank you, sir.'

'And I'm promoting you to Acting Sergeant. I want you to lead a squad with grenades and bayonets and get the Jerries on the run.'

I choked on the cigarette.

'Bloody gas got you has it? Poor chap. You've been through a hell of a lot but I know I can ask this one thing more of you.'

I fought for breath.

'It's by way of being a desperation move, I suppose. But ours not to reason why, eh? Casualties will be . . . heavy.'

I deserted that night.

11

It was just my infernal luck to desert, making myself a coward on the run, a few months before the Armistice which would have made me a hero. I've done the same thing with shares a dozen times, sold out before the boom. But I'm still here to talk about it and that's the main thing.

Deserting wasn't easy. I did some shivering and finished the schnapps and would've prayed if I'd thought it would do any good. I had my money belt, a good idea of which way the coast lay, a rifle and a pistol and a good pair of eyes. As well I had some bread and German sausage. In the early hours of a very black night I slunk out of the sniping post, moved quietly behind the sentries and worked my way slowly back over the ground we'd covered during the day. That was an advantage, knowing the territory. I had a keen eye for cover so I knew where the woods and farmhouses and other buildings were.

I'd covered a few miles when a bombardment started up an hour or so before dawn. I couldn't tell what it was in aid of but I doubted that it was a prelude to a movement by Mad Major Anthony. How I'd misjudged that man, I should have let the Hun shoot him.

My absence was still probably undiscovered and I kept moving through the dark night which was lit by flashes

84

and filled with rumblings. I was tramping along a winding road when the sky lightened and I kept my eyes peeled for a farm which I reckoned to be not far away. Despite the cold I was sweating from the steady walking in a heavy greatcoat and I was starting to panic at the thought of being spotted alone on the road when the sun came up.

As the sun cleared the eastern horizon (it was damned flat country with no real hills to delay the light) I saw the farm and scuttled along the fence, through a gap in it and over to the barn. The old, ramshackle barn was half-full of hay and I burrowed in behind the wall and the edge of the stack, re-arranged a few bales and built myself a hiding place. I buried my money belt and pistol in the hay, lay down with my rifle for a bedmate and went to sleep.

It was afternoon when I woke up with a furry mouth and a bursting bladder. I relieved myself, ate some bread and sausage and was assailed by thirst. This drove me out into a pallid sunshine to look around the run-down farm. The land seemed to have escaped the direct ravages of the war but soldiers had bivouacked there. The signs were unmistakable – planks ripped off walls and used for fires, broken bottles and empty food tins, copses and other sheltered places fouled. I found a well some distance from the main building and drew up some water that tasted better than brandy to my parched mouth.

The place looked deserted. I kept my rifle at the ready and went up to the farmhouse and in through the de-hinged door. It had been a warm comfortable place once but now it was draughty through broken windows and showed signs of letting in the rain. There was nothing worth looking at in the kitchen, sitting room or parlour in front, just old furniture with empty drawers and tables that hadn't been sat at for a long time. I went up the stairs to the front bedroom which was perched out over the front of the house, supported by posts. The low bed had a straw mattress on it with the straw hanging out and two mice jumped from the straw when I gave it a nudge with my rifle. There was an old sea chest beside the bed. I opened it and saw folded inside trousers, shirts and jackets – the deserter's treasure.

I whooped, put down the rifle and began stripping off my clothes. I'd dropped my trousers to the floor and was about to step out of them when the voice came from behind me.

'Stand right there, chum, and put your hands on your head.'

I did it and turned around slowly. Two men, both barefooted and both pointing rifles at my naked chest.

'Jesus,' I said, 'who're you?'

The one who'd spoken was a stocky, apple-cheeked kid with worried, deep-set dark eyes. He was wearing clothes like those in the sea chest. So was his mate, a fair-haired, blue-eyed giant, well over six feet with shoulders and chest to match. On him the shirt was tight and the jacket and pants were inches short.

Apple-cheeks looked at my discarded rifle and uniform and a grin split across his face showing tobacco stained teeth, shocking in one so young.

'Appears to me we might have something in common, like. Why don't you get dressed?'

I pulled a pair of pants out of the chest and hopped into them; they were loose around the waist but I can still recall the feeling of relief at being out of uniform for the first time in over a year. I pulled on a shirt.

'Feel good?' the kid said.

I nodded.

'Scarpering?'

It didn't take much brain power to work out what that meant. I nodded again. He looked at the crumpled clothes on the floor.

'Shit me, we're a fuggin' international brigade.'

His tone had got friendlier so I dropped my hands. 'How's that?'

86

'Hans here and me're on the same lark. I've had a bellyful of war.'

I nodded vigorously at that. The giant lowered his rifle and smiled; his teeth were pearly white and there was something simple about the look that came over his face. I glanced sharply at the kid.

'Don't worry, he's all right. He's a Hun but he's all right. Quick tempered, mind; he wanted to shoot you on sight but I made him wait. When I saw you drop your pants I thought you might be scarpering.'

'You bet.' I reached into the trunk for a jacket and put it on, also an old scarf which I wound round my neck. 'Could you point the rifle away, please?'

He did and I stepped forward and held out my hand. 'William Hughes.'

'Georgie Witherspoon. This's Hans Steller.'

We shook hands. I picked up my rifle, got a few things out of the pockets of my uniform and stowed them in the new clothes.

'We burnt ours,' Witherspoon said.

I looked at the khaki jacket with the chevrons on the sleeve and the heavy woollen pants, muddy and stained with other men's blood. 'Good idea,' I said.

We went downstairs and I crammed the clothes into the burner of the combustion stove. Steller tapped Georgie on the shoulder and made eating motions. Georgie raised his eyebrows at me.

'Bit of bread and sausage, in the barn.'

We trooped over to the barn where I shared out what was left of the food. They ate ravenously and bit by bit their story came out. Georgie was a Londoner who'd been in the service from the outbreak of the war although in 1917 he was still only nineteen years of age.

'Put me age up, mad I was. Mad to get into it.'

I nodded, implying that I understood, might even have shared the feeling.

'Hans was conscripted,' Georgie said. 'Came up into

the line just a couple of weeks ago. One show was enough for him. I understand a word or two of his lingo, picked it up from some prisoners we took in '16. He ain't a coward exactly, just reckons he's too big and is bound to get hit.'

'He's got a point,' I said.

'Fuggin' right. Well, I packed it in after that last push. We made what, half a mile? And I had to crawl over a pile of dead men this high.' He raised his hand to his shoulder. 'That was it for me. I ducked off, moved by night and found Hans already here. He was asleep. If it'd been the other way around he'd have cut my throat.'

I smiled at Hans who showed the pearlies slowly. 'He looks mild enough.'

'He is, 'cept he wants to go home. That's all he wants and Gawd help anyone who stops him.'

'Not me. My idea exactly.'

'Many Aussies take it on their toes?'

I shook my head. 'Not many, bit of s.i.w., that's about it.'

'Same with us. Have you got a smoke, Bill?'

We lay back in the hay and smoked. Hans didn't understand any English but he'd make a remark or two in his guttural gibberish to Georgie who'd respond as best he could, usually using a bit of mime and hand-waving to help comprehension.

'He says the Australians are fierce fighters,' Georgie said.

I sighed. 'The ones that aren't dead. What does he say about when the war's going to end?'

Georgie and Hans did some grunting. 'Never,' Georgie said.

'That's too long,' says I. 'Did you have a plan of any kind?'

For an answer he pulled out a folded sheet of newspaper. It turned out to be a page of the London *Times* on which was printed a large map of Western Europe showing the state of the war. The paper was more than a year old and some of the front lines had changed; where we lay at that moment, for example, was securely occupied by the Germans on the map. Georgie pinpointed the spot with a grimy fingernail.

'Here's us', he ran the nail south-west, 'we thought we'd make for Switzerland.'

'Schweiz, jah,' says Hans.

'Neutral territory,' I said. 'Good idea.'

'Yes, and our Hans comes from some place near the border on the German side. He says that if he'd been born another couple of hundred yards west he'd have been able to spend his time yodelling and mending clocks instead of getting shot at. Anyway, if we can get there he knows some people who'll help us.'

I was getting to like Hans more and more and I'll say this for him, I never met anyone less likely to rape a Belgian nun and he'd have looked bloody silly in a spiked helmet.

I've often thought since that the story of how Georgie Witherspoon, Hans Steller and I scuttled four hundred kilometres across war-torn France to Switzerland would have made a good film. I near as damn it tried the idea out on Raoul Walsh[12] once but I thought I might have trouble explaining how I'd come by all the authentic detail. In fact we'd have had to dress up the story a little for Hollywood because the reality wasn't all that hard. Oh, it had its scary moments, right enough. It wouldn't have been so hard to keep clear of the Germans because they had other things to think about but, as outlaws, every man's hand was potentially turned against us.

We had to worry about the locals who could have taken us for deserting Germans (well, one of us was, but you see what I mean) *and* all kinds of Imperial forces as well as Americans. The skies were full of airplanes some days and we had no way of knowing whether they spotted us or not or cared. Of course we travelled mostly by night and had as little contact with other people as we could. We got an occasional ride on a hay wagon and now and again bought food in the small villages but mostly we grubbed up potatoes and turnips and stole eggs and, a couple of times, chickens.

But the real trick of staying safe in that country was this – we hid in the churches. Many of the villages and all of the towns had them and it was even possible to plot a course from steeple to steeple in some places. Georgie had done some road travelling in England, hop-picking and the like, and he knew the dangers of sleeping rough.

'Get a chill and a fever a couple of times and you're finished,' he said. 'You get weak and you need rest and good food and that's what we ain't got. We'll last twice as long if we can sleep under a roof most nights.'

So we slept in crypts and cellars and naves and door-ways and if a sexton or some other church official sur-prised us the odds were good he wouldn't cause any trouble. Our worst moment came somewhere near where the borders of France, Germany and Switzerland meet. We were making for Basel and the only question was whether to approach it by land, water or railway. As it happened each of us favoured a different method: I was for road, Georgie was for rail and Hans was for water. We drew straws and Hans won. The big blond ape (we were all heavily bearded by this time) grinned and made rowing motions. I looked at Georgie.

'That's different,' I said, 'if he's going to do all the work.'

Georgie talked it over with Hans and came out of the conference happy.

'It sounds like the goods. City's divided in half by the river, boats going backwards and forwards; if I can't get

90

through in a place like that I'm a Dutchman.'

'That's what you might be next,' I said.

You see we'd gone through it with Hans who reckoned that you could get identity papers in Switzerland for a price. I'd given them to understand that I could wire for money when we got to a safe place and that I'd provide for them too. (I hadn't let them see my money belt; they were both good chaps but temptation has a wicked sharp edge.)

Somewhere south of Strasbourg we stole a boat from a slipway. Hans literally picked it up and carried it to the water with Georgie and I doing little more than steadying the thing. I could see what Georgie had meant about him wanting to get home. We had a small supply of food and water, three rifles, one pistol and perhaps a couple of dozen rounds of ammunition. We'd been on the move for nearly a month and thought of ourselves as desperate men. To desperate I could safely add frightened.

It was late July and hot. On this account, and through my perhaps excessive caution, I was for continuing the policy of moving at night, but Hans paid no attention. He was the boatman with the local knowledge and that put him in command although he had little sense and no judgement. Come to think of it, those qualities were never uppermost in other commanders I've known, like von Stroheim and Ronald Reagan.

We got into the boat, Hans flicked the oars through the water and we were underway.

We made good progress through that day and I have to own it was pleasant, lying back there in the boat, smoking and yarning with Georgie while Hans put his back into it. For form's sake we both took a turn at the oars but I wasn't too good at it, Georgie wasn't much better and Hans could read the river currents like a book so we left it to him. We pulled in at night because even a brute like Hans will tire if you work him long enough in the sun. He was an alarming shade of red, I recall. Tied up to a tree with its branches neatly overhanging us and only the stillness of the river around, that night was the calmest I'd spent since being offered the opportunity to commit suicide as an Acting Sergeant. Tomorrow, south to freedom!

A German boat patrol had other ideas. We were skipping along in mid-stream; Hans was complaining about his sunburn but it didn't seem to be slowing his stroke any. There was a mist clinging to the river banks and, suddenly, out of this whiteness, comes a long-nosed, low-slung motor boat with a steering wheel set up high behind a windshield and a machine gun mounted on the front. A man appeared by the gun, held up a megaphone and shouted 'Halt!'

'Christ,' I said. 'What d'we do?'

But Hans had already shipped his oars; he jerked one free of the rowlock and laid it across the boat. He smiled in the direction of the patrol boat while he fumbled under a canvas cover to cock his rifle. I held my breath while the Germans – the black cross on the side made the identification – approached. There were three men aboard, one near the gun, one steering and one standing by the side. The latter and Hans made conversation while our boat wallowed beside the other. Hans conveyed something to Georgie who whispered to me:

'They think we're smugglers. They want to see our papers and to search the boat.'

'We're sunk,' I said, which was perhaps not the best thing to say.

Hans' interrogator had turned nasty and was reaching for a pistol in a holster when Hans swung the oar and knocked him into the water. In one smooth movement Hans had his rifle out and he shot the man who was reaching for the machine gun. He swung around, put a shot through the windshield, and the man at the wheel yelled and dived overboard. The first man floundered in the water and grabbed at a rope trailing from the patrol boat; Hans reached down and crushed his skull with the rifle butt. He dug the oar in, pulled a few strokes clear of the patrol boat and took a bead on the man, about twenty yards away and swimming towards the west bank; he was maybe a hundred yards distant. Hans fired twice; there was a scream, two arms flew up and the swimmer sank.

'My God,' Georgie said.

I said nothing.

Hans rowed like a demon.

12

Hans propelled us downstream as if we were motor driven
and if any alarm was raised about the de-manning of the
German boat, we never heard anything about it. Late in
the afternoon we rounded a bend in the river and Hans
stared at the banks, rowed a little further, stood up and
shielded his eyes while looking to the west. He sat down
and nodded solemnly.

'Schweiz,' he said.

Georgie and I whooped, clapped him and each other
on the back and nearly upset the boat. Hans smiled
broadly, picked up his rifle and dropped it over the side.

'How does he feel about killing three of his country-
men?' I asked Georgie.

'I asked him that before. He says they were Bavarians,
whatever that means.'

I could understand it; I could never feel that
Tasmanians were fully human myself.

Basel was an infernally dull place but dullness was all
right with me after the patrol boat incident, at least for
a while. The river divided the city as Hans had said and
we encountered no resistance to our landing – no
customs, no papers check. Perhaps the patrol boat was
all there was in the way of a frontier post. Consistent

with our policy, we landed on the south bank which was dominated by some sort of cathedral. Indeed there were more than enough churches and monasteries and the like in the old part of the city, rather depressing really, once the need for sanctuary had passed.

We tied up at a small wharf, left the boat and the two remaining rifles, climbed some slimy steps to a broad, flagstoned walk alongside the river and there we were, on neutral ground and safe from all the bastards on both sides who wanted to kill us. Hans knew the town and escorted us through a warren of streets to an inn where he said he had friends. Friends or no, the place was as welcome to me as a whorehouse to a sailor. It smelled of hot bread and beer and I had my bum on a bench and a tankard in front of me before you could spit. I paid in German money of which I barely had enough to slake the thirsts of the three of us.

By evening we were roaring drunk, bellowing songs and smoking up a storm. The Swiss tend to do their drinking quietly and Hans kept hushing us until he got too drunk to care himself. In the end they got rid of us by ushering us up the stairs to a room near the top of the building where there were two beds and a chair. Hans and I took the beds and Georgie collapsed, giggling and protesting, into the chair. We all passed out within minutes and if there had been any hostiles in the vicinity we could've been taken like babes without a struggle.

When I woke up I had a hangover, my first in a long while, but I was also in a bed, so the two things cancelled each other out. Hans was snoring in the other bed but Georgie was sleeping quietly in the chair, his young-old face in repose for the first time since I'd met him. I lay back, enjoyed the light filling the room and the feeling of relief that several thousand tons of gunpowder, lead and steel weren't seeking me out.

After a doze I felt much better; Hans and Georgie had gone, so I wandered to the bathroom out behind the inn and found soap, brush, razor and towels. Shaved and bathed I went back to the inn to gape at my two mates who'd had their hair trimmed. For the first time Hans was wearing clothes that fitted him. We slapped each other on the back; I produced some French coins and we fell on a huge breakfast of coffee, ham and hot rolls.

After that it was down to the serious business of finding a safe place to stay while we sniffed out the chances for papers. The innkeeper was a fat, cheery soul named Brunt who got into deep conversation with Hans when he went over for a fresh pot of coffee. Hans came back, poured coffee and talked a streak to Georgie who had to keep telling him to go slow.

The gist was this: there were a lot of pro-Germans in Basel but also some of the other persuasion. The land-lord was one of the latter and, as far as we were concerned, we could stay at his inn as long as we could pay the tariff. But he couldn't help us with documents.

'Can't or won't?' I said.

George shrugged. 'Hans says these people worship money. A little down might help him help us.'

Now one of the things I'd learned in my time as a sales-man in Sydney was some simple sleight-of-hand. I'd taken a sov or two out of my money belt and I now proceeded to produce one from Hans' ear. He and Georgie were so impressed by the trick that they didn't ask where it had come from.

'Tell Hans to give it to mine host and in return we want to know someone useful.'

Hans then got into deep confab with Brunt and when he emerged he was minus the sovereign and smiling as if he'd been told that the war was a draw and all was forgiven.

'He's got a name and an address,' said Georgie.

We went out to the street and they took me first to the barber shop where I got the old locks trimmed. Then we went through the winding streets trying to keep pace with Hans' long strides. I'd seen a few old towns in France, but then I'd mostly had my head down and my eyes closed so this was my first real experience of medieval architecture – buttressed, ornate buildings, narrow streets, overhanging houses – I can't say I cared much for it.

The Swiss seemed pale, fattish and oddly quiet. Even their shops and street markets lacked animation. I found plenty to excite *my* senses though, in the way of food and drink and cigarettes. I loaded up on the latter, getting some French, some English and American, and ending up with a bundle of Swiss francs in exchange for my second sov. Maybe Georgie and Hans were getting ideas about my money but they didn't say anything and they certainly accepted the cigarettes.

Eventually we fetched up at a place like a warehouse, not far from the river. Down some steps and Hans hammers at a brass bound door. The woman who opened it was a different stamp altogether from the cheesy Swiss women I'd seen. She was tall, with dark hair and eyes and a splendid figure.

'Ja?' she says.

'What a beauty,' I said quietly to Georgie.

'Do you think so?' she said. 'Thank you, sir.'

I couldn't place her accent (it turned out to be Swedish so it was no wonder), but her English was excellent. I wanted to start talking to her straight away, about the weather and what not, but Hans cut in with the business. He was a single-minded chap, like all Germans. She nodded, replied, took a look up past us to the street and then stepped aside.

'You are welcome. Come in.'

We walked into a huge barn-like room piled high with furniture. We followed her along a path between the stuff, like a jungle track, to a comfortable apartment at the end of the building away from the river. The windows overlooked a park and the room smelled of tobacco and comfortable living. At her invitation we sat down; I produced the cigarettes and we all lit up.

'My father will be home soon,' she said, 'but first, tell me all about yourselves.'

It was an odd thing, but she was looking straight at Georgie Witherspoon as she spoke. Now I'd formed all sorts of ideas about her on first glance; she was wearing a neat dark costume with a long skirt, not like the frills and bows on the Swiss women; she was discreetly made up and had spent some time on her hair. She looked as if she'd be keen on a good time and I suppose I naturally thought she'd be interested in Hans or me – tall, well set-up chaps, dark or fair, take your pick – but here she is making eyes at Georgie. I suppose I should have said a little more about Witherspoon, conveyed his character and so on. But when you're half-covered with hair and mud, on the run and stinking like a sow, not much of the shining virtue comes through. Truth was, Georgie had confidence; he looked like a chap who could get what he wanted. It showed in his walk which was almost a strut, in the way he held his head and the directness of his look. This sort of thing is pleasing to some women and comes well before good looks in their estimation. Georgie wasn't bad looking, apart from his stained teeth, but there wouldn't have been more than five foot six and a hundred and thirty pounds of him. Doesn't matter with some women and this was evidently one of them. I usually got along on stature and good looks but, I'll say this for myself, as long as I'm not drunk, I don't persist when I can see I'm out of the running. That's how it was this time and I concentrated on moving along to the business of getting ourselves safe and having some fun, in that order.

I won't bore you with all the details and, indeed, they're a little scrambled in my mind at this distance in time, but the upshot was that the warehouse held a few million dollars worth of furniture which certain Swiss burghers wanted stored in case the Germans invaded. I'd have stored myself first but that's the Swiss for you. They care about their furniture. Our dark-haired beauty's father, Per Simondsen, was a Swede resident in Switzerland who was happy to do the storing for a fee. He had the space, having sold his stocks of timber to the French and German armies in 1914. He had his fingers in a hundred pies – gun running for certain, trading in medicines, counterfeiting and dealing in forged and stolen documents.

We filled the room with the smoke from American cigarettes and aroma of coffee and the fumes of schnapps while we dealt with Simondsen who was the perfect neutral – he had no preferences either way for French, German or English and the only thing about those countries that interested him was the viability of their currencies.

He stroked his silky fair beard as I spun him a story about how I could wire for money.

'In what form would you receive it, Herr Hughes?'

'Sovereigns.'

'The best,' he breathed. 'I could escort you to the bank myself.'

'You speak excellent English, sir,' I said, just to be saying something while I was thinking.

'It will be the commercial language of the world after the war. We will be ready.'

He glanced at his daughter who had moved on to a sofa with Georgie. I don't think even my sleight-of-hand tricks would've done me much good there.

I gave him a hard, direct look. 'How much for three sets of papers – military exemptions, travel documents, the lot?'

He looked puzzled. 'Lot?'

'How much for everything?'

'Two hundred sovereigns.'

That would've stripped me. I felt I owed George and Hans a lot but not that much. 'One hundred,' I said.

'One hundred and fifty.'

'Done.'

We shook hands; I gave him my last American cigarette and he put it away in his jacket pocket. He was probably going to trade it for herrings and cheese.

I've always said that my attitude to women was sound. As it turned out my surrender of any interest in Maj Simondsen in Georgie Witherspoon's favour saved me fifty sovereigns. The two of them got along like a house on fire and had made plans to marry before my dealings with her Dad had progressed very far. Result? Georgie stays in Switzerland with the fair Maj and has no more need for papers than a ballerina has for boxing gloves.

He was a very fly cove, Simondsen. The next day he took me along to his bank, introduced me to an English-speaking official, and discreetly absented himself while I deposited the contents of my money belt. The Swiss bankers didn't give a damn who you were or where your money had come from so long as it was the genuine item. They gave me an account with a number and were happy for me to supply a name in due course. (I'm told it's the same today or even more so but it's been many a long year since I had any dirty money to hide, worse luck.) When I walked out of that bank I was a man of substance and if I'd been in London, or New York or Sydney, I'd have been a happy man.

As it was I had a sort of freedom only. The next thing to hope for was that the war would end soon and things seemed to be pointing in that direction. We saw little of Georgie in the days that followed so that Hans and I were thrown together more. I picked up a few words of German from him and the folk around and when we got hold of a newspaper we were able to stumble through it together. Hans wasn't a great one for reading. In

September the Allies broke through the Hindenburg line and the writing was on the wall.

Hans and I got a little drunk on the strength of this news and tried to encourage Simondsen, whom we'd gone to see yet again in the seemingly endless document quest, to join in the celebration.

'Why are you so happy?' he said, pulling on that damned beard.

'End of war . . . end of our troubles,' I slurred.

'You don't know much about the law, my friend. Desertion remains an offence even after hostilities. An offence punishable by death in most armies, I believe.'

'Shit,' I said.

'Wass?' says Hans.

I explained it to him as best I could and he took it on the chin like he took everything. He jabbered away and I got the impression that he intended to go to German New Guinea to make his fortune as a rubber planter. I was pretty sure that there wouldn't be any German New Guinea if the Huns lost the war and I didn't think they grew rubber there anyway, but I didn't have the heart to tell him.

'You and Herr Steller will need your new identities whatever happens,' Simondsen informed us. 'Perhaps for ever.'

That dampened the spirits a trifle. We were sitting in a cafe by the river, which is to say we were out in front of the place in the open in the civilised way they have in Europe; the water and sky were blue, the air was warm and the beer was strong and cold, but I had a premonition then as clear as any real life experience. I saw myself wandering the earth for years, hunted and with no place to call home. It hasn't been quite that bad but Christ, at times, near enough to it. The feeling made me angry. I gulped beer and turned to Simondsen – the damned wowser was stirring sugar into his chocolate.

'And when will we have those identities, Mr Simondsen?'

'Tomorrow.'

So it was that I became Anthony (Tony) Grace, South African born, 23 years of age, photographer, heart weakened by childhood rheumatic fever, etc. etc. (That was my first passport; they'd brought the damn things in a few years before. It was British, of course: Sir Somebody Something requested and required that I be allowed to pass without let or hindrance etc. If I were drawing a pension for every passport and alias I've had since I'd be on easy street today.)

Hans became Dieter Schmidt, motor mechanic and citizen of the Federal Republic of Switzerland. He looked crestfallen when he received the papers and I felt mildly miffed. I'd paid for them after all.

'What's wrong, Hans?' I asked.

'Medecin', he said. After some stammered pidgin French and German I discovered that he had wanted to be a French doctor – God knows why.

I showed my passport to Georgie who was sitting in the roof garden on top of the Simondsen building, as usual, hand in hand with Maj.

'South African, eh?' says Georgie. 'Ever been there, Bill?'

I thought for a minute, as I always did when faced with questions like this in case I might reveal something discreditable. I gave myself the all-clear and owned that I had been to South Africa, albeit briefly.

'Pick up the accent?'

I shook my head.

'You sort of clench your teeth and squeeze the words out. Try it – say your name.'

'Tenny Grease.'

'That's it exactly. Corker!'

After that it was a matter of grabbing the papers every day to see how the war was going. Only a lunatic would've left Switzerland while those maniacs (I mean half the nations of the world, the civilised half, too) were out there mauling each other. But they were running out of steam, all except the Americans who hopped in at the right moment on the right side as they mostly managed to do in these affairs, at least up until recently.

They say the November Armistice was pretty well celebrated in London – public fornication and drunkenness and so on – well, there was none of that in Basel. I think the merchants might have run quickly through their balance sheets to calculate the effect on monthly profits and a few wilder spirits might've had an extra half gill of schnapps, but that'd be all. Hans and I tried to get a party going at the inn but had no luck. Georgie and Maj came by for a quick drink before setting off into the mountains to look for a chalet. I suppose Georgie is there still, if he's managed to endure the boredom.

That left Dieter and Tony, drunk as skunks in the bar, contemplating their future. There were a few other people about, not all of them Swiss which was unusual. I gazed at a pair of women with liquor-dimmed eyes and wondered when I'd next be murmuring sweet nothings to a member of the fair sex and getting my just reward. Hans nudged me and I realised he was asking me where I would go.

I felt a foolish grin slip over my flushed face. 'Home to South Africa, I suppose.'

One of the two women I'd been looking at got up and walked across to our bench. She was fair and freckled, not my type at all, apart from the swell of her chest under a loose blouse.

'Where did you say home was?' she said.

There was something familiar in the voice but I was

too stinking to pick it up. I knew I had to go on the defensive though.

'Seth Effriker.'

She let out a hoot of laughter and the sound cut through my alcohol fog like a kookaburra at dawn – pure Australian. 'South African my eye. You're an Aussie if ever I heard one!'

13

Her name was Elizabeth Macknight and she was to become my first wife. Had I known that then I would've spat in her eye or thrown an epileptic fit – anything to shake fate from its course. Where are premonitions when you need them? I had no warning though and was probably too drunk to have been aware of one anyway; I mumbled something about a joke and invited her friend and herself to join us.

Over they trotted and I took in their particulars through a haze of schnapps and beer, not to mention tobacco smoke. Elizabeth, as she declared herself to be in a booming voice, was large, red-haired and freckled. She wore a modified Swiss costume – white blouse, black laced weskit and, to my horror, hiking boots under the wide, peasant skirt. Her companion, Patricia Greenacre, was smaller and darker, much more to my fancy, and similarly got up. I introduced them to Hans, stumbling over the new name and making a complete mess of my own alias.

'Really?' bellows Elizabeth. 'I'll have to take both of those names with a bag of salt.' She looked around for a laugh and got a big one from Patricia although I could only manage a weak grin. Hans, lucky chap, couldn't be expected to get jokes in a foreign language, even bad ones.

Bad jokes were Elizabeth's stock-in-trade along with, as I was to learn to my cost, beaver-like persistence, insatiable curiosity and indomitable courage. She and Pat, as she shyly asked to be called, were both nurses in a field ambulance unit. They were taking a spot of leave in Switzerland when the Armistice broke out.

'End of the fun for us,' Elizabeth lamented. 'It'll be back home to tennis parties and bridge after supper, eh, Pat?'

Pat nodded solemnly and sipped her sweet white wine. She gazed at Elizabeth who was scraping mud out of the cleats of her right boot while waiting for her beer to arrive. Despite my adventurous life to that date, I was still in the dark about the Sapphic persuasion, and I wouldn't have been able to interpret Pat's behaviour towards Elizabeth even if I'd been able to see things in single image and understand more than about half of what was said. I was in no trouble with 'another beer?' or 'what about a bite to eat?' which was the sort of thing Elizabeth was coming out with, but Pat's murmurings about edelweiss and telegrams passed me by.

Somehow or other we spent a few hours in the company of these two women. I must have kept up my end of the conversation because Hans' English was rudimentary as I've said and I think he was still sulking about not being a doctor. I remember plates of food being set before us which must have sopped up some of the booze. Eventually Hans fell asleep in his chair, Pat went off to bed and Elizabeth and I were left alone in the smoky parlour of the inn. She'd unlaced her weskit and loosened the neck of her blouse and I felt extra heated by the sight of the rise and fall of her big bosom. She seemed to get excited by the same thing, or maybe it was excitement at my reaction. In any case we staggered up to my room, practically groping each other on the stairs.

'Is your heart up to it?' she says, unbuttoning my shirt and plucking at the hair on my chest.

106

'Eh?' I'd forgotten the rheumatic fever story, you see, which I must have come out with at some point.

'Your heart . . . kept you out of the service. Oh, you're so big.'

I think she meant my shoulders. I was down below her shoulders by this time, nuzzling away at her breasts and trying to get up inside her skirt.

'Wait, wait.' She had my trousers and her own underthings, including the boots, off in no time – well, she was a nurse and practised at these things – and then she was under me on the bed and I was ploughing away, not caring that her thighs were nearly the size of my own and her buttocks were soft and spreading like understuffed cushions.

It had been a highly charged day, one way and another, and I slept like a dead man after I rolled off Elizabeth. When I woke up it was morning and there she was, dabbing at herself with a towel.

'What are you doing?'

'Had a douche,' she boomed. 'Don't want any accidents, do we? Especially with you wandering around not knowing what your name is and how you spent your childhood. Not too keen on Newcastle, are you?'

'What? What?'

She dropped her skirts over those ghastly boots; came across to the bed and gave me a slightly slobbering kiss. Her breath was like a dog's bowl but I don't suppose mine was any better. 'You talked in your sleep, lovey. Don't worry about it. I got what I wanted and you did too. Fortunes of war.'

I hadn't the least idea what she was talking about, brain still fogged, you see, but I certainly wasn't used to being treated like a raped maiden. I raised myself up on an elbow and immediately sank back with a groan. She was over at the bureau now, writing on the back of an envelope.

'Here you go, Tony or whatever your name is.' She

flicked the envelope on to the bed. 'Look me up when you get to Australia. I have to run or little Pat'll be throwing a faint.'

She opened the door and looked back at me with what could have been fondness or maybe she was thinking about her breakfast. 'Prepare yourself for a shock though if you turn up at the old place – very different Elizabeth there.'

I nodded, regretted the movement, and put my head gently into the pillow while she closed the door. After a while I eased up gently, ungummed my eyes and read what she'd written: 'Elizabeth Macknight, The Gables, Church Street, Brighton, Melbourne'. Thoughts of Sydney flooded into my head and I felt a wave of home-sickness sweep over me. The harbour, the beaches, riding in Centennial Park, beer picnics in the Botanic Gardens. I folded the note and put it where I could recover it later. This was not on account of Elizabeth Macknight – I'd keep the Murray River between her and me and even a whole state might be safest, Queensland might be the go – but out of the blind sentimentality of youth. Later I had reason to wish I'd burnt it.

It was time to be on my way. Georgie was staying and Hans didn't have far to go but with every passing day I felt more like a fish out of water. (I wouldn't even have minded a second tussle with Elizabeth but she and Pat left to rejoin their unit on the morning after our en-counter.) I bought some clothes, maps and other neces-sities and paid a visit to the Simondsens to check on some details about the identification papers.

'And where are you going, Herr Grace?' Simondsen asks with an ingratiating smile.

'England eventually. I've got a rail ticket as far as Paris; Calais and a boat after that.'

He frowned. 'I know how to get from Paris to London. Let us see, you are a photographer, aren't you?'

'That's right.'

'Come with me. I can sell you an excellent camera.'

As well as being a river port, Basel was also a major rail head, all quite undamaged by the war, of course. You couldn't say the same for the tracks and signals and stations across France. They sold me a ticket for Paris in Basel all right, but it was often touch and go as to whether I'd make it. The train was damnably slow and frequently interrupted. It sat in a siding for an entire day at one stage and I had to keep to my seat or lose it. You needed a royal bladder for train travel in those conditions.

There was the cold to contend with too. I'd bought a heavy coat with a fur collar and some thick gloves but cold winds seemed to be attracted to railway platforms and it took liberal doses of rum to keep the blood liquid. All Europe seemed to be on the move that winter; crowding into the train were displaced Frogs and Fritzes, Poles and Russians getting away from the Bolsheviks, and probably some Bolsheviks getting away from others, too; demobilised soldiers of all kinds; Scandinavians heading south and Italians going north. I even saw one Chinaman, fat as a pig and carrying a huge two-handed sword.

In fact the cold worked to the advantage of shady characters like me, and I've no doubt there were plenty of others travelling at that time who could well have been sitting in a cell; we all rugged up and muffled ourselves to the hairline so that unwelcome identifications would be hard to make. I was travelling with a fair bit of money on me and I made sure that anyone I didn't like the look of saw that I had a pistol in my pocket. I didn't have any trouble.

I also had a camera and I fell into the habit of snapping pictures from time to time. I did this at first to lend plausibility to my identity but, as I say, it became a habit which I've kept up ever since. You may think I'm over-precise with some of my descriptions of people and places, but you see I've still got photos dating from 1919 and I've refreshed my memory with them here and there. [Browning's photograph collection has survived. The pictures were kept in no particular order in three wooden boxes that had once contained bourbon whiskey. They are amateur work which show some improvement in technique over more than sixty years. One expert I consulted described them as 'energetic'. Ed.]

We finally got to Paris some time before Christmas and I booked into a hotel in the Rue des Écoles, not far from the University. I've never been attracted to universities, although I've played college professors in my time and it's been said that I've managed to appear as foolish as the real thing, but you generally find good boozers and eating places nearby. This was certainly true in Paris after the war. The place was going full barrel, loud and brassy and open for twenty-four hours, just the way I like it. The best thing though was the cheapness; I'd converted some of my war loot into francs and whatever the exchange rate was I doubt it's been equalled since. You could get a meal with wine for a few cents and everything (and I mean *everything*) else was just as cheap.

I really let off steam in Paris. I rid myself of the memory of Elizabeth Macknight with half a dozen small dark French women who mightn't have been to the Sorbonne but had certainly had a sound education. I rampaged in Montmartre and the Boul' Mich', got into drinking contests with Americans and generally made a swine of myself. It was all a bit of a fraud really; I played the fool

110

and spent money as if there was no tomorrow partly because I lived in fear of somebody recognising Corporal Billy Hughes. I waited for the tap on the shoulder or the sidelong glance and in my soberer moments I even scouted a few lanes and flights of steps and gardens around the hotel in case I should need to make a sharp getaway.

The worst thing was the dreaming: I'd wake up, alone or in company, streaming with sweat and trying to deny that I was Browning or Hughes or Grace. My accusers varied from Captain Thorndike to Georgie Witherspoon to Flinders, the faggot guard at Long Bay. I'd wake up shouting, 'No, no, not me!'

'Doucement, chéri, doucement,' Yvette or Mimi would say and I'd have a brandy and try to get back to sleep. I decided in the end that it was being among foreigners that created the anxiety, that plus the sight of so many uniforms. London was the place for me, grey and foggy London where they spoke a civilised tongue and the only uniforms I'd be likely to see would be on the Guardsmen at Buck house.

Besides, I'd almost run out of money.

14

In 1919 (don't ask how I spent the New Year's eve, I can't recall a thing about it), there was none of this EEC nonsense on entering England. If you were white and from the Empire you strolled along to Customs and lesser breeds just had to muddle through as best they could. Customs was a pretty relaxed business too; there was no comment passed about my pistol, for example.

I'd been practising up on the South African accent and my papers were in order so no-one looked at me twice. Currency was a bit of a problem, not this pettifogging about maximum and minimum amounts carried, but simply my lack of the stuff. When I got off the train from Dover at Victoria I had precisely three pounds and two shillings to my name. My visits to the capital when on leave (God, it seemed as if it had happened in a different life) had given me a bit of knowledge about the place so I took myself off to Kings Cross where the cheap hotels were. Installed in a small room which was over-heated and made noisy by a service elevator that seemed to rattle up and down behind my bed, I contemplated my future.

I should have known then that the right place for me was in movies: in what other occupation is it considered acceptable, even necessary, to lie about your age, name, background and talents and pretend to be what you're not while behaving like a selfish child? But I didn't know it and thought I should set about earning a living. I confess I had it in mind to save enough for a passage back to Australia. This unadventurousness nearly finished me or perhaps it made me – you'll have to judge for yourself.

Bolshevism was the great issue of the day. The papers were full of it with every poor devil who went on strike being accused of it (Australia would have been ripe for the take-over if that had been true), and every employer shedding tears for the Tsar. I even read about an expeditionary force that went into Russia after the war to set things straight. Australians present too; probably along for the vodka.[13] A lot of good it did them. There was heavy unemployment in London in the aftermath of the war and a few Reds among the ranks I daresay, but the English workman proved to be as docile as ever.

I tried selling some of my European photographs in Fleet Street but got nowhere, too frank I suppose. My only real talent was for straight shooting, literally not colloquially, and there was no market for that. When the funds got really low I sat in my hot, noisy hotel room and looked at the service pistol for which I had three rounds. I was contemplating robbery not suicide but I didn't have the nerve for either. Instead, I pawned the gun in a place near Euston Station and took the proceeds to the pub. It was lunchtime and busy but I wasn't hungry. I bought a pint of the thin, tasteless stuff they call bitter and hunched over it with a cigarette. After a few puffs and draughts I looked around and almost fell flat – I was standing next to Georgie Witherspoon.

I steadied myself with some more tobacco and alcohol and looked closer. It wasn't Georgie but the dead spit of him, maybe a little younger. He was smoking a Senior Service and sucking down lager, looked prosperous enough in a rough, working-class sort of way. I wasn't exactly looking like a toff myself – I still had the fur collar

113

coat but it had taken a lot of wear. My boots weren't very sound. Browning's rule is, *friendship is no barrier to a touch.*

'Excuse me,' I said to him, 'your name wouldn't be Witherspoon, would it?'

'S'right, mate. Eddy Witherspoon at your service. Who might you be?'

'Ah, Tony Grace. I knew your brother in the war. Georgie. How *is* the old Georgie?'

He glanced slyly around him, touched my elbow and drifted off to a quieter part of the pub. I followed him instinctively; discretion and the avoidance of wide open ears were second nature to me. Witherspoon watched me butt out my Woodbine and offered me a Senior Service, which he lit with a flash lighter.

'Thanks. Brother, are you?'

'S' right. Three years between me and Georgie. Kept me out of that fuggin' war.'

'Lucky you.'

'You bet. When didja last see Georgie?'

I hadn't thought that far ahead but if I hadn't been able to think on my feet I would've been dead long ago. ' '16, would it be, or early '17? Somewhere in France. I was with the Canadians and we did some drinking with the Tommies. Good bloke, Georgie. Did he come through all right?'

Witherspoon looked so sly that his eyes disappeared into slits. 'In a manner of speakin'.' He drained his lager. 'Buy you a drink?'

We bought each other several drinks and with the oiling of his tongue Eddy let the story slip. The family had been harassed by the authorities ever since Georgie's desertion (which had made him a hero with his nearest and dearest, by the way); their natural concern for his welfare had been set at rest by a postcard from Switzerland.

'Reckons he's got a corker of a missus.' Eddy leered at

a faded streetwalker who was resting her weary anatomy on a stool nearby.

'Good for him,' I said. 'What's your game, Eddy?'

'Drivin'. Want a job?'

It was as simple as that. Eddy worked for what must have been one of the first limousine services in the world. All arranged by telephone too, nothing is as new as you think it is. I'd done a little driving around Sydney (the more senior of the Robespierre men had cars) but was no expert. Still, it was an easier age – no tests to pass, practical or theoretical, just a half crown to pay and you were on the road.

Eddy and I got very thick. He introduced me to the manager of Green's Motor Services, gave me my first lessons in piloting the big Vauxhall Tourers and Sunbeam 16hps around the narrow London streets, and gave me a daily guide to the best pubs. I even boarded with the Witherspoons in Camden Town and, gradually, took on the identity of Tony Grace, South African, and relaxed my vigilance.

Mrs Witherspoon was a gigantic fat woman with scarlet, crooked lipstick and a totally criminal outlook on life. She was into everything – fencing, betting, abortions, lease-breaking etc. All services for a fee, no grassing guaranteed. She sat in her front parlour in the little terrace house she'd occupied all her life and ran her operations without benefit of books or accountants. She sized me up within seconds of our first meeting.

'You'd 'ave some sorta nick-name, wouldn't you, Tony?' she says.

I thought back over a few I'd had, all uncomplimentary. I shook my head.

'One'll come to me, don' you worry. Me it was named "Cricket" O'Mahoney.'

'I don't quite see it,' I said. 'A cricket-playing Irishman. What . . .?'

She laughed; her dewlaps shook. 'No. He killed eleven men in the Troubles. You saw Georgie after he scarpered, didn't you?'

I denied it but she made me feel very uncomfortable. She grinned and the lipstick got even more crooked. 'Don't worry about it, boy. Just keep your nose clean and your hands off the customers and their bloody goods. I've got an interest in that firm.'

It was like being at school again, or in the army or worse, and I felt like backing out of her presence. I needed a bracer and Eddy was never loath to have a drink.

'She's a one, ain't she?' he said as we waited in the local for the drinks.

'Whatever that means. Where's your father?'

The beer came (I was getting a taste for it), and Eddy shook his head. 'I think she done him in,' he muttered.

It wasn't a bad life, hanging around the depot in Golders Green and going off to pick people up and take them where they wanted to go, wait as often as not, and bring them back. I suffered a bad case of envy almost every day, especially when some old buffer would provide the service to send some young stunner shopping, but the tips were handy.

It was a useful couple of months I spent with Green's. For one thing I overheard a lot of interesting conversations from the front seat. Stuff on finance and shares (never did me much good), politics (they were carving each other up at the Paris Peace Conference at the time, preparing the ground for Hitler), motor cars, clothes and food and drink. It was an education and helped me to play a wide variety of characters – from brothel keepers to bishops – in the movies.

We carried a few celebrities. I remember driving Kipling and his wife around one day but I can't recall that they said or did anything interesting. Somerset Maugham I took to lunch, in the Sunbeam I mean. He just sat there from the West End where I suppose he had a play

116

running,[14] to Swiss Cottage, and when we arrived he said, 'Th-thank you, d-driver', and gave me a pound. Jimmy Wilde, the 'Welsh Wizard' was a bit more lively; he did some singing and talked a blue streak, but it was in Welsh and I couldn't understand a word. Driving along one day, I caught sight of a face I knew from photographs. He was getting out of a big, black car and having difficulty keeping the top hat on his head. He was small and sallow, about the same colour as the people he used to rant against as 'the yellow peril'. The Hon. William M. Hughes, Prime Minister of Australia. Just over from Paris for the day, no doubt. I would've run him down if I could – the bastard almost got me killed.

I didn't see any of Maugham's plays in the West End or anyone else's for that matter. My main entertainments were the pubs, the music hall and the cinema. I saw one and two reelers and films which I'd seen before in Australia, like *Birth of a Nation* and Fatty Arbuckle pictures like *Oh Doctor!* and *Goodnight Nurse.* I had an occasional fling with girls Ma Witherspoon could vouch for, but living in London wasn't nearly as cheap as in Paris. Dinner and a show cost a lot; wine was a ruinous price and cigars had to be rationed. I was making good wages at Green's and the tips were good, but I wasn't making much progress towards saving for a passage back to Australia. I should say that I intended to go first class; no six weeks of steerage for me, and it was necessary to make the grade with the people I might want to impress on the trip and after.

So I was stalled; I even felt that I was going backwards. I was eating and drinking too much in that damned English cold and putting on weight. I was in a foul mood, for the above reasons, when I got the call to take the actor, Harry Southwell, from Grosvenor Gardens in South Kensington to Mecklenburgh Square. Actor? I'd never heard of him and it wouldn't have been the first time I'd struck someone without a shilling to his name raking up the hire price somewhere just to make an impression where he was going.

Southwell was a smallish, nervous-looking type with a voice that contained an odd mixture of Welsh and American intonations. His hair was grey which made it hard to judge his age within ten years. As I later found, he was Welsh-born, but had spent some years in America. He had an Australian wife but I never heard him say a good word about Australia; perhaps that was part of his trouble.

He sat in the front seat, which was unusual, and smoked nervously. We passed a cinema where *The Heart of a Texas Ranger*, a Tom Mix film, was showing.

'That's rubbish,' Southwell snapped. 'Have you seen it?'

I said I had and agreed that it was rubbish although in fact I'd enjoyed the film. Disagreeing was no way to get tips.

'I could write better,' Southwell says, 'and direct better, too.'

Just to keep the conversation moving I ventured that I'd done a bit of film acting myself. Southwell looked interested.

'Where was that?'

'Oh, in Australia, before the war.'

'Is that a fact now? Say, that's interesting. My wife's an Australian.'

I nodded and he fell into a brown study for the rest of the journey. He directed me to an imposing front door along the square but he didn't seem too sure of himself as he alighted. He didn't give me a tip either. I was about to drive off when he stuck his head in through the open window.

'Say, have you ever heard of Ned Kelly?'

I was exasperated and said the first thing that came into my head. 'Kelly's my middle name. We're related.'

I opened the throttle and roared off leaving him there with his hat in his hand and one foot up on the white marble step. I thought no more of it and was surprised a day or two later when I got an invitation to meet Mr Southwell for a drink in The Green Man at Notting Hill Gate. The invitation was in the form of a note delivered by hand to Green's depot. It added that I would hear 'something to my advantage'.

I showed up after work with a fairly heavy thirst at the appointed time. Southwell was drinking scotch and soda, a sight which cheered me up at once.

'You know me,' he said as soon as I had a glass in front of me, 'what's you name?'

'Tony Grace.'

'Tony Kelly Grace?'

'Ah, well . . .'

'You said your middle name was Kelly.'

'That's right, but . . .'

'Oh, I get it.' He took a pull on his drink and smiled. 'You look like a fellow that's been around. Well, it's none of my business as long as that's straight goods about you being in films in Australia and a Kelly.'

'It is,' I said. 'I wasn't a lead player or anything of course, too young . . .'

'Sure, sure.' He got out a packet of Fatimas which I hadn't smoked since Switzerland and lit us both up. 'Nothing's what it seems in the movie business. You know Tom Mix, son of a cavalry officer, war hero and all?'

I nodded.

Southwell leaned closer. 'I happen to know that his father was a lumberjack and that he never saw active service. Oh, he was in the army all right, but he deserted in nineteen oh two.'

My heart almost stopped. I carried the whisky to my mouth slowly so that my hands wouldn't shake and had a slug. 'That so?' I gasped.

'Yeah. Anyway, here's why I wanted to see you. I was meeting some fellows the other day to raise money to make a film here.'

'What sort of film?'

'Robin Hood.'

'Good idea.'

'They didn't think so. It's no go.'

'Bad luck.'

'Maybe not. My wife has been at me to go out to Australia. She says the movie business is big out there and wide open to the right man.'

I sipped my scotch feeling the beginnings of excitement. 'That could be so,' I murmured.

'She's told me all about this outlaw, Ned Kelly. Be a great film, she thinks.'

'It would,' I said. I racked my brains for the details – horse stealing, police killing, the fire at the Glenrowan hotel and a rope over a beam. It didn't sound too promising put like that, but I nodded and blew smoke affirmatively. 'Great material,' I said.

'I've got a proposition for you. Why don't you come out to Australia with me, help me raise the money, advise me on how to do things out there? Look you, I don't know a damn thing about Australia and my wife isn't much better informed. Can you ride?'

'Yes,' I said, 'but why me?'

Southwell drained his drink. 'You know, you remind me a little of Tom Mix . . .'

'Eh?'

'Don't get me wrong. You look a little like him and let me tell you – he might be a slippery, lying son of a bitch but he's a great rider and everything he's touched as turned to gold. I've got a feeling about you . . . Tony. Another drink?'

120

He held up two fingers to the barmaid to indicate doubles. I watched the generous measures of whisky go into the glasses and thought that Harry Southwell was a chap I could work with.

'I'm your man,' I said.

15

We travelled by P & O but I can't recall the name of the
ship. I was aboard the damn things so often in following
years that they all tend to blend together. I've got a photograph of this one; very arty, all funnels and railings, but
it was a foggy day and the angle cut out the name. It
doesn't matter, they were all the same – cramped cabins,
smelly smoking rooms and stodgy food. You'll have
gathered that I wasn't travelling first class. I never *did*
manage to travel first class by P & O; I always seemed
to be on the run or short of cash, or both.

It was late April or early May of 1919 and I'd have
travelled aboard anything that wasn't a troopship. Some
ships offered private passages although they were basically troopships. They were still ferrying survivors from
the madness home and the last thing I wanted was to run
into an old comrade at arms. Nothing like that on P & O:
in first class it was all people resuming colonial posts and
holdings and public school boys and Oxford and Cam-
bridge men going home; in second class we had the better
type of migrants, representatives of commercial firms
with interests in South Africa, Rhodesia and Australasia
and some odds and sods, like a small touring theatrical
troupe and a few clergymen. Who the riff-raff in steerage

were I didn't care to know.

Southwell was paying the passages. He'd made some money in America writing scenarios but probably less than he implied. He also knew less about producing and directing than he implied, but who was I to talk about exaggerating experience? Anyway, I had some money saved but I soon whittled that down at cards. It was illegal to gamble on board of course, but try telling that to a Malay planter when he's holding a straight to your two pair. After wasting too much money at drinking and gambling I had to find other recreations and there wasn't much to do except talk to Southwell and his wife, Annette. She was a pretty little thing who danced well. I'd always been a bit of a clodhopper on the dance floor before then, but Annette straightened me out so that I could glide along with the best of them. That was a useful talent later, too.

Another man might have got jealous at the amount of time I spent dancing with his wife but not Southwell. He could dance already, he said, and he left us to it while he scribbled away in his cabin. He had got hold of a book called *Dan Kelly, Being the Memoirs of Daniel Kelly (Brother of Edward Kelly, Leader of the Kelly gang of Bushrangers), Supposed to have been Slain in the Famous Fight at Glenrowan*,[15] and he spent hours poring over it. I took a look at it myself; it ran the line that Dan Kelly had survived which was all rubbish. Southwell said he needed a 'hook' for the story and that this could be it.

When he could be drawn out of his cabin and sat down with a whisky or two, Southwell was a fund of information about Hollywood and New York and he really whetted my appetite for those places. We'd be cruising along within sight of the West African coast and Annette would coo, 'Wouldn't you just love to land on a coast like that, Tony? Face the harshest nature has to offer and survive?'

I'd grin manfully, but privately I'd be thinking of the

parties in Manhattan or sitting around a swimming pool in California with some of the under-dressed beauties Harry would tell me about when Annette was out of the way.

'What a time they have,' Southwell would say. 'At weekends, mind you. They're too pooped through the week. But at the weekends they really let go.' A sip of scotch and up went the glass. 'An ocean of this stuff.'

'I thought they had prohibition,' I said. It was one of the things that had decided me against going to the States when I was feeling low in England.

'It's on the way. But I bet you wouldn't know it in Santa Monica on Saturday night!'

I soaked up as much of this as I could get and also Southwell's technical knowledge of films which wasn't a lot. He soon found out that I knew a deal less than him and I sometimes wondered whether he regretted our arrangement, especially when I was a little vague as to the exact whereabouts of places like Glenrowan. I bluffed along as best I could and tried to spend more time with the three other chaps in my cabin – a couple of Yorkshiremen who were going out to South Africa to work as engineers in the goldmines and a Scot who was going to try farming in Western Australia. But their conversation was about dredges and water tables and sheep and I found it hard going. Things were a little strained when we steamed into Cape Town.

'Ah, the old Table Mountain,' I intoned as I stood by the rail with Southwell and Annette. A good number of the passengers were leaving and there were a few people getting on. I was keeping my eyes skinned for a likely-looking woman who might make the rest of the journey less dull.

'Is this where you're from, Tony?' Annette asked.

'Ah, not exactly. More up country.'

'Let's go ashore,' Southwell says. 'We've got all the rest of the day. I want to stretch my legs.'

I wasn't keen; my knowledge of the town extended barely beyond the wharves; I couldn't speak a word of Afrikaans and I knew there were a hundred and one blunders I could make. But I had to look like a man of action for Southwell's sake and, as it turned out, it was lucky I didn't skulk about in the smoking room looking for a worse card player than myself, as was my inclination.

It was a fine warm day and the town had the smells you got then and don't now – horses, fresh country not far away and human sweat. We've covered the sweat up with chemicals. We've done the same to the other smells, come to think of it. Annette looked pretty in a light frock and wide-brimmed hat and Southwell was proud of her as he squired her around, stepping well clear of the blacks I noticed. I had a tropical suit which I'd had made in London. I'd lost weight on board ship because the food was so dull I often couldn't be bothered eating it. The suit hung a bit loosely and I felt untidy in it. I had a solar topee pulled well down against the sun and possible identification. What I'm trying to say is that I was feeling pretty depressed when Southwell proposed that we take a buggy trip up the mountain a ways to see the sights.

'Don't look so glum, Tony,' Annette said. 'You can point out the sights to us.'

That didn't help. Things got worse when we found that the rascally Indian who hired out buggies to tourists only had a two-seater available. So, here we are, under a hot African sun, Harry and Annette with their bums comfortably on a seat and me astride a nasty-tempered black stallion that started at every blade of grass. I was a good rider but anyone would've looked an amateur on that nag. Southwell, who'd seen the great Tom Mix make horses turn cartwheels, wasn't impressed.

That experience put me off touristing for life; ever since I've made it a point never to see the sights of a place I might be visiting. The road up the mountain was winding and dusty and other riders and drivers were impolite. My stallion pulled and heaved and snorted. It was harder work controlling him than lumping coal which *looks* hard – I've never tried it. I was soaked in sweat by the time we reached the top and Harry and Annette had ridden up like nabobs, sheltered under Annette's parasol. It was sheer misery trying to fob off questions like, 'And what's that place over there called, Tony?' I made a botch of it and Southwell was looking at me very oddly when we prepared for the descent.

'I hope you know more about the State of Victoria than you appear to about the Cape,' he said.

I'd never been south of Gundagai.

Halfway down the hill a dog shot out of the bushes at the side of the road and ran straight across in front of the Southwell buggy. The horse shied and bolted; my black bastard reared and almost threw me as the buggy swerved in front of us and then he was off too, bolting down the hill in a cloud of dust as if he was determined to dump me under the wheels of the buggy.

I yelled and hung on. The yell seemed to push the horse harder. The road was pretty wide and clear but the bends were sharp; the buggy got around the first one and then there was a long steep stretch to the next. I looked up and caught a glimpse of Harry pulling at the reins and Annette's sheet-white face. My horse gained on the vehicle and drew level; I was clinging for dear life as the ground shot past. There were some skull-crackers of stones by the side of the road, too.

I'll never know how it happened but my horse suddenly propped, reared back as if a giant hand held it; I went sailing over its head and I landed, splayed out like one of those insane free-fall parachutists, on top of the horse pulling the buggy. I suppose I screamed; I know I grabbed hair and leather and pulled. The bend ahead was practically an S and the terrified horse couldn't have made it. My arms were loose in the sockets when the beast slowed, swerved, grunted and came to a halt. It must have been a hundred in the shade but I was shivering like a Covent Garden whore on a winter's night.

And that wasn't the end of my heroism. I slid down off the horse; Southwell jumped down from his seat and came towards me. A clatter of hooves and my stallion comes bowling down the road towards us. Blindly, I reached out and felt the reins slap into my hand. I hated the bloody nag so much I gave them a vicious tug and it threw up its head and stopped. Southwell gaped at me.

'That was the greatest piece of horse work I've ever seen, bar none. Do that for the cameras and we'll be rich.'

I felt moisture in my pants but maybe it was only all the sweat trickling down into my socks.

16

Nothing was too good for Tony after that. The word went around the ship and I could've stayed drunk on free drinks from the Cape to Singapore. I didn't because I didn't want to undermine the hero image by blundering drunk into the wrong bedroom or, worse, confessing in my cups to my abbreviated war. The adulation was heady enough and I basked in it, as well as the sun, all the way to the Straits.

Luckily the old Africa hands had got off the boat at the Cape so my new notoriety didn't prompt awkward questions about my background. The hero-worship yielded nothing in the way of a sexual dividend, unfortunately. The few attractive wives were close-watched by their husbands and the only daughters around were a trifle too young. One of the Etonians showed a little too much quickness in producing a match or being on hand for deck quoits (and the shower bath afterwards), and I had to accidentally trip him down a flight of steps. Iron steps too, a painful landing.

At Singapore I almost jumped ship. I'd never seen such women as the ones who paraded around that town under parasols and with silk wrapped around their narrow haunches. Some of the eyes I gazed into promised unbelievable depths of sin and I had to shake myself like a wet dog to stop from following them for miles through the shops and markets. The long abstinence had a lot to do with it and perhaps the heat, but I can't remember feeling so randy before or since. The ship lay over for three days which was enough to get me in a fine lather over the slanty-eyed Chinese wenches and the chocolaty Indians.

The ship was really lightened now with all the people for the *F.M.S.* and adjacent parts getting off. I was sorry to see them go as the rest of the voyage promised to be even duller. They were great story-tellers, some of those gin-soaked Malaya hands. The more approachable ones used to spend time in the second class and I heard some fine old tales of unfaithful wives, desperate card games and wily natives. If I'd scribbled them down I could have anticipated old Willie Maugham's success with his stories, but I didn't bother. Life is full of missed opportunities.

In any case sex was on my mind more than literature. Towards the end of the second day in Singapore I was feeling almost ill with the strain. I was having a drink on the after-deck with Annette. She tapped me on the arm with her fan.

'Tony! You haven't heard a word I've said.'

'Eh? I'm sorry, Annette. The heat. Would you like another drink?'

'No. It is *not* the heat. It's hotter than this in Sydney and you know it. I know what's the matter with you.'

I was peeved. 'Do you, by God?'

'Yes. I am a married woman, after all. I understand men.'

Hello, I thought. Could this be it? Damned difficult, but she's not a bad-looking little thing and Harry would rather scribble than screw it appears. I smiled at her non-committally.

'Have you made the acquaintance of Mrs Barnes, Tony?'

'Can't say that I have.'

'She is a lady travelling first class . . .'

I got her drift. 'Alone?' says I.

'No, not alone. Her husband is with her but he is . . . that is, he was hurt in the war.'

'Hurt?'

'Yes.' She waved her fan in a movement that might have meant almost anything. 'You know.'

'Ah, yes. Poor chap.'

'Mrs Barnes confided in me, perhaps she sensed a kindred spirit.'

'You don't mean that Harry . . .'

'No, no, of course not. It's just that Harry is frequently preoccupied with his work. Women can sense these things.' She snapped her fan shut. 'This is the modern world. That ghastly war, made by men, is over. Times are changing. Women . . . Mrs Barnes would like to make your acquaintance.'

And that is how I was saved from an almost certain dose of Singapore clap or a steady decline into insanity across the Indian Ocean, or both. Nancy Barnes was a thin, dark, intense woman with hard, glittering eyes and sharp features. She was wearing a cloth-of-gold dress like a modified sari which, after the fantasies I'd been enduring, was no bad thing. She ate me up with those eyes on our first meeting and I felt that her long fingernails were curving like meathooks, waiting to bite into my flesh. Ordinarily this would be a bit off-putting for Browning but at that particular time I'd have taken her on if she'd had stainless steel teeth. (I know what I'm talking about; I had a woman with stainless steel teeth once, in Russia. Just the once, but still it's not every man who can say he's put his head into the lion's mouth as it were.)

Annette Southwell got us together over a drink in the first class saloon and then she quietly slipped away. Nancy and I were both suffering from the same fever and we both knew the cure. I bought her a gin, lit her cigarette and our burning eyes locked (well, it *was* like that, and it's no worse than some film scripts I've read).

'I saw you in the Orchard Street market,' Nancy said. 'I thought you were going to rape that Chinese woman.'

Such plain speaking was uncommon with well brought-up women in 1919, but it was welcome to me. I grinned. 'And her daughter.'

She sipped gin. 'Yes, she wasn't young. You've no objection to women older than yourself, I mean as lovers?'

I judged she was about five years older than me. 'None,' I said.

'Good.'

That was about it for preliminaries. We couldn't go to her cabin or mine and the first time we did it was in a lifeboat. She'd equipped the thing already with a rug and a pillow and a bottle of wine and we climbed in, already tearing at each other like fighting cats.

The moon was up and the sight of her small, hard breasts made me groan and pant to be rid of my trousers. She was skilled and co-operative and we were soon going at it hammer and tongs, shaking the boat so much that I thought it might spontaneously launch itself from the davits.

After, we lay back and sipped wine while looking up at the southern stars.

'Were you in the war, Tony?' says she.

'Yes.'

'So was my husband. He had his testicles shot off.' Her hand was cradling mine as she spoke. 'And this is all I ever want to say about him to you. Do you agree?'

I did, most heartily. The truth was that after we'd finished I did feel a small pang of guilt about cuckolding a man who couldn't strike back, as it were. I felt the same pang once or twice again. But Nancy's formula of no discussion on the husband subject helped considerably. After a bit, I began to feel that I was probably doing the poor chap a service in keeping his missus happy.

At first, we had trouble finding places, especially in the daytime when the lifeboat was out. But I mean morning, afternoon and night because that's the way it was. After a while Nancy located an empty cabin and a steward with an itchy palm and that problem was solved. I don't know where Mr Barnes (I never even discovered his first name) got his money from but there must have been plenty of it and he was generosity itself towards Nancy. She bought drinks and cigarettes, meals and snacks in the cabin and kept the steward happy. I occasionally wondered if she was keeping him happy in another way too, but I can't honestly believe she could've found the time, let alone the energy. It's possible, though; she was a remarkable woman.

It was as well we had these diversions because there were some damned dull stretches on that cruise. The nuts and bolts in the ship rattled in the same way day after day and the monotonous beat of the engines was enough to send you crazy. Exotic country, of course, if you care for black beaches where you can't swim for crocs and sharks and flights of brightly coloured, squawking birds you can't eat. The nights were often as hot as the days and Nancy and I worked ourselves into a fine sweat. She preferred sex to be vigorous.

'Bull me, bull me,' she'd say, and I had to do it standing up and bullocking her back against the wall or the door. Astride a chair was one of her favourites and, indeed, she liked almost anything except the good old missionary position. She particularly liked to do it while wearing an item of clothing – stockings and shoes, a blouse or slip – and I own I developed a taste for this. She had slim, well-muscled legs that seduced me utterly, especially when silk-covered, and to nuzzle her hard nipples through a thin, lacy blouse . . . well, I was young and I thought myself a hell of a fine fellow.

I was well up to the work, that I must say. I took

exercise every day on the deck, didn't drink over-much and my young lungs seemed to be able to cope with the forty cigarettes a day. The sea air probably helped. Added to all that, a real spice and stimulus, was the mutual knowledge, that it was all going to end, forever, at Fremantle.

The ship headed south from Singapore for the Straits of Sunda but first we put in at Batavia in the Netherlands East Indies. A worse combination than the natives of these parts and the Dutch is hard to imagine. I've scrubbed most of Batavia from my memory – only recollection of the heat and the dust and the present Nancy Barnes bought me remain with me now.

It was a dirty, noisy little place with a lot of people bartering and haggling over nothing at all as far as I could see. I went ashore with Annette and Nancy, making sure that I kept a lot closer and paid my attentions to Mrs Southwell rather than Mrs Barnes. It was hard to keep up the pretence; Nancy was wearing a light dress that seemed to float around her. She had turned darker under the sun, not for her the obsession with the fair English complexion, and she looked mysterious and exotic with gold bangles and jewel-studded open weave sandals that she'd bought in Singapore. I knew every inch of her body but that didn't stop me panting at flashes of exposed flesh or feeling an urgent response when a breeze pulled her dress tightly across her body.

'Stop it!' She hissed at me when I was crowded up against her at a street fruit stall. 'There are other people from the boat about.'

'Why are we here? We could be in the cabin. The ship's almost empty.'

'I want to buy you something.'

133

After some hours of searching she found what she wanted in a filthy little shop in which half of the merchandise seemed to be covered with chicken dung. It was a cigarette case, gold, flat and with a beautifully smooth spring action that years of neglect hadn't harmed. Intricately etched and embossed on the front were the figures of a man and a woman performing the sex act in a highly imaginative and just barely possible position. You had to look very closely to see the figures and even closer to see what they were doing. I forget what she paid for it, a lot for Batavia at that time.

Nancy showed the case to Annette when we got out of the shop.

Annette stared and raised her eyebrows.

'Appropriate?' she said.

'Entirely,' says Nancy.

She gave it to me with a smile and a squeeze of the hand. We went back to the ship and that night we discovered that the position *was* possible and had a few highly rewarding side benefits. I kept the cigarette case for twenty years. It entertained a lot of people (some of them women, I have to admit and I only parted with it very reluctantly when I needed the money desperately, after I'd got the sack from *Gone with the Wind*).

Nancy and I maintained our rapid fire rate for the rest of the journey as the ship moved south along the west coast of my native land. I tried to find out more about her but I gleaned very little. She was English, born in India. One night she dressed in a sari with paint spot and nose jewel and we had an amazing time, a sort of Kama Sutra party you could've called it. She'd met her husband in England where he was flying planes in the RAF. She'd read everything, especially in the pornographic line, and had an ambition to be a doctor.

She got off the ship at Fremantle. We'd had our farewell the night before and I didn't see her that day or ever again. I've thought of her often though. I've wondered whether she ever became a doctor and I've wondered how long her husband lived and if she continued with the same methods of satisfying her natural urges. If she did, there have been some damned lucky fellows down there in Western Australia.

17

After a stop in Adelaide which looked like a pretty little place, green hills close to the town, perhaps a few too many church spires for comfort, we went on to Melbourne. It was a grey, wet day in July when we arrived, damnably cold and more like London than California, or so Harry Southwell said.

'Say, where's all this sunshine I've heard so much about? The only thing you could film in that would be *The Phantom of the Opera.*'

It looked as if a cloud was sitting on top of the city; grey mist swirled around the wharf as the baggage went ashore and we prepared to submit ourselves to the officials.

'It's winter, Harry,' Annette said.

Harry pulled up the collar of his astrakhan coat which he'd resurrected from one of his many trunks. 'Winter? They don't have winter in California.'

I was interested to hear that; always hated winter myself. I was more keen than ever to take a look at Hollywood. The words – Hollywood, Beverly Hills, Malibu – already had a shining quality for me; they must have shone pretty brightly for Harry at that moment too because he didn't like anything he saw around him.

'No wonder you quit this dump, Annette,' he said as he handed over his passport.

'I'm glad to be back, Harry. You'll see, the gardens are lovely and Cup Day is such fun.' She was a game little thing, Annette, and often stuck up for herself. The passport official could hear the local accent in her voice (although, like Harry's, it was overlaid with English and American) and he slipped them through the entry procedures smoothly. I was a different kettle of fish.

'You're a photographer, Mr Grace?'

'Yiss.'

'Not much call for 'em here.' He flipped a page in the passport. 'Born in . . . Basutoland?'

'Yiss.'

'Hmm, sounds native.' He peered closely at me. 'Both parents white?'

I was still darkly tanned from the cruise. I drew myself up to the full six two. 'Uf cuss.'

'All right, don't get y' back up.' I reached for the passport and he slammed the stamp down on it, missing my fingers by a fraction. He grinned. 'Welcome to Australia.'

Harry had a sense of style. As soon as we landed he sent a messenger to telephone for rooms at the Menzies Hotel and to organise us a taxi. We pulled away from Port Melbourne with the car loaded to the last inch of the springs with luggage. It was an emotional moment, or should have been – my homecoming. But this was a strange city to me; I was calling myself something other than my baptised name and the rain was sheeting down. I could have been in Chicago.

Harry got busy on the telephone as soon as we arrived. He ignored me and Annette both and we went to the bar to talk things over.

'What now?' I said.

'Harry will call up everyone who might put money up to make a picture. He's very good at that sort of thing.'

'Who?'

She sipped her drink. 'I don't know. He never tells me anything about his business.'

'And what will you do, Annette?'

'Oh, shopping, look for a house if we're going to be here long enough. There'll be plenty to do.'

'What about me?'

She looked me over appraisingly. 'You do look dashing, Tony. You'll look wonderful on film. Can you act?'

'I don't know. And my name's not Tony.'

'No, I thought not. You've been slow to answer to it a few times. And you're not South African?'

'No.'

'Well, you can drop that awful accent. You only remember to use it some of the time anyway. Where are you from?'

'Sydney.'

'What's your real name?'

'Richard Browning.'

'Well, it's a nice enough name. Have you done anything so terrible that you can't use it?'

'Of course not,' I said, thinking: *Different matter for a chap named Hughes.*

'Don't get on your high horse. D'you know much about the Kelly gang, T . . . Richard?'

'Dick,' says I. 'Not much.'

'Well, you'd better bone up. Harry will be calling a press conference pretty soon; you'll have to be there and you'll have to be able to say *something*!'

Melbourne had one of the best public libraries in the world at that time. It was said that the first purchase had been all the works mentioned in the footnotes of Gibbon's *Decline and Fall of the Roman Empire*. Whether that was true or not, they certainly had a big Kelly collection – books and pamphlets, the report of the Royal Commission on the Kelly outbreak, newspaper articles and the like.

It was a strange occupation for a chap like me, to be

sitting in a vast circular reading room under the eye of a supervisor, who sat on a sort of podium in the middle of the room able to look down all the 'spokes' of the wheel – which was how the tables were arranged if you get my drift. I kept at it because I wanted to make good in the picture game and because I found the Kelly story interesting in itself. Who knows, I might have been related to the Kellys. There were certainly enough convicts and scoundrels on both sides of the family to have made it possible. I've studied up on a few things in my life since – mostly card tricks I'll own, but also the antebellum South for that animal Selznick's lousy picture and on French Morocco for *Casablanca*[16] – but I don't remember any reading I did with more enthusiasm than that on the Kellys. Then, of course, I did it young and sober in the Melbourne Public Library, later it was with cigarettes and bourbon in the Garden of Allah and such places. Well, both methods have their points.

I didn't just do research. I wrote off to Sydney for my birth registration and applied for a passport in my real name. All the functions of the Commonwealth Government were in Melbourne then (they should have left them there in my view, instead of creating that fly-blown money burner in the middle of nowhere they call Canberra), which made things easier. In those days you could get yourself identified by your bank manager and I soon got on good terms with the Bank of New South Wales in Collins Street. I had some money saved from my work in London and, as a well-dressed associate of Mr Southwell, I was *persona grata* there if not at Government House. That passport with my likeness and real monniker on it gave me a feeling of security.

Harry got on with the business of raising money and interest in his film. The Kelly story had been filmed before, in 1906, but when did that ever stop a film-maker, from that day to this? (I have the dubious distinction of having worked on all three versions of *The Mutiny on the Bounty*. I've heard talk of a fourth and I wouldn't be surprised if they call me in for that, too.) Not that Harry didn't encounter some opposition: it was a busy time for films in Australia; I think a dozen or so were made in 1918, and competition for production cash was fierce. Apart from that, there was a wowser spirit still abroad that persisted in Australia, so it seems to me, until the 1970s. (The last time I went back, in 1975, things had changed so much that half the men in Sydney were in drag.) In 1919 this wowserism took the form of an objection to bushranging films, as if most of the pictures made in the country to that time weren't on this theme and half the people descended from lawbreakers. Harry got around this somehow, with a combination of Welsh and Yankee slickness which was never on such fine display as at the press meeting he organised some time in late August.

We'd moved out of the Menzies into a house in Fitzroy by then and Harry summoned the gentlemen of the press to meet us in the Fitzroy Gardens. I was got up in the uniform of a trooper in the Victoria Police, vintage 1880, and I had to put a cross-grained chestnut through a few smart paces. Luckily, I'd been practising out at the Caulfield racecourse and I was able to put on a pretty good show of jumping and turning on a penny piece. Harry had suggested some shooting but I'd drawn the line at that. I was never as keen on shooting after 1917 as I had been before although I retained the skill.

It was a cold day in the park but Harry had provided hot rum which is all that is ever required to get a good press. He oiled the bowler hats and cloth caps up and threw the meeting open to questions.

'Why d'you want to make a film about the Kellys?' asked the man from the *Argus*.

Harry had been in Hollywood long enough to know that the way to answer a question is to ask one. 'Where would Ned have been in 1915?' he said.

Perhaps they were a little too well-oiled; the *Argus*

man, a heavily built fellow who looked as if he belonged on the wharves, certainly was. He blinked and I had to step in with the answer.

'At Gallipoli,' I said.

'Right,' says Harry.

That set them buzzing, not that it stopped them drinking. The man from the *Bulletin* took off his cap and scratched his head. 'Do you mean that Ned Kelly should be seen as a national hero, Mr Southwell?'

'He would've been, if he'd been alive in 1915.'

Double talk, you see, but the sort of thing a journalist can get his teeth into. I was standing a little apart from the tight group of men because I had to attend to the horse from time to time. One of the writers, a little weasel-faced fellow, sidled up to me with his notebook at the ready.

'I hear you saved Mr Southwell's life, Mr Browning?'

'Where did you hear that?' says I, gruffly.

'From Mrs Southwell.'

Clever Harry. Although Jimmy Wilde was always the real 'Welsh wizard' for mine, the claim Harry Southwell laid to the title wasn't without foundation. He plied them with more rum and when one of them finally asked who would play Ned Kelly in the film Harry waited until all the tin cups (an authentic bush touch, you see) were lowered before he answered.

'Godfrey Cass.'

Well, it doesn't mean a hill of beans to you now, but it meant something then. Cass had been a famous stage actor for a good few years and his name was likely to attract investors and the public. One of the reporters then piped up with a very sensible question: 'Why not Mr Browning for the part of Ned?'

'I am considering Mr Browning for a variety of roles.' He smiled and dippered rum into the nearest cup. 'In fact he may play a variety of roles; he will certainly be involved in the trick riding.'

There was some more buzz at this; Harry later told me that in Hollywood films it was common for the one actor to play several parts, but it was unknown in Australia at that time. The remark about the riding should have alerted me to what was in store, but I was young, puffed up with pride at the attention and, truth to tell, I'd had a few cups of rum myself by this stage. So I just preened and patted the horse and accepted a cigarette. The foxy little scribbler who'd questioned me before buttonholed me again.

'Were you in the war, Mr Browning?' says he, pencil poised.

'Er, yes.'

'In what capacity.'

'Ambulance driver, British unit.'

'You saw action in France?'

'My word I did. Excuse me, I have to deal with this horse.'

I think it was that brief exchange which reconciled me to not taking a leading part in the film. Too many interviews with long-nosed characters like him and I could've been tying myself in knots and prompting embarrassing questions in the wrong quarter. The meeting broke up with Harry promising further startling announcements from Southwell Screen Plays, as he'd styled his production company, and further outdoor entertainments.

The horse was stabled in North Carlton and Harry and I set out to walk there for the exercise. We waited while a tram rattled past and crossed the road to walk through one of the gardens that ringed the northern part of the city.

'What're these announcements, Harry?' I said. 'You've already made the great koala announcement.' I got a bit of fun kidding Harry about that – he had a koala bear as the emblem of the production company. God knows whose idea that was.

'I'm going to make five pictures, Tony. Five.'

'Dick,' says I. 'Better get this one underway first. How's the screenplay coming?'

'Slowly. There's so much to get in. I need your help on that, Tony.'

'Dick, Harry, Dick. Okay, boss, whatever you say.'

'Your American accent is terrible, most actors' voices are terrible. Thank God there's no sound with pictures.'

'How could there be?' I said. 'That's impossible. Steady, boy.' This was for the horse which was shying at a small dog scampering on the grass. 'How's the money side of things looking?'

Harry glanced sidelong at me. I hadn't been paid for three weeks and this wasn't the first time I'd reminded him of it. 'Looking better; let's do some work on the screenplay tonight. I'll give you a cheque tomorrow.'

That was Harry; nothing for nothing and damn little for sixpence.

18

By October Harry had the money and the weather he needed. As it turned out, my ignorance of the geography of Victoria didn't matter because the film was shot in a makeshift outdoor studio just up the road in Coburg. There were some location scenes around Melbourne, particularly the Glenrowan Hotel sequences, but we never got closer to Kelly country than the south end of the Sydney Road.

Harry's notion of a script was a bundle of cards, several copies of a card for each scene, which he handed around to the players and anyone else involved. The handwriting wasn't always easy to understand and sometimes people got the wrong cards and the result was a shambles. Harry had had less experience at film directing than he said; in fact sometimes I thought perhaps he'd had none. He wore the right clothes, plus fours, loose coats, berets etc., and seemed to know how to act like a director but not how to be one. There was some experience available: among the leading players were several members of a theatrical family by the name of Inman and they seemed to have a few clues. Godfrey Cass I'm not sure about; he was wooden, but so were nearly all actors in those days.

Part of the problem lay in the scenario and there were two reasons for this. One was that Southwell had tried to pack it all in – Ned's early misfortunes, the fight with 'Wild' Wright, run-ins with the police, Kate Kelly and the coppers, Stringybark Creek, the robberies and escapes, the death of Sherritt, the Hotel fire, the siege, the capture of Ned, the trial and hanging. Harry had no sense of selection; if there'd been a story about Ned in his cradle we'd have filmed that, too. His second mistake was in calling on me to help with the story. I found the whole Kelly tale bloody depressing and I tried to lift it in spots with a little humour.

I had the police fall off their horses and a few other touches like that (I think I was influenced a little by Mack Sennett). I worked hard to get a love interest between Ned and a squatter's daughter going but I encountered a fair bit of resistance to that. Something of it got into the film but I think the overall effect was confusing. I remember I wanted to keep the shots where the corpse of Joe Byrne, which the police propped up against a wall for the photographers, kept falling down. I laughed fit to kill myself and I thought it would be a good tension breaker, but I was over-ruled.

We had the usual technical problems, perhaps not quite as many as I saw forty years later on *Cleopatra*, but enough. There were equipment failures, torn costumes, sick horses and bad weather. The whole crew absented itself on Melbourne Cup Day which was something Harry hadn't anticipated. Nor had I. I turned up with the horses for the day's work and there was the set, all flapping black cloth and creaking, tacked-together timbers, and Harry wandering about and not another soul in sight.

'Where the hell is everybody?' Harry moaned. 'We've got big scenes today.'

I looked around and then I remembered how quiet the roads had been. 'I remember now. It's a holiday.'

'A holiday?' shouts Harry. 'What is it, the goddamn

King's goddamn birthday again?'

'No, it's Cup Day.'

'What's that?' Harry was working night and day on the picture, never seeing a newspaper.

'A horse race.'

'Christ, what a country!' I was mad myself – I could've gone to the races.

By the end of the shooting, horses were the last things I'd have wanted to see, racing or playing the violin. I was at it day after day, setting up the riding scenes, rehearsing the actors and nursing the bloody horses. I didn't have to duplicate my leap from one running horse to another which must have been one thing Harry couldn't manage to cram into the script, but there were other things like jumping fences and running up rabbit-holed hillsides that were quite dangerous enough for me. I took a few spills but considered myself lucky to get off without breaking bones.

Harry was paying up more or less on time by this stage and I was well-fixed for money. I learned the truth of what he'd said about Hollywood, that picture-making left everyone too tired for mischief through the week but the weekends were a different matter. Melbourne was a pretty lively place in those days as people recovered from the depressing years of the war. The liquor trading hours were still restricted so there was a lively sly grog scene accompanied by gambling, good-time girls and a lot of cocaine. It amuses me now to hear young people ratting on about 'coke' as if they invented it – Melbourne was awash with the stuff in 1920. You could get it at certain suburban chemists and from a couple of dentists and doctors – some of the latter at the best addresses.

Things were organised then as now, with the police heavily involved as suppliers and protectors. It was rough too. The rival gangs fought over the territory with bottles and knives and guns. Two gang leaders shot it out at the intersection of Swanston and Little Collins Streets (which is like doing it at Broadway and 47th), and I've seen big, tough hotel-keepers go pale when Squizzy Taylor walked in. He created much the same effect as Dutch Schultz and, of course, he ended up much the same way. [17]

Harry and Annette kept a pretty sedate house in Fitzroy. We'd go back there after work on Friday with a few of the crew and cast and have a few drinks but it was lights out around eleven. That grog would've picked me up and made my rattled bones less sore, so I'd kick on with a few pals until the early hours. With luck, we'd find a few girls in one of the late night places and stay overnight with them somewhere and head off to the beaches or the hills on Saturday. There were bottles and borrowed cars and rugs and sandwiches and, as like as not, someone sick and crying by the finish of the weekend. It was all harmless fun and wasn't Harry going to make five films and weren't we all going to be rich?

Although it must have been the worst organised production since Lumière set the whole business going, [18] I learned a lot from the making of *The Kelly Gang*. (The Lumière reference shows you that I learned something about the history of the cinema, too.) The studio at Coburg was an old warehouse with a deep backyard; it had lofts and fences and other things useful for filming. We blacked out the windows with tar paper for night shots and used the natural light for everything else. It was before the days of smog and clear days were *really* clear so that you could shoot from soon after dawn until late in the afternoon. It had to be a pretty obtrusive moving shadow to worry a director in those days.

The greatest difference between a movie set then and now was the noise. No-one worried about noise in 1919 – dogs barking, things falling to the floors, voices, nothing mattered. A carpenter could shout for a hammer in the middle of filming Aaron Sherritt's dying words to Ned (there were a lot of liberties taken with the historical truth), and no-one gave a damn. Later, when I was in Hollywood, I often saw three movies filming in the studio at the same time with a steady roar of instructions and equipment noise going on throughout. We were spared that in Coburg, but no-one used to the hush of the modern movie set would have credited that we were making a film.

There were fewer hangers-on, too. All those girls in boots you see nowadays, carrying clipboards and performing minuscule tasks for the director and actors, are a modern necessity. We had the basic team – actors, director, one woman for make-up and wardrobe, a props man and two cameramen. They would have an assistant if they were lucky.

Fortunately, we did have a stills photographer. I say fortunately because it was the holder of this office, Helen Hawes, who became my especial friend during the filming of *The Kelly Gang*. Helen was an unusual woman: she was about forty and having tried unsuccessfully to be an artist in her twenties had turned successfully and profitably to photography. She did portraits of the rich inside and outside their houses and they paid her well. She took pictures of the poor, exhibited them in tiny places where no-one went, and the cognoscenti said she was a genius. She was happy.

I recall one day, after we'd coupled furiously on a rug on a hillside overlooking the bay at Mount Eliza, I stroked her long, slim flank and asked her why she smiled so much. She reached up and gripped my moustache in her long, strong fingers. She was a long, strong woman – built slender but with whippy muscles. Her hair was a chestnut colour, possibly naturally so, and her eyes (I think) were green.

'You will find, my poor Richard, that there are two

sides to your nature. Reconciling the needs of the two sides is the problem of life. He or she who reconciles them is happy. I have, so I smile.'

'What two sides have you reconciled?'

She stretched. She was wearing only a thin shirt, having shed her stockings, underwear, shoes and long skirt. Everything was almost within reach, but I was tired after a lot of wine and our fun and games. 'The artistic and commercial,' she said. 'Do you understand?'

'I think so. What about me? What're the two sides to my nature?'

'That, Richard, dear, is something you have to find out for yourself.'

'You mean I have to find them and then . . . what was it again?'

'Reconcile them, yes.'

'It sounds like hard work.'

'It is.'

I lay back and looked up through the waving gum trees at the blue sky and tried for some answers. I think it was the closest I ever came in my life to self-examination (I don't include the endless sessions with psychiatrists later, that was all sham and show), and do you know what I came up with? Nothing. Not a damn thing. I still don't know what the two sides to my nature are or how to reconcile them – that is, unless they're lust and laziness which don't seem to need much reconciliation.

Helen's job was to take photographs of the scenes before they were shot so as to ensure that costumes, hair-do's and such were consistent in consecutive scenes. This was unusual professionalism for *Kelly* and a little out of place given the other shortcomings. I appear on a grey while galloping up a hill and on a chestnut when coming down it – my mistake, I admit, but no-one picked it up.

I kept a couple of the pictures Helen took, they knock mine into a cocked hat, and it brings it all back to me to see the troopers on their horses (me, heavily bearded,

149

in the middle); Godfrey Cass, his knees buckling under the weight of the ploughshare armour; Harry Southwell as Sergeant Steele, bending over the fallen outlaw with a mind to blow his brains out, which would have made a better ending in my opinion.

We filmed the sequence where the outlaws attempted to de-rail the train full of troopers on a stretch of track just outside Melbourne. It was lucky that the de-railment failed, I doubt if Harry's budget would have run to the real thing. I had to jump a horse out of a box car and I did it after making damn sure of a soft, level landing. The crew whooped as I landed and I feared for a moment that I might have to do the stunt again but Harry was beaming as I rode up.

'Terrific, Dick, you looked as if you really meant business.' It was a knack that came in handy often, appearing resolute when I was terrified to death.

That was almost the end of my duties. I helped to dint the armour but after that I was at a loose end and I own I was not always sober around the set. Helen and I used to sneak away occasionally and I think Harry was on the point of firing me when a chance came for me to boost my stocks with him. We were using a pub out along the Geelong road to do the early Glenrowan Hotel scenes and the moment came for the troopers to open fire and break a few windows. Do you know that not a man on the set could be confident of putting a bullet through a window at a hundred yards? It was child's play to me; I loaded up the .303 and peppered the windows from top storey to bottom while the cameras ground and the crew cheered.

Then it was into the pub for a few celebratory drinks and a bottle to keep us merry in the coach back to town to film the scenes in which the hotel burned down. A special wall with two windows had been built out from the back of the main building where the interiors had been filmed. The plan was to set a fire at the base of this wall on the inside, get some flames licking up and take some shots in through the windows. Then the 'interior of the hotel' scenes – where the outlaws ranted about injustice and drank themselves silly – could be intercut with shots of the burning wall.

I was given the job of setting the fire; God knows why because, after the pub and the coach, I was in no fit state to do anything. Maybe after the shooting episode they thought I had the necessary steady hand or perhaps, as a forty plus a day smoker, it was just that I always had a match. Whatever the reason, I was given the job and I couldn't get the fire to start. Maybe the wood was wet. I'm no bushman as I said, so I resorted to the townsman's trick of splashing a little kerosene around. This did the trick; the fire flared up most satisfactorily and the cameraman got the footage he needed of burning boards and tongues of flame licking at windows.

When the filming was over I beat the fire out where it had taken hold on the walls, mostly on the fresh paint, and stamped it out at the base. I wandered off to find Helen while Harry was attending to a few last details; the actors were getting their make-up off and so on. When movie people assemble you can bet there will be one life-of-the-party type who'll be able to lift the company's spirits up to hilarity and beyond. On *Kelly* this was Sam Kerr, a roly-poly, white-bearded actor who played a couple of genial parts in the film by dyeing his beard and wearing and not wearing a hat. Sam had been to the pub, got some bottles and was giving out with spritely tunes on a harmonica. I grabbed Helen and put into practice some of the steps Annette Southwell had taught me on the boat. Pretty soon what would now be called a 'wrap' party was underway.

More bottles were procured and people drifted in from the streets. A fiddler arrived from somewhere and Harry was persuaded to give him a few bob to do his stuff. It was bush dancing at which some of the actors and others were uncommon good. I picked it up quick enough (jigs and reels sum it up pretty well; you'll find it anywhere drunken Celts gather), and whirled Helen and others, male and female, around and jumped and shouted with the best of them. It's a pity the camera wasn't rolling; some of that action would've livened the film up considerably.

I don't know whether someone smelled something or whether 'flames shot into the night sky as the inebriates cavorted' (I'm quoting the newspaper report from memory now), but the music stopped and everyone started to yell 'Fire!' and to run. My instinct was to head for the street but Helen pulled me towards the fire. The free-standing wall was engulfed and the flames had spread to the main building which was roofless with a lot of light timber and tar paper lying about. The up-draught was terrific and the place was going up like a bonfire.

Harry had to be restrained from rushing into the building and only stopped struggling when a cameraman told him there was no film inside. Harry jumped up and down on the spot screaming at the fire.

'Bastard,' he yelled. 'Son of a bitch!' Suddenly he stopped and whipped around. 'Is anybody getting this?' he shouted.

Nobody was; a great fire went to waste along with a lot of costumes, props and greasepaint. Two fire engines arrived with a clanging of bells and a lot of shouting through a loud hailer. The horses calmly backed and filled until the machines were in position and the firemen got busy with the hoses. Before long the Southwell Screen Plays studio was a blackened shell emitting little hisses as drops of water fell on hot ashes.

'Any idea what could've started it, Captain?' Harry asked the fireman with the most buttons on his coat.

The man twitched his mountain sheep moustache and looked disapprovingly at the gang of film folk who were standing around. Most of us were holding glasses or bottles; we had cigars and cigarettes in our dirty, sweaty faces and some of us weren't standing too straight. He sniffed loudly and spat, walked back out of the lantern light and returned with a tin can. 'Yes, I have got an idea,' he said. 'Some idiot has been splashing kerosene about.'

19

The fire episode terminated my relationship with Harry Southwell. My name was omitted from all credits which I thought a bit vindictive given my sterling efforts with horse and gun, and there was even talk for a while of a prosecution for negligence or something such. I knew that horse wouldn't run, but I had to leave the Fitzroy house, which had been a comfortable billet, and move in with Helen Hawes. This was something I'd been trying to avoid for weeks but my expulsion after the fire ran me out of excuses.

Not that Helen wasn't an obliging and easy woman to live with. She had plenty of money for one thing which was agreeable. Harry hadn't paid me all he owed me (something I got used to in the film business, but I was mightily put out then), so my pockets had plenty of air in them.

'What would you *like* to do, love?' Helen asked me one morning. We were lying in bed in her loft in Carlton. From the window I could see out across more tree tops than roofs. Melbourne was in the grip of a January heat-wave; the night had been scarcely cooler than the day and we were very sweaty after the morning grapple.

'I don't know. Go to Hollywood and get into films?'

She laughed and pulled a cotton nightgown over her head. 'You're a funny creature. You say I don't know and then come out with something quite specific. Do you *think* before you speak, Dick?'

'No. Does anyone?'

'I do. I'm going to make coffee. When I come back we'll have a serious talk about the future.'

What she meant was that *she* would have a serious talk about the future, first to herself, then to me. That's how it was when she came back with the coffee.

She opened with: 'Why don't we go into partnership? You can take photographs. I've seen them.'

Opening with a question and an assertion, you see. Out on the court; I win the toss; my serve.

'Yours make mine look silly,' I said.

'True. But I could teach you to be good enough to do the society stuff, or some of it.'

'What d'you mean, some?'

'Have you ever had a good look at my society portraits?'

I slurped down some coffee; she made very good coffee, too. 'Hmm,' I said.

'Notice anything?'

I ran my mind's eye over an album she'd shown me. 'Moustaches,' I said.

She leaned across and kissed me. I like the smell of coffee on a woman's breath in the morning, it arouses me.

'Hands off. Clever boy, Dick. Men, mostly men.'

'Men have the money.'

'That's not why I get the work. Follow me?'

I looked down at the rumpled bedclothes and up at her fine breasts sticking through the thin cotton. I couldn't help it.

Used goods, I thought, *very used.*

'Shocked, Dick?'

'No. You mean I could . . .?'

'Exactly. You see, society people are divided up two

ways: there are rich old men with young wives and rich old men with old wives.'

I *was* shocked. Here she was telling me that I should bed down the young wives and grab the portrait fees while she did the same for the old buffers. What she failed to consider was male solidarity; imagination may not be my strongest suit, but I could easily conceive myself as an older man taking good care of a young wife or as having a wife who was a bit past it. Helen's proposition didn't attract me and I laughed it off. She looked puzzled but she'd got used to my easy-going ways and no doubt thought she'd return to the attack again.

Have you ever noticed how women set about trying to change men about as soon as the shoes are together on the floor under the bed? You were strong and masterful at first, or funny and a tonic to the flagging spirit, but after a while this becomes domineering and irresponsible. The woman who's drunk with you and screwed with you from dawn to dusk and back to daylight becomes a mass of problems which are all, somehow, your fault. Oh, everything will be all right, if you'll just change into a male version of her!

Well, I had other ideas. I could see myself spending what remained of the summer pleasantly with Miss Helen Hawes of Carlton and Brighton (she had a nice little seaside place a few miles out of Melbourne), but after that I'd get a bank together somehow and be off to Americky, quick smart.

So what was I doing a month later, tossing around in bed in a Toorak mansion with Gwendoline Cavendish, wife of Sir Thomas of the same name? Well, I told you I was given to lust and laziness. Helen wore me down by putting her idea to me at every opportunity and, truth to tell, this helped me to get a little tired of her faster than I ordinarily would have done. The remedy for jaded lovers, or one of them, is fresh bodies. Anyway, since she as good as said she slept with every greybeard who commissioned a portrait it would've have been priggish of me to shy away from the under-attended wives.

Helen instructed me in camera technique so that I got reasonably proficient at the portrait. This was useful in my later brief stint as a private eye in Hollywood – for real I mean, not in the movies – and taught me enough so that I could get by at developing and enlarging. She also arranged the meeting with Lady Cavendish, who was an under-attended wife if ever there was one.

I presented myself at her front door one hot February morning and was told to go around the back by the morning-suited servant. Perhaps I'd had an early morning bracer and was feeling brave or perhaps the servant was smaller than me, I can't recall. Anyway, I stood my ground and insisted on seeing 'Lady Gwendoline'.

One of the first things she did was put me right on that. (Sir Tom just being a baronet and her not the daughter of a peer, she was just Lady Cavendish.) I didn't see why, or why it mattered, but jumped-up judies like Gwen are very strong on that sort of thing. After a bit of a fracas Gwen arrives wearing a dress that made her look something like a mushroom – it was all billowing, layered silk, very fetching, and eminently photographable and peel-offable. As it turned out, Gwen was game for both. She soothed the servant and escorted me across the green lawn (lawns everywhere else in the city were brown) to a sort of pavilion at the end of the garden.

She was a pleasure to watch – not tall but beautifully made and a lovely mover. Contrary to what you might think, the real aristocrats slouch and mooch along mostly and it's only the people who've had to make something of themselves that study movement. Gwen was a graduate with beautiful carriage of her finely shaped, blonde head,

157

big firm breasts and just a suggestion of ladylike movement of her behind.

Another servant followed up with a tray on which there was champagne in an ice bucket and some food I don't remember. She scarcely looked at me while the servant was there but when he'd gone she turned her big, blue eyes on me and parted her lips.

'Let's do the photograph quickly,' she said.

As I discovered, that was the only thing she had a mind to do quickly. I set the camera up, arranged her by a table with some flowers, ducked under the cloth and got a couple of quick exposures without any hitches. She was starting to drop parts of the dress almost as soon as I got my head out into the light. I barely had time for a gulp of champagne before she was clawing at my loose artistic tie and trying to get her hand inside my shirt.

'The servants?' I gasped.

'No,' she said. 'Not for hours.'

She was right; we got down to it right there, on and around a padded cane lounge with the sunlight flooding in over us and an occasional frond or leaf getting in the way. She was a mobile, active lover who liked to make use of all the fittings on hand. It must have been three quarters of an hour before I could draw breath.

She lay back on the lounge, naked except for a black velvet band around her throat, and held out her glass for champagne.

'You are splendid,' she said. 'It's rare to find a man with stamina.'

I nodded modestly and poured. To tell the truth I was having a little difficulty, not in performing, but in finishing off if you get my meaning. Very unfamiliar situation – titled lady, servants, house like a castle – it was holding me back, but Gwen wasn't complaining. I got down a glass or two and wondered how the business end of things had been arranged.

'Er, should be a fine portrait, Lady Gwendoline.'

She burst into laughter and that's when she set me straight on the title. 'Sir Thomas is seventy-three,' she said. 'He can't satisfy me.'

I almost said something like: 'He's probably been at it forty years longer than you, nothing to be ashamed of,' but I just did some more nodding and pouring. I was still in fine fettle, you see, and she wasn't really interested in small talk.

'Come here,' she said. I went across and she found a new use for champagne.

Some time later she was sitting in a big wicker chair tearing the petals off a rose. 'Of course, there will have to be other sittings.'

'Eh?'

'More sittings. I'm not sure that this place is the right setting. Some interiors perhaps. You can do interiors, can't you, Richard?'

'If the light is right.'

'There's wonderful light in the master bedroom.'

There was, too, as I found out a few days later and confirmed on another couple of visits. She must have fixed the servants good and properly because a blind butler and a blind deaf mute maid couldn't have failed to understand what was going on. I enjoyed it well enough – the four-poster bed was another novelty – but I remained a trifle nervous. There were a few portraits of the master of the house around and he looked like a pretty capable old gent, seventy plus or no. Added to which, Gwen wasn't really much of a conversationalist: she'd worked in a teashop before catching Sir Tom's eye, and clothes and society gossip occupied her mind when it wasn't on sex.

She was selfish about sex, too, only caring for her own pleasure. After our second indoors bout I suggested to Helen that the job was done. We weren't on good terms by this time; I think she was jealous or perhaps just annoyed at the exhausted condition I'd presented in.

159

'Very well,' she said. 'I received the fee today. She appears to be very satisfied.'

That decided me. I was happy to bed a woman in lieu of payment for a meal or a warm coat or to worm my way into a place to lie low, but this was different. Outright whoring it felt like, not for Browning. The problem would be how to discourage the lady. I mulled it over but I couldn't exactly ask Helen for advice. As it turned out, the cold back she presented to me in bed, three nights in a row, helped provide the solution.

The next time I presented at Toorak Gwen had come up with the idea of a session in the billiard room. This raised my nervousness level considerably; the walls were lined with hunting trophies and other evidences of Sir Tom's abundant manhood. When Gwen draped herself across the green baize in stockings, that neck band and garters she'd had sent from Paris, well, I was nervous and I'd been denied for three nights. I advanced ardently enough, too ardently. The partly clothed female form has always had a powerful effect on me and this time I reacted too powerfully, much too soon.

She'd dropped her head back on the table; she raised it now to see what was holding me up, although that's the wrong expression. Her big blue eyes went wide in disgust.

'Get out!' she hissed. 'Get out!'

I collected my clothes and camera and got. I was driving a smart Chevrolet at the time, parking it in the street near the entrance to the house. As I was unlocking the car a Rolls came down the road and made a stately turn at the gates. I caught a glimpse of the man in the back. It was Sir Thomas Cavendish, sitting straight and tall. I could see the jut of his jaw; I could almost hear the clink of his medals. I started the Chevvy and got out of Toorak in record time.

I thought about it on the drive back to Carlton. The traffic was light, still horse-drawn a lot of it, and driving was still relaxing. People actually went for drives to think and relax. It's hard to believe. It seemed unlikely that Cavendish's arrival was a coincidence. The man worked like a fiend and Gwen had said that it would take an earthquake or the declaration of war to get him away from his desk.

The concerned, guilty look on Helen's face gave me the answer.

'You told him?' I said.

'Yes.'

'Why?'

'I love you.'

Damn funny way of showing it, I thought, to put a man within reach of the horsewhip. But I've always been a sucker for women who say that they love me; I love them back for at least an hour afterwards and Helen and I made things up in fine style for the rest of the day in the loft.

20

There was no more talk of Dick screwing for his supper after that, and I fancy Helen wasn't doing much in that line either. We were happy, in fact, lazing around town in the cooler parts of the days and nights and going down to the seaside at Brighton. There was none of this strutting around the beach with a piece of string around your waist that you see nowadays. Helen had a rented cabin in the ti-tree scrub at the back of the beach and we used to change into very modest costumes before venturing onto the sand.

I'd learned to swim in the Oakhampton creek so the mild waters of Port Phillip Bay had no terrors for me. Helen wasn't a swimmer; she hoisted up the skirt of her swimming costumes (women wore things like tunics which covered their chest and came down to mid-calf) and paddled in the shallows. We did the things lovers do – walked along the beach at dawn and dusk, threw stones into the waves, wrote messages in the sand. I wasn't altogether easy about it: if I'd had to put all my hopes and plans into one word on the sand it'd have been 'Hollywood'. Helen's word I felt sure would have been 'marriage'.

Summer gave way to autumn. We ate in the Chinese

cafes of Little Bourke Street, sipped iced drinks in the backyard of the Brighton bungalow and made love in the Carlton loft. I still didn't have any money to speak of and in March *The Kelly Gang* was offered to the public.

It was a curious experience for me; I suppose I felt like all those novelists I met later whose books had been adapted for the screen. If the movie was a failure they took no blame but they cashed in if it was a success. My name appeared nowhere on the credits of *Kelly* but I would have blown my trumpet loudly enough if it had been a hit. It was a lamentable flop.[19]

Most of the critics regretted the film's subject. Fresh from a time when a couple of million people had been slaughtered, newspaper scribblers got up in arms about glorifying outlaws who'd been the cause of the death of a few rascally policemen. Southwell had anticipated this problem by putting a long homily at the beginning of the film about the perils of a life of bushranging, as if anyone was going to take to it in 1920. This probably helped to kill public interest before the story got underway, but there were other problems.

Helen and I sneaked into the show one day in the city. I was wriggling with boredom within a few minutes and the thing ran for two hours. Helen had to hiss at me to sit still.

'It's terrible,' I whispered.

'You look lovely on your horse.'

Well, that was true enough and I suppose I managed to hold my seat just by waiting for the scenes I was in. Even so, it was hard work. The acting was broad and over-emphatic, the sets looked ill-lit and crude and the sequences were long and boring. There were a few successfully dramatic moments, like the close-ups of the death of Aaron Sherritt, and the shattering of the windows in the Glenrowan Hotel, but overall the film showed up Harry Southwell's deficiencies as a director glaringly. At one point I burst into laughter along with everyone else in the theatre.

'What's wrong?' Helen said.

'Read the title,'

She pulled the spectacles she was generally too vain to wear out of their case and hooked them on. The title read: 'Oh, dear, Ned, you are so dear to me, dear.'

'Jesus,' Helen said.

That led to an outraged 'Shh' from the woman sitting next to her and a sharp reply from Helen which brought the woman's companion into it so that soon everyone sitting around us was hissing and groaning. The music stopped and the attendant threatened to eject us. Helen and I sat through the rest of the film, hand in hand and suppressing giggles.

Out in the soft night air we walked back through the parks towards Carlton. The leaves were thick on the ground and we scuffed through them, still laughing at the film. I collapsed on to a thick bed of leaves and imitated Godfrey Cass's gestures as the fallen Ned. Helen bent double with laughter.

'You should be a comedian, Dick. You'd do marvellously.'

I climbed up a little grumpily; I was thinking of heroic roles myself, swords, muskets, distressed damsels to be comforted on and off the set, that sort of thing.

'What's wrong?' Helen took my arm as we resumed our walk.

'Nothing.'

'This film business is silly, don't you think? I thought it might be a nice change and lead to something, but after that . . .'

She burst out laughing again, no doubt remembering the trial scene in which the judge had born an uncanny resemblance to a spaniel.

I clammed up. There's nothing better than being happy with a woman, that is, when she bounces along with you, shares the fun and doesn't get moody. But the trouble

164

is that women don't understand that men have difficulty expressing their feelings and needs and they have no talent for guessing what's on a man's mind. Then they trample on your hopes.

Helen clutched my arm tighter. 'Never mind, love,' she said, not having the faintest idea what it was I was minding. 'I've got a lovely surprise for you. Something that'll really cheer you up.'

'What?' I said.

'A surprise. Wait and see.'

That was my mistake. I *did* wait; I should've started running.

I fiddled about with a few things, considered trying to set up a limousine business like Green's in London, thought about throwing in with a bookie, but somehow I couldn't feel right about going into business in Melbourne. I missed Sydney for one thing, although I wasn't in a hurry to get back within reach of 'Wild Bill'. The Long Bay matter would have long blown over and I supposed there wasn't much chance of being recognised as William Hughes. I'd changed a good deal and the majority of the chaps who'd known me as a soldier were beyond the reach of any court. I started to think about Sydney as a staging post to Los Angeles.

Meantime there was Helen's surprise. It turned out to be a fancy dress party to be held in one of the plusher houses in Brighton. The residents were on an overseas trip and Helen had somehow contrived the use of this white pillared edifice with a ballroom, oak staircases and chandeliered ceilings set in an acre of rolling lawns and sculptured gardens.

She told me all about it one night in Brighton over brandy. I was still muttering darkly about a future in the movie business and Helen told me that there would be some film people present.

'Who?' I said.

'Oh,' she said airily, 'Raymond Longford, Lottie Lyell.'

That's interesting, I thought. 'Who else?'

She named some sporting figures like Lewis, the jockey who'd taken Artilleryman first past the post in the 1919 Melbourne Cup, Tommy Uren, the boxer, and others. 'A very mixed group, darling,' Helen said, 'and I've excluded the two categories you dislike most.'

I was getting pretty keen on the idea by this time and the brandy was going down extremely well. I gave her a hug and we exchanged a kiss that promised well for later on. 'What two categories d'you mean?'

'Politicians and clergymen.'

I laughed and gave her another squeeze. She was dead right there and I appreciated her thoughtfulness. She was a nice woman, Helen; she certainly tried to please me in the small things while pleasing herself in the big ones.

I must be frank. I was a bit starved for company and fun; Helen held the purse strings and was keeping a fairly tight rein on me as well. Oh, in the nicest way: 'Let's go out, dear; here, you hold the money' and all that, but I was still under the thumb. A big bash might give me a chance to kick over the traces a little and, besides, I might meet someone useful and get a leg up.

So I was ready for anything when the great night arrived. It was late April or early May and the year was on the turn, just the time for this sort of thing. A little cool so that the dancing is welcome, but not so cool that the women are covering their arms and chests and presenting you with so many hooks and eyes and buttons and laces that it's hardly worth the trouble. Helen had done the thing in style, hired the best catering firm with the best drink johnnies and prettiest little snack servers you ever did see. She was looking magnificent herself; she'd spent the day at the hairdressers and a king's ransom on something low cut and black with red trim. I fancy I was up to the mark in my wing-collared soup and fish.

The old drunk (or bore, when he wasn't drunk) Scott Fitzgerald hit the nail on the head when he called the 1920s the Jazz Age. It was all the go in Melbourne as early as 1920, I can tell you, and Helen had hired the hottest orchestra available, Bunty Browne's Scorching Six, to kick things along. They set up in the ballroom, close to a supply of booze and where they could also be heard, through an open set of floor-to-ceiling French windows, out on the terrace. Bunty Browne was a six footer who must have weighed well over two hundred and fifty pounds. Standing up, trombone in hand, he looked a formidable figure and it occurred to me that his popularity at affairs like this might reflect the fact that he would be damned useful as a bouncer if things got rough.

Guests started to arrive around nine and I greeted the first few suavely enough; after that, their faces began to blur and I didn't bother. I have to confess that I got fairly tanked fairly early. I hadn't seen French champagne of that quality and in solid supply since my days at Robespierre's and I'm afraid I sampled it too freely. That was a mistake as it turned out; if I'd had clear vision I might have been able to take evasive action.

Helen's friends were mostly young and mostly rich people who knew other young, rich people. They were all experienced at having a good time and a party in a ballroom was just their style. The music blasted out and the heels were kicked up and the levels in the punch bowl and bottle went down the way they will when the booze is free, the woman are pretty and the talk is loud. Some of the women *were* pretty, by God, and I began to get an idea why Helen hadn't trotted me around to her friends' houses more than a trifle. There were a few good fellows there, too, chaps from the best schools in Melbourne and between dances it was most pleasant to smoke a cigar out on the terrace and listen to male talk about stocks and shares, horses, real estate and that sort of thing.

The Scorching Six seemed to know all the latest numbers and Bunty whipped them into a frenzy with his little dances up in front; for such a big man he had a light, airy step; he'd cut up for five minutes and then go on with his tromboning not a whit out of breath. In other company all that booze and jazz could have made things pretty willing by midnight; you'd have expected a fight or two and the odd scream from the shrubbery, but this was the Melbourne upper crust and they seemed to set limits on themselves. I heard a few voices raised in anger, once when I danced a little too long with a very fetching redhead in a green silk dress, but there were always cooler heads around. A few of the younger bloods staggered into the garden and came back a trifle pale, but no carpets were ruined.

'Are you having a good time, darling?' Helen was at my elbow, fresh from a dance, looking slightly flushed and with her bosom heaving.

'I am,' I said. I was, too, and looking at her I was thinking that I'd have an even better time later on if I could just slow down on the grog and perhaps get a bit of coffee into me.

'That's good.' She took my arm and steered me out to the terrace.

'Hold hard,' says I. 'We've scarcely had a dance, you and I. I want to try that . . . what is it . . . Melbourne rag. Ho, Bunty, play it again, I . . .'

'Not now, love. Later. There's someone I want you to meet.'

'Meet? Oh, you pearl of a woman, you. Someone in the film business is it, someone to give old Dick a dashing part?' I sketched a few parries and thrusts as she drew me across the terrace.

'No, darling. Though there *is* a man here who might be able to do something for you if you've set your heart on it.'

'Hollywood,' I muttered.

'Yes, we might. Who knows.'

I heard that, I thought. We, she said, we. So that's the way the wind was blowing. It sobered me a fraction I fancy. I'd been thinking of Browning the lone wolf in Hollywood, not Browning the tied-down one-of-a-pair. I drew in a deep breath of the night air; there was a tang of the sea in it and a touch of new-mown lawn. The lights blazed from the house and the jazz drifted through to the terrace in gusts of happy sound. I was standing stock-still in one of those rare moments in which I analysed life. I was thinking that I should be happy having such jolly times with this beautiful woman who was now pulling me by the arm, jerking me out of my reverie, dragging me across to where another woman stood in the shadows.

'It's such a coincidence, darling,' Helen was saying, 'that you should know each other. One of my oldest friends. It's amazing.'

'Who? What?' I said.

We were over near a low wall between the terrace and the garden. A large blonde woman was standing there raising a cigarette to her mouth.

'Richard,' Helen said, 'I'm sure you remember Elizabeth Macknight.'

21

It had happened this way: during one of the periods of coldness in our relationship, Helen had gone through my things and discovered the envelope on which Elizabeth had written her name and address. This had puzzled her. She'd known Elizabeth from school days but had lost touch with her over the war years. She renewed the acquaintance, but I suppose you don't sit down over the first cup of tea in ten years and start flinging questions about men out of the past. As she later reported it to me, Helen had sidled up to the matter by asking Elizabeth if she'd seen the film of *The Kelly Gang*.

'Yes,' Elizabeth replied. 'Rubbish!'

'Did you recognise anyone in it?'

'No.'

'One of the actors knows you.'

'Ooh, who?' Elizabeth was totally screen-struck.

'Richard Browning. He played a trooper and other bits; he was a member of the jury.'

'I've never heard of him.'

Helen laid it out for her then – the envelope, the dashing, moustachioed six foot two inch Browning, but Elizabeth still disclaimed all knowledge. You see what this means, of course. She must've been leaving envelopes in chaps' bedrooms all over Europe, no doubt hoping that she'd strike it lucky with one of them.

I've always suspected that she swore some dark oath to the effect that the first of her overseas lovers to re-appear would get the treatment. However, she must have played it very cunning with Helen. Polite interest, appar-ently, was all she displayed and she passed off the en-velope as 'the sort of thing one did for those poor boys who were dying over there, so far from home'. Dying? I'd never been fitter apart from being paralytic drunk. Horseshit!

Anyway, there we were, two years later and she recog-nised me instantly. I'll say this for Elizabeth, when her own self-interest was involved her mind was as quick as lightning.

'Richard! Of course, how wonderful to see you.'

'Er, hello.' I looked around, wishing the terrace would stop spinning and the garden beds wouldn't jump up and down. I must have had some mad idea that I could escape because I tipped my hat to Elizabeth (although I was bare-headed) and started to wander off. Helen grabbed me.

'Now you and Elizabeth have a lovely talk, dear. People are starting to leave and I must see them off. Hasn't it been a *heavenly* party? It still is . . . don't go, Elizabeth, will you?' Her heels clattered across the terrace and she was gone. I looked blearily at the woman who'd put out her cigarette and was waiting for me to light a new one. I fumbled a match alight somehow.

'How have you been keeping . . . Tony?'

'Er . . . all right. You?'

'I'm well. I'm glad to see that you came through it all right – the war, I mean.'

'Yes.' Her image was blurred and unsteady. *Christ*, I thought, *why can't the bloody woman stand still*. 'Er . . . about that Tony thing, I . . .'

'No need to explain. They were dreadful times. Isn't Helen a wonderful girl?'

She said this in what I later came to know as her acid voice. She adopted it when she was saying the complete opposite of what she was thinking. She wasn't aware of the habit but it helped me to cope with her, not that I ever coped well. At that moment I was thinking that Helen *was* a wonderful girl, *the* most wonderful girl, except why didn't she come and rescue me?

'Wonderful girl,' I said. 'Where is she?'

'Sit down.' She pulled me down onto a seat that ran along the wall and sat down herself. I remember being surprised at the strength of the pull. Then it all came back to me – that ghastly outfit, the boots, the douche . . . I struggled to get up but I was too drunk to co-ordinate body and legs properly. 'You stay here and tell me everything that's happened.'

She proceeded to tell me everything that had happened to *her*. I won't pretend that I grasped it all then, given the condition I was in, but I got the gist and heard more later. She and the dreadful Pat had re-joined their nursing unit and been transshipped to England. Believe it or not she'd hung around looking for more wars to go to and she actually went to those parts of Russia where the Bolsheviks were still mopping up and sundry odds and sods were still shooting at each other. (No doubt she left envelopes in a few cavalry officers' bedrooms here and there.) She'd not long returned to Australia and she was setting about establishing a series of private hospitals. Her family had money, you see – and that was about the only thing she said that interested me.

But she was also doing things as well as talking. In my befuddled state it took me a while to realise that she'd put her hand inside my trousers and was getting to work with her strong fingers and firm palm.

'That's my boy,' she crooned. 'You're a fine boy, I remember you.'

It will sound strange, but it was oddly pleasant. The

sight of Helen and all the other lovely women around had made me randy enough but I was in no fit condition to do anything in the least energetic about it. Elizabeth had hit on just the right strategy for the occasion. Besides, she didn't look too bad herself: big, of course, with wide white shoulders and a magnificent bosom that was mostly on display. The bigness continued all the way down unfortunately, but it wasn't easy to see that in the shadows with her wearing a stylishly cut full-length dress. I put my hand on her left breast and we sat there squeezing away happily with the breathing becoming a touch more rapid.

'What business are you in, Richard.' Squeeze, squeeze.

'Oh, films, you know.' Squeeze.

'Papa adores films, he's often talked of putting some money into films.' Squeeze. 'He'd *love* to see his name up on the screen.'

Now, *that* was interesting. A closer look and I could see that the jewellery Elizabeth was wearing hadn't come cheap and I struggled to remember the address she'd written on the envelope – The Turrets, was it? The Buttress? Anyway, it was something that sounded like money. From some inner well of strength I collected my thoughts. I took my hand off her tit and gently removed hers from my crotch.

'Elizabeth,' I croaked. 'We mustn't, not now, not here.' I tried a kiss and landed fairly close to the mark.

Her breathing rate seemed to increase. 'You're right. Oh, where, when?'

My mind raced or stumbled ahead. 'I'll telephone,' I gasped. 'That's it, I'll telephone. I still have your address, of course.'

'Oh, Tony . . . Richard, have you? Have you really?'

'Yes.'

'And have you thought of me?'

Had I but known what was in store I would have

wished for a rusty nail to stick into my bum at that moment and for tetanus and lockjaw to strike instantly. But I didn't. 'Yes, I have,' I said.

It was all a terrible mistake, really. I just thought I could keep the lady company occasionally, meet her father and discuss the film business, perhaps enter into a mutually beneficial business arrangement. Before I knew what had happened, the whole thing had got out of hand.

I admit I was indiscreet about the meetings with Elizabeth. It never occurred to me that Helen would have the least suspicion or that, if she did find out, that she could imagine that I would prefer Elizabeth to her.

I'll confess it was a nice change though. We met the first time in the Carlton loft when Helen was away on a photographic assignment, and plunging around in all that soft, white flesh was like, well . . . like skiing, I suppose. The next time was in a room in one of Elizabeth's private hospitals. Not a very conducive environment you might think, but you'd be surprised at the things you can do on one of those high, narrow beds.

Then Helen found out. It was Elizabeth, of course, who got the message to her, although I didn't find that out until later. Helen, who'd originally been happy to have me bedding down the millionaires' wives, reacted completely differently to my infidelity with her old school chum. In the first place she threw most of my things out of the loft window. I ran down to retrieve the first lot and she pelted me as I stood there in the laneway.

'Bastard!' she shrieked. 'With that fat slug, you bastard.'

'Helen, love . . .' A shoe hit me and my hip flask came sailing down to land with an ominous tinkle on the bricks.

'You vile louse!'

I raced up the stairs and back into the loft – into a hail

of matches, collar studs and the like.

'Helen, it was an accident. Just the one . . .'

'Liar. Look!' She shoved an enormous pair of lace knickers at me. 'I only wanted to make you happy. You seemed so lonely, with no friends, no family. An old friend . . . nurse or something . . . the bitch!'

'Love.'

'Don't! Get out! Get out! You nothing! No talent, nothing . . .'

I gathered a few things of mine that were strewn around, stuffed them into a bag and stalked out.

A fine gesture, but it left me high and dry. I had less than twenty pounds in the bank, the clothes I stood in and carried, and that was all. The car was Helen's. I should have gone straight to the railway and caught a train for Sydney, or signed on as a deckhand on a vessel bound for anywhere. Almost anything would have been better than what I did. I went to Elizabeth.

First, she took me into her office in the hospital. This was her new establishment in East Melbourne. it was an old house, set in small but pleasant grounds, and designed to care for a certain category of old people – rich ones. She got me a drink and sat with me on the couch. She was wearing a modish dress, white and blue, starched and with just a suggestion of the nursing profession about it. In my shaken state her cool efficiency was very welcome. She kissed me on the cheek.

'Poor boy.'

'How could you have left your smalls there?'

'I'm terribly sorry. I was so excited.' She clutched me and let me feel that soft, warm bosom. I sighed and put my hand on her knee. I needed a bed for the night and time to think.

'Well, what's done is done.'

'Yes.' She stroked my cheek. 'Richard, I think it's time you met my father to talk about your film ideas.'

Elizabeth always had wonderful timing. She got up and

175

locked the office door. I had another drink and we smoked a cigarette. Then we tested the couch springs.

Cameron Macknight had had a charmed financial life. He was the son of a wool baron who'd avoided all the pitfalls – over-extension into drought-prone country, over-borrowing from banks, splurging on city mansions and trips 'home'. The solid fortune the father had handed down to the son had consolidated on the land and in the Melbourne property boom of the 1880s. The Macknight character was an interesting blend of adventurism and caution (Elizabeth had it in full measure); they knew when to buy and when to sell but also how to insure. Cameron Macknight once explained to me how he got in a no-lose situation in the war. I didn't grasp the details, but I gathered he was in a position to profit from the expansion of her industry if Germany had won, and was in line for massive reparations when she lost.

I picked these points up over tea, coffee and soda water at The Gables. I never saw a stronger hater of drink than Cameron Macknight; there were a number of fine drinking rooms at The Gables – dens, billiards room, conservatory and so on – and not a drop to be found in any of them. Elizabeth and her sister Daphne were enthusiastic, semi-secret tipplers; Mrs Maud Macknight was a drunkard. It was not a happy family.

The night Elizabeth introduced me to her family I felt I had stepped into a play by one of those crazy Norwegians. (I've never seen one of these things, about ducks and women called Gabbler, but I've heard of them.) I walked through the huge entrance doors, all togged up properly and with peppermint on my breath, to be met by a reeling, lurching woman who tried to take my hat although I'd already given it to a servant. Down a magnificent staircase comes an old, white-whiskered, pale-faced codger with rabbit trap jaws and with a steel rod for a backbone.

'Maud,' he hissed. 'To your room.' Then he lifted his voice a little. 'Daphne!'

A woman built on the same lines as Elizabeth, although younger and bigger, appeared from a doorway. She strode across the elaborately tiled floor, took the shaking woman by the arm and led her out of the presence of the master and me. Macknight stood on the second stair from the bottom; he wasn't a tall man but this gave him elevation.

'I must apologise, Mr Browning. My wife is unwell.'

I'd seen 'Wild Bill' in a like condition many a time. 'My sympathies,' I murmured (this was the sort of thing I'd picked up from Farnol in Long Bay.) 'I'm delighted to meet you, Mr Macknight.'

'Yes. Now, where is Elizabeth?'

The servant, a lean, dignified number in a black suit who'd witnessed everything but betrayed no signs of having seen anything, coughed politely. 'Miss Elizabeth is in the library, sir.'

'Good,' said Macknight. 'Show Mr Browning through, Manning. I'll see to my wife and join your promptly.'

Manning steered me towards massive oak doors. He threw them open to reveal Elizabeth sitting at a table with a glass of sherry in her hand. Later, I came to realise what brave behaviour this was. The library was for show, of course: floor-to-ceiling books of incredible dullness to judge by their uniformity, size and bindings. There were four chairs set around a low table on which stood the sherry decanter. I glanced back at the open door and walked quickly across to peck Elizabeth's cheek. She smiled and poured me a glass. I reached for my pocket but she stopped me.

'Papa detests smoking. Don't, if you want anything from him. He dislikes drinking, too, so be careful to be moderate.' She giggled, a fairly nauseating sound to come from a person of her size. 'It would never do for him to find you in the state in which I found you – on our first and second meetings.'

I smiled. Elizabeth had a knack of making me feel uneasy by referring, in a seemingly light-hearted way, to some of my less dignified moments. I looked at the chair settings.

'Will your mother be joining us?'

'Hardly. Sit down, Richard. Don't be nervous.'

'I'm not nervous. But if I can't smoke I can't sit still.'

'You'll have to learn. I did. Papa permits Daphne and me to have sherry and wine. Me, because I was so brave in the war and Daphne because she takes such wonderful care of mother. But he would never allow us to smoke.'

I sat down. 'Sounds like you don't have much fun around here.'

'Don't sound so grumbly, dear. No, we don't. Apart from seeing films, Papa's idea of fun is to make more money this week than last.'

'He's got a point. It's certainly no fun to make less.'

She sipped her sherry (I'd put mine down in a gulp) and smiled. 'Display that sort of wit on that subject and you'll get along famously.'

Oddly enough, we did. He was a scoundrel, of course, a corrupter of public officers, an unscrupulously low tenderer for public contracts who then had a hundred reasons why the costs had to go up, a sweater of labour and a rack renter. But what man in his position wasn't? His wowserism was hard to take but he was no hypocrite – no mealy-mouthed Christianity for Macknight. The Gospel according to Mammon, that was his style. For some reason he was keen on films, and when I told him I'd put the shots through the hotel windows he was mightily impressed.

'Could have done with you in the Western District in my father's day,' he said.

'How's that, sir?'

'Aboriginals.'

We were sitting down to dinner by this time, Cameron, Daphne, Elizabeth and yours truly, climbing outside an indifferent roast which the girls and I were washing down with an insipid claret. Washing is hardly the word: sipping the stuff I was. Macknight drank iced water.

'Richard is interested in making his own films, Papa,' Elizabeth said.

'Oh really, my boy. What subject?'

I'll swear it flashed into my head just then. 'Pioneer dramas, sir. The struggle for the land against the blacks and the elements.'

'And the miners and agitators,' Elizabeth chipped in.

'Pass the potatoes, please,' says Daphne.

'Splendid!' Macknight cried, thumping his fist on the polished teak. 'Just what the country needs!'

'You made a wonderful impression,' Elizabeth told me later as she was farewelling me out on the gravel path that swept around the house. I'd have a good tramp from there just to get to the gate.

'D' you think so?' I was sober of course and able to judge my own performance critically, which wasn't usually the case after a feed with the rich.

'Oh yes. Oh God, Richard, I wish I could have you tonight.'

She had this uncomfortably direct manner, quite took the fun out of things. I was living in a hotel in South Yarra, over the river from Elizabeth's East Melbourne hospital. Although she was a few years older than me, Elizabeth, who lived at home, was obliged to *be* at home every night. Macknight had the most rigid ideas of female behaviour and she was dependent on him for operating capital.

Compared with Daphne in the wood-panelled, baronial dining room, Elizabeth looked positively sylph-like under the Brighton moon. I took the risk of eyes watching from

179

the house and kissed her energetically. 'Tomorrow,' I said.

'Oh, yes, yes. At 11 o'clock, Richard. At the hospital, at 11am precisely.'

You see what I mean about her ability to take the fun out of it?

22

Things moved along very rapidly. I met Macknight several times more (the next time I was at The Gables, for lunch, Mrs Macknight gave me a shovel and tried to get me to work in the garden). Macknight's club, at least the one he took me to, was the Horatian which was progressive enough to have screened films for the enjoyment of its members. Good food, too, although it was damnable to have to work your way through a three course lunch without a drop to drink. It was an even greater agony to have to go two or three hours without a smoke.

Brown Knight Screen Productions Ltd was formed with a nominal amount of capital from me and a heavy subscription from old Cameron. By chance, I kept the original company papers and had them looked at much later by a film lawyer who told me that it would have been impossible for me to have made a penny out of Brown Knight, no matter how successful it might have been. I mention this to forestall any possible sympathy for Macknight in the light of my own behaviour.

It was getting cold in Melbourne and I began to see some of the pleasures of working on the production side in films. Warm clothes for one thing, long cosy lunches in well-heated clubs and chop houses and the company of amusing people, especially aspiring actresses. Not that I got the chance to do much in that line. Elizabeth kept me on a very tight rein: she'd leave me alone to pursue sports in which she had no interest, such as horse-riding and target-shooting, but when there was dining out to be done, or drinking or party-going, Elizabeth was by my side.

Just once, she persuaded me to try bush-walking which was her only outdoor activity. A party of us, all wrapped up against the autumn winds, trudged for miles through the Dandenong hills, startling lyre-birds and wallabies and, in my case at least, removing large patches of skin from the hands, face and feet. Back in town (I had a nice little flat in St Kilda, courtesy of Brown Knight, by this time), I rested my tired body in a deep bath while Elizabeth made me a hot toddy. After that she used some sort of embrocation which, she said, contained goanna oil. I must say it was very restorative, and, as Elizabeth was none the worse for the walk, we had a spirited romp to finish the day. That was the thing about Elizabeth – she would do and say the most terrible things to me and follow them up with something most agreeable. The terrible soon began to outweigh the agreeable however, until she landed the most painful blow of all.

Everything seemed to be going splendidly. Brown Knight's first production was to be *The Squatter's Dream*, an epic tale of triumph against nature, primitive man and officious bureaucrats. Cameron's vision was of a film stretching from convict days to the present (something on the scale of *Intolerance*); it would have underlined the criminal nature of Australian society apart from the land-owners. In the Horatian he used to get quite heated on the subject.

'A constant battle against the riff-raff, that's the story of Australia, Richard.'

We were on first name terms by now. 'Yes, Cameron.'

'We need a scenarist who understands that.'

'We do.'

That was one of the early problems; Macknight had a mass of material in the form of letters and diaries of his pioneer forbears which he wanted to use as the foundation of the story. The Macknight clan had settled in the Western District where they'd slaughtered the Aboriginals, torn out all the good timber and turned half the land into a rabbit run. No scenarist I contacted displayed any real interest in *The Squatter's Dream*, still less in the clan Macknight. One chap, a sharp-eyed Gallipoli veteran who said he'd got through the war by telling jokes in the trenches, *was* interested in the theme but only as the subject for a comedy. I couldn't see old Cameron buying that.

My greatest coup was managing to convince Cameron that the film should be set in New South Wales.

'Better weather, better country,' I told him one day in the Horatian.

'Hmm.' He looked out the window; Collins Street was being swept by gusts of wind-driven rain and the sky was the colour of lead. 'Place is full of wobblies,[20] isn't it?'

I didn't know what he meant, but I shook my head. 'Not in the film business.'

'I don't know.' Like many Victorians, Macknight was impossibly parochial, seeing Sydney as a seething den of vice. The non-parochial ones made their way up there as fast they could.

'Harry Southwell's moved his operation there,' I said. To anyone who really understood the film business this would have been an argument against what I was proposing. Southwell failed time after time, but Cameron, you will remember, had actually liked *The Kelly Gang*, mainly because of its anti-bushranging homilies and the (to him) satisfactory ending. Southwell was aces with Macknight.

'Do what you think best, Richard. I'm sure there must be a good temperance hotel in Sydney where I could stay.

How are you and Elizabeth getting along by the way?'

'Oh,' I said absently, 'First rate.' I really wasn't listening, having won my point. I suppose I was yearning for a brandy and a cigarette. I *should* have been listening; I should have been analysing every word and gesture. But I was well off guard. I hadn't seen such a lot of Elizabeth in recent days: she was subtle that way, able to space her appearances and intrusions out to make them unobjectionable. Besides, she was beavering away, making plans and contacts. So she told me. Poor fool that I was, I thought this was all to do with her expanding private hospital racket.

I was busy, you see, trying to learn the film production business on the run. There were technical people to consult, theatre owners to talk to, the press to deal with (there was a particularly aggressive outfit called *Picture Show*, reporters for which could turn up at your door at any time of the night and day), and politics at every turn. New South Wales, I learned, was in the grip of a socialist administration that would probably only want films about heroic miners and factory workers to be made. I gave *The Squatter's Dream* the working title of *Australia* to help get around these problems.

One problem looked intractable. Cameron Macknight refused to have his name associated with a film which showed the consumption of alcohol.

'But Cameron,' I protested (we were in the den at The Gables at the time, drinking tea), 'some of those pioneers were hard doers, bottle of rum a day men.'

'No drinking.'

'At least we could show the workers drinking. Drunken shearers and the like?'

'No drinking.'

I left it there, along with the question of the scenario and some insurance matters and negotiations about the price of film stock. I own I let the whole matter drift somewhat; it was agreeable to go riding out along the Geelong

Road or have a game of billiards in the Horatian when I could get away from Elizabeth. I was well and truly tired of her by this time; her conversation was mainly about the hospital business which is not something a man wants to talk about before or after dinner, and she was already up to the old female trick of trying to change me.

'Have you considered brown suits, Richard?' (I customarily wore blue or grey.)

'No. Don't like brown.' (I didn't tell her the reason for this which was that the shade reminded me too much of army uniform.)

'You should, it would suit your colouring. Do you think the velvet on the lapel of that topcoat is quite the thing?'

'I'm a film producer, must look the part.'

'A *gentleman* film producer.'

And so on. The truth was I could see no future for Brown Knight Productions. I'd had a good ride and even managed to skim a little of the operating capital off into my bank account. After a while I converted this to gold and acquired a money belt as I had in the dark, dangerous days of war. I extended the horse riding, pistol shooting and billiards playing and tried to ease myself out from under Elizabeth. (If you consider that the wrong expression just think about it for a moment. I can assure you it's not.)

A short conversation with Daphne one day put me on my guard and forced me to make departure plans. I'd run into Elizabeth's sister in the city by chance. She was buying cream buns and I seized the chance to pump her a little. I took her to a cafe and ordered coffee. She looked around, extracted one cream bun from the bag, and ate it in two bites.

'These are for mother,' she said, jaws working. 'It's almost the only thing she eats.'

She'll be lucky to see any of that lot, thinks I, but I just nodded. Daphne's conversation was almost exclusively about her mother and food, as Elizabeth's was about hospitals and clothes, and their father's about radicals and grog. 'Here's the coffee,' I said, 'Sugar?'

'Three lumps. When are you and Elizabeth getting married, Richard?'

I almost upset the table but I fought for control. 'Oh, I don't know. Has Elizabeth said anything about it?'

'No, but she's getting her trousseau together.'

'Oh?' I sipped coffee wishing it was brandy.

'Lilac silk.'

I shuddered. Daphne leaned across and touched my hand. 'I do believe you shook with passion, Richard. Just like in the novels. Oh, Elizabeth is so lucky!'

I was trembling now, and turning pale I fancy. I got out my cigarette case, opened it somehow and got a cigarette to my mouth.

'Can I have one?'

Daphne leaned forward eagerly. Flesh flowed across the little table and I had a vision of the size Elizabeth might reach if she abandoned all dietary restraint as Daphne had. I fumbled a cigarette out for her and lit it. She puffed luxuriously.

'Father would kill me,' she giggled.

I smoked in nervous puffs thinking of Macknight as my father-in-law, holding the money bags. I imagined the wedding with Daphne supporting Maud Macknight in a corner and the aftermath – enough lilac silk to make a parachute and, in the fullness of time, old Cameron promising the children a thou apiece if they signed the pledge.

'Drink up, Daphne, have to run.'

It was the douche bag that had caused me to feel secure. I knew that Elizabeth was still using it and in those days the most popular method of trapping a man into marriage was to get yourself in the family way. Of course old Macknight would have ranted and preached but there were conventions about that sort of thing – the worst hellfire and brimstone vilifiers became doting grandparents after the knot was tied and the pup was dropped.

Still, Daphne didn't have the wit to invent anything and women have an instinct about these things anyway. It was time to settle pressing accounts and head north. I scooted off to Spencer Street and bought a ticket on the night train to Sydney. Then it was back to the flat to throw things into bags, collect any cash lying around and leave time for a few stiff ones before the train left. I had an arrangement to meet Elizabeth that night and a braver man might have turned up and faced the thing but not I. The thought of her as Mrs B. was just too much to stomach. I rang The Gables and left a message with Manning that I was indisposed.

I'd finished packing and was just shrugging into my greatcoat when there was a knock at the door. I opened it and there stood Elizabeth, filling the aperture, a vision in blue velvet.

'Elizabeth, I . . ., ah . . .'

She brushed past me. 'No need to explain, Richard. My, you can pack quickly when you've a mind to. Give me a drink and a cigarette.'

I was so thrown I just set about obeying; I unshipped the brandy bottle and poured two stiff ones. She puffed smoke at the ceiling and stood with her back to the cold fireplace. 'I gather you had a chat with Daphne today?'

'Er, yes.'

'I knew you'd be reluctant but I didn't think you'd be this quick off the mark. What, leave poor father in the lurch? Desert me?'

'Elizabeth, I don't think . . .'

'We're getting married, Richard.'

Maybe it was the alcohol and nicotine, or perhaps it was the mere sight of her, all pale and boneless-looking, but I found the courage somewhere for a spirited reply. 'I'm hanged if I will!'

She smiled and reached into her handbag. Slowly she put down her cigarette, lifted her glass and finished the brandy. 'You'll be hanged if you don't,' she said. 'Have a look at this, Richard dear.'

She passed across a small magazine, roughly printed, six or so pages. It was open at a page that carried a photograph. I peered at it. Twenty four men in military uniform. Smiles and grim looks. Names listed underneath. The room spun and I heard a roaring in my ears. The man at the back on the extreme right was Lance Corporal William Hughes and Blind Freddy could tell that it was me.

23

Of course I tried to bluff it out, said it wasn't me, couldn't be me, too young, different coloured hair and so on. But she had me dead to rights.

'What else could you have been but a deserter? Skulking around in Switzerland. Tony Grace of South Africa, I ask you.'

I flopped down into an armchair and drew my hand wearily across my face. 'I've told you about that. It was a secret mission, very hush hush.'

'Nonsense. You can hardly be trusted to order dinner. Secret mission! Bosh! You were on the run from the Australian Army and you know what the penalty is for that, don't you, Richard?'

I do believe she'd been looking forward to this conversation. As I found, there was no end to her deviousness – she might even have put Daphne up to tipping me the wink. Still, I wasn't going to fall in a heap. I took some more brandy and thought about it. Elizabeth threw her cigarette in the empty fireplace and looked at me. Odd thing was, her look could only be described as fond.

'You've no proof,' I said.

'Oh, but I have. I recently met a gentleman who was badly wounded in the war. Leg wounds, very severe. He can't move around much but his mind is keen. Very keen. He's writing a book about his war experiences and do you know, Richard, he can remember every man who was ever under his command. Remembers their names and faces and mannerisms; it's quite remarkable.'

My mouth was dry and I reached for the brandy again. Elizabeth extended her glass and I topped us both up.

'Oh, yes?' I said. My necktie felt tight and I'm sure my hatband would have felt the same if I'd been wearing a hat. My temples were throbbing.

'Thank you,' she took a ladylike sip. 'Yes. I think you'd be interested to meet him. I should add he has very good eyesight. I think he fancied himself as a rifle shot and took an interest in men who displayed the same talent. His name is Thorndike, Richard – Major Wilfred Thorndike.'

I gulped the spirit down and felt it burn my throat. 'He's here, in Melbourne?'

'Yes, under the care of a friend of mine. I won't say where.'

I think that was as close as I came, before I turned thirty, to breaking down and blubbing in front of a woman; I did it often enough in later years, Christ knows. There didn't seem to be any point in further denial but one thing still puzzled me. I finished my drink and had another; well, it wouldn't be the last time I'd be drunk when a train pulled out with an empty berth. I remember one time in San Francisco . . . ah, memories. 'Elizabeth,' I said, 'If you know I'm a deserter and a scoundrel, why the devil d' you want to marry me?'

That look of fondness she wore became stronger. She took a few steps, bent down and kissed me. 'Because I love you, Richard.'

I'll never understand women.

It was downhill all the way after that. To Elizabeth it was all perfectly reasonable: either I'd marry her or she'd inform on me to the authorities and I'd be executed for desertion, or imprisoned until I couldn't do her or any other woman any good. This monstrous proposition, the sort of thing that no man would serve up to a woman, was to her a blueprint for action and, indeed, happiness. I got her drunk a few nights later (not as easy as it may sound, I was near-paralytic myself with the effort) and teased some of her further thinking from her.

'I'm worthless, Elizabeth,' I moaned. 'Worthless.'

'True, Richard,' she said with a steadiness well beyond me, 'but marriage will improve you.'

There it was, you see – the old story of a man being changed by the love of woman. I never saw it happen, either in life or, convincingly, on the screen. It was all very demoralising; I looked back on all the difficulties I'd had since, well, since Dudleigh really, and it seemed that I'd finally been run to earth. I think it was kind of tired, defeatist thinking that made me go along with the marriage plans. I trembled at the thought of Thorndike sitting there, somewhere in the city, probably unaware of his role in the scheme of things, set like a bomb to blow my life into fragments. I had no doubt that Elizabeth was capable of having me arrested, either in bed or on the run at some train station or port. She'd drop names into her conversation, Judge This and Commissioner That, to let me know that she had influence. I had no friends and couldn't influence people. I was licked.

The marriage preparations were truly horrible. Elizabeth excelled herself at lining up a tame minister (she was as pagan as me), sending out invitations and organising a reception that seemed designed to let the State of Victoria know that Elizabeth Jocelyn Macknight was getting married. One of her hardest tasks was to persuade Cameron that alcohol was an essential part of the wedding breakfast. She succeeded and I knew that if she could manage that it was useless to resist her in anything else. I smiled, bought clothes, met friends of the family, attended afternoon teas and felt the ring in my nose and the shackles around my feet.

Occasionally, I broke out. I recall a couple of monumental drinking bouts at this time and losing at poker twenty pounds that Elizabeth had given me to buy flowers or some such nonsense. She smiled sweetly and forgave me. She seemed to think of nothing but the day itself, and not a minute beyond into the certain hell she was preparing for us.

Five days before the ghastly event I shook myself from my torpor and took action. I tried to the best of my ability to locate Thorndike. I broke into Elizabeth's private office and ransacked her correspondence looking for a clue. I followed her on a couple of expeditions here and there, only to find that they were connected with the nuptials. I bribed a maid at The Gables to tell me about callers and telephone messages. Had I found Thorndike I believe I would have despatched him on the spot, so it was as well that I did not.

Perhaps the lowest point I reached was when I found Helen Hawes' name on the guest list.

'You're not inviting her, surely?'

'Why not?' Elizabeth smiled in a fat, complacent way I had grown to hate. 'She's one of my oldest friends.'

I thought of Helen's lean body and the inventiveness of her love-making. Something of this must have showed in my face because Elizabeth was calling her a whore within seconds and I was snarling something back. Then it came out that Elizabeth had contrived Helen's discovery of our early clandestine sessions.

I was aghast. 'I can't go through with this, Elizabeth.'

'You must.'

'I'll go to gaol rather than marry you. I've been there before.'

She smiled that maddening smile again. 'I know you

have, dear. I also know other things about you. You have problems that you're not aware of.'

'Like what?'

'Like a child with a mother who is reputed to be one of the stupidest women on the south coast of New South Wales. This woman has a vengeful father who has sworn to give this child a father or to bring it half-way to orphanhood.'

'What are you talking about?'

'His name and hers is Ryan.'

'Jesus.'

We were in my flat; I was sitting in an armchair and Elizabeth was by the window looking out at St Kilda Road. It was raining and car and carriage wheels swished on the road. I would have given anything to have been out there, drenched to the skin, but heading north. She let the curtain fall and came across to me. Her cool hands moved on my hot temples.

'Whatever you may think of me, Richard, I'm not a south-coast cow girl with dung on my boots. And I'm not stupid. I want you to succeed and I'm sure you can . . .,' she paused but kept smoothing my hair, ' . . . with papa's help and mine.'

'Yes, Elizabeth.'

She had a point in a way. One of the benefits of the marriage nightmare was that it deflected attention from *The Squatter's Dream* (sorry, *Australia*), and therefore from my own failure to do much towards the production other than feather my nest in a small way and learn a bit about the business. I suppose I had dreams of a towering success – a Brown Knight Production that would take the world by storm and make me enough money to be able to thumb my nose at petty authority.

I hadn't been sleeping well. I was pursued by phantoms – Les Darcy came skipping towards me wearing his boxing outfit; then I was in uniform, sniping away at the Germans who turned into sausages as my bullets struck them; I saw the man Hans Steller had sent to the bottom of the Rhine surface, streaming with water and blood. But that night, Elizabeth and I slept together in the flat; I was full of brandy and dreams which made the reality seem bearable. Just.

I won't bore you with every detail of the wedding. It was ghastly throughout. It rained for one thing; Elizabeth and Daphne got wet on the way to the church and looked like nothing so much as beached whales, pale and blubbery with their wet finery draped around them like seaweed.

Although more than half a century has passed, I can still see us standing in front of the altar with the Anglican clergyman (old Cameron's father had traded-in Presbyterianism on a more bankable Anglicanism years before) got up like a schoolmaster in drag. I can still hear the meaningless words ' . . . honor and obey . . . death do us part' and smell Elizabeth's heavy, sickly-sweet perfume. (My mind races on to my other weddings – on board ship with a dypsomaniacal captain who lusted after my bride, in a whorehouse in Reno where the bride had slept with everyone, man, woman and child, in the room etc. etc. . . . all dreadful, but none so bad as the first.)

After the religious ceremony came the civil horrors. The rain had eased to a drizzle and we bundled into motor cars to travel to the speechmaking and slobbering at the Exhibition Hotel in the city. This must have cost Cameron a month's takings: there were flunkeys to do everything from wiping the mud off shoes to keeping the glasses filled. Macknight seemed to go into a trance at the sight of so much booze. I spoke to him a couple of times but he was somewhere else in his mind.

I had presented myself as an orphan to the Macknights.

Of good family to be sure, but scattered – a mighty land-owner in Western Australia, a timber miller in New Zealand, South African connections. As a consequence, my side of the banquet hall was a mere pocketful of acquaintances – an amateur jockey (a gentleman) who'd done a little work on the Kelly film, a few knights of the green baise from the Horatian and a couple of people to whom I'd given a guinea to cover the hire of a dress suit. Helen Hawes hadn't come, of course.

Somehow I got through the speeches: an uncle of Elizabeth's, a member of the upper house of the State parliament, extolled her virtues although he'd only seen her twice before since her birth. I mumbled a response, said something appreciative about the ghastly pile of silver and crystal that constituted the wedding presents, thanked Cameron and Maud for giving me their daughter (I almost choked on that), and essayed the only humour on the occasion.

'When can a Scotsman see a joke?' I asked.

Stony faces.

'After the surgical operation.'

Stonier faces.

I stumbled from the dais and, in the vicinity of the ladies' toilet to which I had mistakenly made my way, I bumped into Mrs Macknight. Like all drunks she had found a way to get hold of her poison and time to consume it. She gripped me by the arm, looked blearily up at my face and tried to remember who I was. I was none too sober myself by this.

'Richard, mama,' I said. 'Your son-in-law.'

Her vision seemed to clear and her grip intensified; I carried the bruise for weeks. 'Get drunk and stay drunk, young man,' she said. 'That's the only way. They're devils!'

I was well on the way to putting this advice into practice and normally I would have continued on that course. But something about her face; its puckered, robbed-of-life intensity, sobered me. I went to the lavatory, washed my hands and face, straightened my clothes and looked at myself in the mirror. Despite all the disappointment and dissipation, I was still a dashed handsome fellow – clear-eyed, well, reasonably so, square-jawed and with a full set of teeth and head of hair. Who were these bloody Macknights to get the better of a Browning?

It was still the champagne and brandy talking, of course, but not altogether. I stood at the back of the dining room and looked at them all. Amazing how many secret tipplers there must have been among that sober-sided lot. How many hypocrites. I wager that if I'd been able to do blood tests and genetic scans (not that such things were available then), I'd have found a good few whelps that didn't belong in the litter.

I re-joined the gathering with the feeling in my heart that I was in the midst of mine enemies; I had lost a battle perhaps, but there was still the war to be won.

24

Elizabeth could only spare a week away from her burgeoning business (she was forever opening new buildings, new wings, hiring and firing staff and trying to get a better deal on bed linen), so the honeymoon had to be local. We went to a town called Warburton, past those bloody Dandenong hills we'd hiked through in what Elizabeth had begun to call our courting days.

I've still got a photograph of the place we stayed at – a huge Victorian guesthouse, all porches and dormer windows and wide balconies. It was called The Green Gate and I suppose it had one, I don't remember. What I do remember is the vile food, huge amounts of stodge three times a day, and the sheets, cold and hard as iron.

We had the Victoria and Albert suite naturally, a couple of big rooms with a balcony looking out over the hills and a fireplace more suited to a maid's attic. It was impossible to get warm in that room, either by sitting close to the fire, getting into bed or pouring brandy down your throat. I pursued the latter course mostly while Elizabeth spent a lot of time sitting in bed with enormous shawls wrapped around her brawny shoulders making calculations on a notepad.

Outside it was either raining or there was an icy crust

on the ground. We went walking (again trying to get warm) but Elizabeth had gained weight fast in recent weeks and was still gaining so that she didn't have the sprightly step of yore, thank Christ. There was a lot of simpering from maids and knowing looks from waiters and others; Elizabeth bloomed (she loved the food) while I must have visibly waned. I overheard remarks like, 'She must be keepin' 'im 'ard at it. Poor chap's wore to a frazzle.' Truly a miserable time; seven days felt like seventy.

Back in town Elizabeth threw herself into her business and left me pretty much alone in the daytime although she watched me like a cat at night. I kept a tight hold on my small gold reserves and didn't have much ready money by this time, Brown Knight Productions being somewhat stalled. I suppose Elizabeth reckoned that without money I couldn't find mischief. God knows I tried; I hung around the clubs drumming up a few bets on billiards (at which game my straight eye made me a flashy performer) and then at the races trying to increase the stake. The results were indifferent. I got to know a few fellows in a like fix – good chaps, knew their wine and horses but always strapped for cash. I recall one of them envying me my well-heeled wife.

'You're on easy street, Browning. God, I'd change places with you!'

'Today?' I said. 'How about tonight!'

'Steady on, old chap.'

'You don't understand, it's a misery being tied to a woman you don't love.'

He laughed at that and ordered another bottle. 'I met a fellow the other day who said it was a misery being with a woman he *did* love. He felt he wasn't worthy of her, couldn't live up to his good opinion of her. Did you ever hear such claptrap?' He drank deep and rapped the glass on the table. (We were in a wine shop in Fitzroy,

198

low place, but the wine was fair.) 'Remedy's the same in both cases.'

I was getting sick of his prosing and spoke sharply. 'And what's that, pray?'

He rubbed his red nose with a nicotine-stained finger. 'Be off, dear boy. In your case with the family silver or whatever you can lay your hands on.'

I knew he was right but he didn't know about the threat that Elizabeth held over me like the sword of . . . [Browning's voice fades here; he was evidently trying to recall the name 'Damocles' from his interrupted education. Ed.]. I went back to the flat deep in thought. We were living in the flat temporarily while Elizabeth looked for a house. She wanted something near the hospital in East Melbourne, which narrowed the field somewhat. Also, she was too busy to spare much time for the task. At least she hadn't wanted us to live at The Gables.

I threw myself into an armchair, lit a cigarette and opened the paper. There was nothing of interest in the sporting news and I was idly looking at an article about the different states co-operating on a Murray River irrigation scheme (that *was* news, the states had never been able to agree on anything, even on a standard railway gauge to run between them) when I heard the letter slot open and clatter closed. I heaved myself up, went to the door and retrieved the letter.

The postmark – Newcastle – set alarm bells ringing and the writing was vaguely familiar. I opened it and found a short note in my mother's uncertain hand. I've watched enough television to know that what happens to you in your early years, early days even, affects you for the rest of your life. And from what I can see, there's not a damn thing you can do about it, even if you later come to understand *exactly* what happened. I know that my fear of my father has affected me. I still jump when I see an old photo of someone who looks like him or hear a voice like his.

So even out-living him hasn't helped. Of course it was much worse when I was younger; everything about him scared me – and letters that were written in his house scared me as much as knives or bullets. I can recollect this one, more or less; it read:

Dear Dick,
 Father and I have heard of your whereabouts through a friend who showed us a copy of the Melbourne *Argus*. You are a very cruel boy to stay out of touch for so long and to become married without telling us. However, we want to say that all is forgiven and we would wish to see you soon. Father is not well and you would not want it on your conscience not to see him at this time.
 We are still in Newcastle at the same address. Please write to us or better still come to visit with your bride or both.

Your loving,
Mother

Newcastle! The thought of going anywhere near the place terrified me, but present circumstances needed desperate remedies. A plan began to form in my mind.

Elizabeth came home tired and I was attentiveness itself. I'd been out to the shops and had bought some wine, biscuits and cheese and a lemon cake which was her favourite variety. I proposed a supper in the flat and an early retirement – this with the best I could summon in the way of a leer. She ignored that but welcomed the idea of the food being to hand. I helped her off with her boots and slid a stool under her feet.

'I'm so tired, Richard.'

'You work too hard, love.'

'It's a pity you don't work harder.' This was a new line with her – poor Dick's laziness. I found it galling and usually snapped back but this time I was conciliatory.

'The production is on schedule. You can't rush these things.'

'If you say so,' she said wearily. 'Pour the wine.'

We had a glass and some of the food, me keeping up a light line of chatter, her sighing from time to time. I was trying to look serious and concerned, not an easy thing for me to do, being a light-hearted chap. She seemed more than usually preoccupied and so it was that we simultaneously opened our mouths and said: 'What's the matter?'

'You first, dear,' I said. 'More wine?'

She nodded and I poured. 'Pat's back,' she said flatly. 'You remember Pat – from Switzerland. When you were Tony Grace?'

This was said in a malicious imitation of the Afrikaans accent. I wanted to brain her but I smiled and nodded. 'Yes, I remember her.'

'She's a damn nuisance.'

'Oh?'

Elizabeth flushed. 'Well, we were just girls and there were no men around, no whole ones anyway. D'you understand, Richard?'

I sipped my wine and shook my head.

'You must have heard of schoolgirl crushes?'

'Vaguely.'

'It must happen in boys' schools, too. I'm told it happens in prisons. You *must* know something about it!'

I was beginning to get her drift. 'Ah,' I said.

'Stop saying "ah" and "oh" and say something useful.'

'She's pestering you to . . . renew your friendship, is that it?'

'Yes, and more. She wants to help me in the business. The trouble is, she's damn good at that sort of thing. She's got ideas that would double . . . Oh, but you're not interested.'

In truth I wasn't and the evening wasn't turning out at all as I'd planned. I'm not much good at handling other people's troubles, usually because I've got too many of my own to spare the brain power or whatever it is you apply to troubles. I was well and truly stumped by this one and I sat there dumbly looking at her as she scoffed biscuits and swilled wine. My appetite had fled and it looked as if I wasn't going to have to get my strength up for a bedroom tussle.

'Why can't you just send her packing.'

'It's not as easy as that, she . . .'

'She's not blackmailing you?'

Elizabeth picked up crumbs with her forefinger. 'To operate private hospitals in the State of Victoria you have to be of impeccable moral character.'

'You mean . . .?'

'Well, married, for one thing, if you're a female.'

'I see.'

'I suppose you do. But that was only one reason; I am fond of you, Richard.'

I acted hurt and poured myself another glass to cover my whirling thoughts. On any other occasion I'd have been delighted – the biter bit and all that. Here's Elizabeth, who's blackmailed me into marrying her so she can make her money and, either as a cover for herself as she runs after the nurses or as a means of averting temptation, having the screws put on her by one who knows all. It was rich. But I couldn't see what good it would do me.

I shrugged. She looked at me angrily. 'You don't care!'

'Not much. I've got my own problems.' I pulled out the letter from my pocket and smoothed it on my knee. 'See here, Elizabeth, I wasn't being quite straight with you when I said my Mama and Papa were dead. I've just had a letter. Looks as if I'll have to go up and see the old chap.'

I passed the letter across. She read it rapidly and then stared off into the distance, as if she wasn't just a few feet away from the hunting scene wallpaper.

'I knew about your Novocastrian origins, of course,' she said, 'and you've never given off the air of an orphan, dear.' She clicked her tongue. 'This is perfect.'

'Eh?'

'I'll leave Pat in charge of things for a while. She can get everything running smoothly but she's bound to be indiscreet with one of the nurses. Then I'll be able to get rid of her.'

'I don't follow you.'

'God, you're slow. I'm coming with you, Richard.'

25

Well, never let a few obstacles interfere with a good plan, as General Custer said, referring to the Indians. I'd made up my mind to go to Newcastle and if I had to take my blushing bride along with me, so be it.

She made her arrangements and I made mine. These mainly consisted of turning everything of value I could lay my hands on into gold coin and collecting together useful items, like my passport and some of Helen Hawes' photographs of myself in the Kelly film. Quite apart from my long-term plans, I was very keen to get out of Melbourne. The winter seemed colder than in England (though not as bad as in France, nothing could have been), and day after day of heavy skies, whipping rain and icy winds will depress the most ebullient spirit.

Departures have always made me happier than arrivals. I was feeling fine when we boarded the train at Spencer Street. Even the length of time it took to get Elizabeth's cases and hatboxes aboard didn't upset me, nor her fussing about rugs and windows in the carriage. I got her settled and went out onto the observation platform for a smoke. I was well rugged up in my British warm, with gloves and a thick woollen scarf I had won in a billiards game. A train pulled out from the adjacent platform and I saw the steam jet out and the wheels turn and I understood why no film director has ever been able to resist that shot of the turning wheels.

Then it was our turn. The steam enveloped the platform workers and all those poor devils unlucky enough to be staying behind. I flicked my cigarette end out onto the track and watched the city lights move past. It was eight o'clock; I remember hearing the sound of the hour striking over the noise of the wheels. The tram tracks ran parallel to the railway and at right angles up the wide streets of Melbourne which are laid out in a square pattern. The wind whipped at me and I ducked back inside the car. I never saw 'Marvellous Melbourne' again.

Elizabeth kept up a steady stream of complaints as we cleared the suburbs. Unlike me, departures upset her – she worried about things left undone, loose ends that might unravel while she was away. There were two or three other people in the compartment – two women and a clergyman I think, or perhaps it was two clergymen and a woman – in any case, little chance of a good conversation or a game of cards. I listened to Elizabeth express her doubts about the Sydney weather until I could bear it no longer.

'Do shut up, Elizabeth!'

'Why, Richard . . .'

'Talk about something else.'

'What?'

'Anything.'

'Tell me about your parents.'

'No.'

'Your mother sounds . . . forgiving.'

Unlike you, I thought, but I said nothing.

'Tell me about your father.'

I said nothing still but must have changed colour and expression.

'Why, Richard,' she crowed. 'I do believe you're afraid of him.'

I went outside for a smoke.

Standing at the end of the corridor, I lit a cigarette and considered the question of my attitude to 'Wild Bill'. Was I afraid of him? Probably. He stood a couple of inches taller than me, had developed extraordinary strength in his mining days and sometimes let me feel the effects of it. I mean in a sidelong sweep, not a full-bodied punch. I don't believe I would be here in full possession of my faculties (well, most of 'em) if he had landed one of those punches on me as a kid. He was reputed to have killed a man in a bare knuckle fight on the diggings. Yes, I was terrified of him.

But it wasn't just a physical matter. I wanted to please him and felt I never could. Could never be brave enough or selfless enough or noble enough. So, of course, I abandoned all three of those qualities. I see it all clearly now with the wisdom of this much hindsight, but then, as a mere twenty-four year old, I only had glimmerings. I think I was beginning to understand that I was the man I was because my father was the man *he* was – but I simply blamed him for the bad parts of my character and took credit myself for the good.

I lit another cigarette and had a couple of swigs of brandy from my flask as a protective against the night air. The train was rushing through the country now; an occasional firelight showed in the distance but the night was very dark and the interior of the train felt like the whole world. You'll think I'm being fanciful if I say that the wheels of the train were saying 'Hollywood, Hollywood' to me. You'd be right; despite the brandy they were just clacking along. I had my feet on the ground (so to speak) and I knew what I was doing.

Back in the carriage I smiled at Elizabeth who had her head buried in a copy of the Government gazette – probably trying to pick out the most corruptible officials for future reference. Her eyes came up and she saw my expression.

'Why are you looking like that, Richard?'

'I'm looking forward to introducing you to my father. I think you'll be afraid of him, too.'

That gave her something to think about. I tipped my head to one side, cocked my hand up under it, elbow on the window, and let myself drift off to sleep. One of the clergymen (or was it one of the women) was already snoring.

In those days you couldn't travel from Melbourne to Sydney by rail without interruption. The 'statesmen' who'd been in charge in colonial days had never been able to agree on a standard width for the railway. One state had one width and another another. The result was that you had to get down at a place called Albany. [Browning's memory failed him again here; the changeover took place at Albury. Railways were never a major interest of Browning's. Ed.] We reached this place some time after midnight and changed trains. This involved stomping across an icy, windswept platform and waiting while the baggage was transshipped. Elizabeth grumbled, naturally, and in the way of Victorians, accused the colonial New South Wales politicians of being the cause of the gauge dispute, and the present bunch of being responsible for the slowness of the change.

Half-stewed from my not infrequent nips of brandy I stared out the window and ignored her. The train started and we ran briefly beside the Murray River, that same one they were talking of co-operatively using for irrigation, some hope. The steward came in and pulled down the bunks; we were in a two-berth sleeping compartment now and could hope to get some rest on the seven or eight hours of the journey that remained.

'Good night,' said the steward, although it was morning.

'Good night,' I said and that was all the exchange between us. You won't believe me, but tipping was unheard of in Australia in those days. If you'd tried to tip a fellow like this he would have felt insulted, like as not, and given you a straight right. It's not everything that has changed for the best.

If you've been reasonably lucky in your life, you'll have made love in a narrow bed while a train rattled along the tracks. I have, more than once. It's a very romantic feeling and has practical benefits, too – the motion is convenient and deep and restful sleep afterwards is guaranteed. But there was nothing like that on this occasion. Elizabeth settled herself on the lower bunk, read her gazette for a while and fell asleep. I tossed and turned in the top berth until there was no course open to me but to finish the brandy.

I slept long and deep. When I awoke the sun was up, we were somewhere west of Sydney, not too far out, and Elizabeth was sitting up, brushed and washed and reading the morning paper.

'Breakfast,' I mumbled.

'You were snoring,' Elizabeth said primly. 'I've had mine. You'd better hurry along to the dining car or you'll miss it.'

'Where did you get the paper?'

'They came on board at a place called Liverpool. Quaint, isn't it, all the English names up here.'

She was ignoring the fact that she'd grown up in Brighton, Victoria, the way she ignored everything that didn't suit her. I grunted, checked my pockets for cigarettes and money, and left the compartment. I made the dining car just in time and settled down to a breakfast I don't care to remember – I wasn't to retain it for very long, anyway.

208

I left money on the table, lit a cigarette and got up to go. As I did so a man came into the dining car. He was a big fellow, well built, square-jawed and with sandy hair. He was wearing a police uniform which delayed my identification of him. But when I'd registered that fact and made allowance for it, plus a few years and few pounds in weight, I knew who he was and I had to grip the table to stay upright. Jack Henderson of the Liverpool training camp, the troopship *Wisden* and the muddy hell of France.

I had to go past him to get out of the carriage. Somehow I got my legs moving. I held my hand up to my face with the cigarette in it and shielded my features as much as I could. He was intent on looking for a seat. *I'm going to make it*, I thought. Then the bloody train lurched; I had to grab for a handhold, he did the same and our eyes locked.

'Hughes!' he shouted. 'You cowardly bastard!'

I pushed past him, stumbled through the door and pushed it back savagely at him as he regained balance and came after me. I almost ran through the narrow, bucketing passage; I swayed and hit my shoulders on both sides. Through the connecting door, across the shifting floor that covered the coupling, and into the next carriage. I bumped my knee excruciatingly but kept going. There was a mirror at the end of the carriage and I saw him practically fall through the door and charge after me. Time slowed down: I saw him reach behind his back and pull out a truncheon. His pale eyes started from his head as he came on.

I went through a rattling, half-open section over the coupling between this carriage and the next and tugged at the door. It was locked. The baggage car. I was trapped in a space six feet by six, open to the wind but with no hole big enough to jump through and with one of the toughest men in the 1st AIF bearing down on me. He threw open the door and fear confronted hatred.

'Hughes,' he spat, fighting for breath. 'Corporal bloody Hughes.'

'Jack, I can explain.'

'Deserter! Worse than a scab!' He swung the truncheon and it landed on my shoulder. I sagged in time to take some of the weight out of it but I knew what I'd feel if it landed on my head.

'I got lost.'

'You ran out on yer mates.' He was playing with me now, feinting with the stick, waiting for me to commit myself to a movement so he could clobber me in the right way. I was sobbing. I held my hands in front of me.

'Jack . . .'

I moved to my right although I hadn't meant to. I couldn't move again and he had me as a stationary target. His arm cocked and I waited for my head to explode.

The train went into a bend and swung wildly; the end carriages whipped around and our section bucked and heaved. Jack, intent on his prey, lost balance completely – he cannoned into a metal support, cried out and dropped the truncheon. I was still pleading as I bent, picked it up and swung it. With no timing, no finesse, just luck on my side, I caught him across the temple and he dropped like a poleaxed steer.

26

I imagine I was whimpering as I checked his pulse and rolled back his eyelids. The sentence for desertion combined with assault on an officer of the law would be impossibly harsh. If he died I was gallows bait for sure.

But he was unbloodied and breathing regularly. I recovered some composure and my brain began to function in a rudimentary way. *Throw him out*? I thought. No, you fool, that'll make it murder. Hide him? Better, much better. I sneaked a look into the rear of the last sleeping carriage. Still no activity and why would there be any traffic coming this way, except for . . . and there it was – the men's convenience.

I got Jack under the shoulders and dragged him through the door. He didn't move a muscle. Somehow I got the lavatory open and him inside. There was hardly room to turn but I wedged him between the wall and the bowl. I took off one of his boots, closed the door and jammed it tight from the outside by hammering the boot in between the bottom of the door and the floor. I was sweating from the effort and poked my head out for air. I vomited violently before I could make any sense of the landscape. I hadn't travelled the line for a few years but I could see that we were getting close to Sydney. Close enough? That was the question. Then I saw Jack's truncheon; a flick and that was out and over the embankment for some slum kid to find.

I wouldn't claim to be a resourceful man, too panicky, but I did a smart thing then. I got out one of my Brown Knight cards, wrote 'OUT OF ORDER – USE CONVENIENCE IN NEXT CARRIAGE' on the back and wedged it in the door at eye level. A man passed me, heading towards relief, as I scuttled back in the direction of my compartment. I heard him swear and then follow me. He didn't notice the boot or try the door.

Back in the two berth I urged Elizabeth to hurry with the collection of her things.

'Why?' she grumbled.

'I want to be first off.'

'Why? Papa always says . . .'

'Hang Papa. This is an emergency, try to think of me as losing blood from terrible wounds.'

'Why, Richard, whatever d'you mean?'

I didn't answer but the language made enough impact on her to get her moving. I collected my things (I was travelling very light, as always), and kept poking my head out to survey the corridor. Through the window I saw a station sign – Redfern.

'Hurry!'

'I am hurrying. I need a porter.'

'You'll need a doctor if you don't hurry!' I grabbed cases and boxes and shoved others into her arms and dragged her down the passage to the nearest door. I could imagine Jack coming round, gnashing his yellow teeth and throwing his thirteen stone against the door. The train slowed and went into a tunnel. If it stopped it could be the finish. Then we were out in the light and pulling into the Central Terminus.

Elizabeth was practically weeping and I pushed her out on to the platform. She dropped bundles but I scooped them up and collared a porter by showing him a fistful of silver.

'Very sick woman,' I said. 'Get us to a cab as quick as you can.'

'Right, sir!' He threw cases and boxes into his wheeler and started down the platform like a sprinter. I dragged Elizabeth along with me, feeling in my waistcoat pocket for the tickets. Nothing.

'Christ, the tickets!'

'They took the Sydney ones last night, don't you remember? Richard, what *is* the matter?' She was red in the face and gasping. No bushwalker now. 'Aren't we going on to Newcastle by train?'

We were through the gates and I relaxed a little. 'No. I've had a premonition. My father's dying, we have to hurry.'

'Liar!'

'Here we are, sir. Should be a cab along any minute.'

'Thank you.'

'Thank *you*, sir!'

I watched him go and when he was out of sight I gathered up the cases again, ignored Elizabeth's protests, and dragged her off to the nearest tram stop. Police can follow porter/cab driver trails like hounds after foxes; honest folk travel by tram.

Sydney didn't seem to have changed much in the few years that had passed. A little more noise, perhaps, certainly more motor traffic. But George Street was instantly familiar and welcoming. As the tram moved up past the Haymarket I could see down to the edge of Chinatown and then up Park Street to Hyde Park where, in a few hours, people would be sitting out in the sun having their lunch. Sun, that was the big difference. It was the middle of the year but the day was going to be warm; we were both overdressed, Elizabeth particularly. We looked like refugees which, I suppose, we were.

Elizabeth was uncharacteristically quiet. She gazed out at the city, craned her neck to peer up the narrow, crooked streets and let her eyes wander up some of the higher buildings. I wondered if she was impressed, or felt, as many Melburnians do, that Sydney was a higgledy-piggledy mess. The Town Hall was a fine example of the style, surely. I hefted cases, preparing to get off and she turned to look at me.

'Richard,' she said, 'where are the hospitals?'

Martin Place would be the spot, I reckoned – motor and hansom cab stands, flower sellers, newsstands, hustle and bustle even at nine in the morning. I installed Elizabeth with the baggage on a seat near the steps to the GPO and went off to look for a car hire firm. A few enquiries directed me to Gregory's Car and Charabanc Hire Company in Pitt Street. I knew the drill in a place like that. I produced a card from Green's of London and passed myself off as a one-time director of that august firm. I hinted that I was interested in investing in a local company (not setting up in competition, mind you), and could I negotiate a car hire for a trip to Newcastle and return? Insurance? Of course – essential part of the business. Fuel? Customer to purchase at selected outlets, goes without saying. Deposit? In cash, of course, and could a driver show me the operation of the vehicle on the short trip to collect my lady wife? Nothing easier, Mr Browning, sir.

A half hour later, having crossed the harbour on the vehicular ferry, I was pushing the Austin Vitesse along at a good clip up the Pacific Highway. Elizabeth had paid the deposit, I'm happy to say, and she was watching me intently as I drove the car.

'You drive very well, Richard,' she said. 'Could you teach me?'

'Of course, dear.' Promise them anything on the last hand in the game is my motto. I was feeling good, of course, with my coat and tie off, the window half open

214

and a nourishing Sydney breeze blowing through. The back seat was full of our luggage and heavy clothes we'd discarded. We had a reserve can of petrol strapped to the running board, and I'd stocked up with wine, bread and cold meats in Crows Nest. I'd driven the route before and knew the hazards – bad stretches of road, the Hawkesbury ferry which could cause delays and several steep hills which had to be gone up in reverse in the old days. But it was a fine morning and the Vitesse was going like a bird.

There wasn't much conversation between us. Elizabeth, it transpired, was one of those people who can read in a motor car. Myself, I can barely read a map; a minute's concentration on the print and I'm ready to empty my stomach by the roadside. But my good wife read her medical and financial journals, only looking out at the scenery occasionally. The Hawkesbury fishing villages, she owned were pretty.

'But they don't compare with the ones along the Rhine, do they, Richard?'

I grunted something. That's the way Victorians are; rather than admit that Kosciusko is a respectable peak, and far superior to the miserable hills of their state, they'll compare it with Mont Blanc or the Matterhorn. We stopped for lunch once over Peat's Ferry and I still remember it as a pleasant occasion. We had a tartan travelling rug down on the grass, some decent claret and a crusty loaf. I felt quite domesticated as Elizabeth and I puffed on our cigarettes, brushing away the odd fly and looking forward to a cup of tea at the end of our journey.

There was the question of pursuit to consider of course, but I judged danger from that source to be small. Jack Henderson might rant and rave about having seen a deserter, but he only had the name Hughes and a quick, action-blurred description to go on. I doubted that he'd taken in too many details of my clothing and appearance. William Hughes, solitary breakfaster, and Mr and Mrs

Richard Browning wouldn't easily be related and there should not be a warm trail from railway station to motor hire. The fright I'd had confirmed me in the wisdom of my plan, however.

We made pretty good time to Newcastle, considering the state of the road, getting stuck behind greybeards with horses even older than themselves, and Elizabeth's insistence that we stop to take photographs – not, you understand, of the scenery, which she disdained, but of ourselves. I had the Leica old Simondsen had sold me (God knows how I had hung on to it through all the vicissitudes since then), and I kept some of the snaps I took on that drive. They show Elizabeth, bursting at the seams of her modish dress, coyly sitting up on the bonnet of the Vitesse, and me, in shirtsleeves and motoring cap, holding a cigarette and smiling uneasily into the lens.

Newcastle today is said to have some of the best Victorian buildings in Australia. It certainly had a lot of 'em in 1920: look down some streets from the right angle and you could swear you were in London, or perhaps Birmingham if you were feeling depressed. The place depressed me as I drove in – too many bad memories: I was too drunk, too young behind that pub over there; . . . had my face slapped good and hard by a girl whose name I've forgotten in a house down that street; . . . still owed money to this shopkeeper and that one and several across the road.

The place looked prosperous enough though, as it always did when the mines were working and shipping was busy and all the agriculture in the hinterland was buzzing along. It only took a slump in the price of something or some fool of a radical unionist to call the men out and money dried up in Newcastle overnight. I'd often heard 'Wild Bill' rant on the matter. Thoughts of my sire were contributing to my depression. I'd often had fantasies of coming home in a Rolls, pockets bursting with money, my name on everyone's lips, and presenting myself to him in that fashion. It was a far cry from that – a rented Austin, a fat Melbourne blonde for a wife and about fifty pounds in gold to my name.

It was late afternoon and getting cool; Elizabeth had started to put back the clothes she'd taken off so that when I handed her out of the car at the Terminus Hotel she was swaddled and enormous.

'Isn't it rather close to the railway, Richard?' says she squinting at the tracks.

First complaint of the session, thinks I. 'Best hotel in town,' I grunted.

'I hope the trains don't run too early and late.'

'Couldn't say. Here boy, I'll take a paper.'

'Oh, do let's get on, Richard!'

'Yes, dear.'

It was the same story at the desk. 'No higher than the first floor, if you please, and well away from the railway.'

'Yes, madam. Room with bath?'

Never high on my list of priorities, but tops with Elizabeth.

'Of course!'

'Do you wish the laundry service, madam?'

Here she was good enough to consult me. 'We'll only be here one night, won't we, Richard.'

'Could be two,' says I. 'Better get the smalls washed, just to be on the safe side.'

She huffed and puffed at that and at the close confinement of the elevator, the darkness of the corridor and everything else until we were settled in our room. It was big and airy, looked out towards the city's park and monument and had a decent carpet on the floor. I kicked off my boots, wriggled my toes luxuriously and settled down to look at the paper.

'Richard!'

'Yes, Elizabeth?'

'Don't you think I have been most forbearing?'

'I don't follow you.' I put the paper down; hopeless to persist when she was in one of these moods.

'I haven't asked you why we got off the train in such haste, why we couldn't take the train and why we had to drive up here, at some cost to myself, may I add.'

'You haven't, that's right.'

'Nor do I know why we are putting up in this miserable hotel instead of going at once to your parents' home which, you tell me, is commodious. Unless that's another of your lies?'

'No, biggish place, as I recall, not The Gables but . . .'

'Well, my patience is at an end. Why, Richard? Why? Why? Why?'

I couldn't give her all the answers, of course; I had to improvise and embroider. Some of it was God's truth.

'On the train I was recognised by a chap I knew in the army.' I uncorked one of the bottles of wine we'd brought, located a glass on the bureau and poured. I held up the bottle enquiringly but Elizabeth shook her head. 'Had to stay clear of him for reasons you well know.' I let that sink in: if someone else blew the whistle on me as a deserter Elizabeth would lose her hold. She saw the point at once and remained silent. 'Chap was a policeman,' I went on. 'Could've mounted a search and so on, hence the motor.' She nodded. 'As to my parents, well, it's delicate.'

'They're not . . . undesirables?'

'Are to me, particularly my Pa, but, no – you'd find them rough but presentable, especially my mother. Damn rich, too, unless Pa's affairs have gone downhill which I don't think for a moment they have.'

'Well then?'

'I'm under a cloud don't y'see. Black sheep and all that. I have to spy out the land – check on the old chap's

218

health, see who's hanging around the place, find out how I'm regarded. That sort of thing.'

'Why?'

'You want a warm welcome, don't you? To be treated like a daughter?' I drank some wine and put on my boyish, confused look. 'Besides, when we . . .'

'When we what?'

'Well, children and all that. Bound to happen and there's a solid inheritance at stake here – for you and yours, I mean ours and mine, I mean . . . you see what I mean?'

I swear she blushed and I knew that I'd hit the right note. I wished I'd hit on this line of approach earlier but, there it was, better late than never. I knew how to handle Elizabeth for the little more time required.

'I see, Richard.' She sounded thoughtful and looked docile. I went across and planted a kiss on her slightly sweaty forehead.

'Now you just have a rest. We'll have dinner here. I'll go out later to sniff the air and by tomorrow I should know how to tackle 'em. Just leave it to me.'

She smiled and nodded. I buried myself in the paper and heard her ferreting around for a while. Then the bed-springs creaked and I could concentrate on my reading. I ignored the news and the sporting pages. 'Shipping' was the section I was after. Tiny print but I had sniper's eyesight. There it was – sailing on the 4.30am tide for San Francisco, the US merchant vessel *Sternwood*.

27

Meticulous planning at some crucial points in my career (and damn good luck at others) has kept me alive this long. Certainly, I'd planned things out in Newcastle in 1920. For one thing, I'd made sure that my valise with a few things like papers, clean shirt, razor and underwear remained behind in the car when we checked into the hotel. Elizabeth, only concerned about her own paraphernalia, didn't notice. Point two: I didn't let her sleep for too long. Just when she was ready to go deeply under, I roused her, forced her to accept a glass of wine, and took her downstairs for dinner.

Here, I was lucky. The dinner was a heavy affair – soup, roast and pudding – the sort of thing Elizabeth loved and which was guaranteed to bring out the glutton in her. The travelling had sharpened her appetite and, as I was keyed up and not hungry, she managed to score food from my plates as well as her own. We had a bottle of claret and there again I was abstemious and let her do the work. After brandy and the sort of weak, milky coffee which was standard in Australia in those days, Elizabeth was ready to continue her sleep.

We didn't talk much during the meal; the dining room was about half full which contributed noise and smoke to the air. I was smoking furiously and Elizabeth had a couple of cigarettes too, which I suppose she felt safe to do so far from home. It all helped to lower Elizabeth's eyelids. She was practically asleep when we got back to the room but I had to fight off an amorous advance before I could get her settled into the bed, pillows plumped and the lights down low.

'Don't be long, Richard,' she murmured.

'No, my love, I won't be long.' And I wasn't, not if you measure time on the generous scale appropriate to human history.

I hadn't meant to go within a mile of the place. I was bound for the docks which I knew like a prisoner knows his cell. I'd spent untold hours playing around the wharves when I was kid, by myself and in company. I knew ways in and out, up and down, hiding places, storage sheds – the works. But something happened as I turned into the road that ran up behind the beach. I felt a pull, and a counter pull, and mixed feelings that I couldn't get rid of in any other way than by turning down another street and driving along the dark road that I'd travelled so many times before.

The family home was a sprawling colonial-style house set in generous grounds overlooking Newcastle beach. The house was bought for prestige not practicality. I was the only one of the children who ever lived in it, really. My two sets of twin sisters were married and away early and my brother Tom lobbed in only occasionally to dry out and touch Mother for some money to start on his next binge. My parents and I, along with a cook and a maid, rattled around in the house. There were a couple of small cottages in the grounds, quite fit for humans, which the dogs slept in.

I pulled up a hundred yards from the gate and, moving like an automaton, I got down and walked towards the house. I don't know what I expected – my father, lying on his deathbed near a window so that I could peer in at his waxen face? My mother, sitting by a lamp, sobbing over her bible? Did I see myself as the prodigal son, forgiven, understood, restored to my proper place in the world? I don't know, all I can say is that the experience was nothing like that.

I walked up the gravel drive. Suddenly there was a howling and baying and the sound of rattling chains and gnashing teeth. I had forgotten the dogs; my father always kept several packs of them chained up at points around the house. When he was sober he'd rush out when the dogs barked, slip them and let them chase the intruder (if the damn things weren't barking at a rat or possum). When drunk he'd stagger out onto the verandah and discharge a shotgun into the night. Very disruptive, either way. This night he was very drunk: I froze as I saw the door open. A wild figure, fully dressed but with his collar askew and his shirt hanging from his trousers, lurched out of the door. Framed against the light as he was, I could see that he'd put on more flesh; he almost filled the doorway.

'Bastards!' he bellowed. 'Be off!'

Boom! Boom! Two barrels out into the still night air – I told you he was *very* drunk. The dogs screamed and pulled on their chains.

'Wild Bill' Browning put his hand into his pocket; he broke open the shotgun and re-loaded. I moved off the path; perhaps a mistake, perhaps the movement caught his eye.

Boom! Boom! I felt and heard the shot whistle past me, inches away. I dropped to the ground but I still stared up at the house.

'William, William, come in. There's nothing there.'

My mother's tiny figure appeared in the doorway. She

tugged at his sleeve and drew him back into the house. The dogs let go a few more howls and then fell silent. The door closed. A light which had come on around the side of the house, possibly in the maid's room, went out. I slithered back on the grass a few yards, got up cautiously and crept away towards the gate, staying off the gravel.

Nothing had changed in six years. My mother was still lying to herself and everyone else as the only strategy for survival she knew. My father, at fifty odd, looked to have at least that long ahead of him. Had I gone to the door he would have greeted me with the butt of the shotgun, if not the barrels.

I went back to my car and drove to the docks.

Port Hunter was a complex arrangement of channels and lights and docking places; vessels of different tonnage were piloted to different berths and there was a variety of tying-up places according to cargo: coal, grain, fruit, everything that could be sucked from the earth was exported.

The *Sternwood's* cargo was wool so I knew where the ship would be docked. I left the Austin in a dark lane a mile or so from the docks and walked through the streets carrying my valise and with my heart pounding hard. It was a very risky enterprise, you see. You don't see? Well, neither did I until I thought it out on that one mile walk. If I'd thought it out clearly before I might have looked for another plan. If I got clean away, that is, went undiscovered until I was out to sea, all would be well. The general rule in such cases was: work your passage or pay for it and be landed at the first port of call. I had enough gold with me to pay my way and a valid passport that should get me ashore without trouble in the US.

But, if I were caught before the ship sailed there'd be

hell to pay. Elizabeth would blow the whistle on me; my assault on Henderson would come to light. Christ! I stopped dead in my tracks as a terrible thought struck me. They might send me to Long Bay where there might be some old lag with a long memory stretching back to the Farnol episode. Old Barton's evil face came towards me in the gloom and I could smell his breath, foul with tooth decay. I considered going back but the prospect there was grim – Elizabeth and a meeting with my father. Not to be endured. I squared my shoulders and tramped on.

The dockyard was surrounded by a high fence but there were poorly mounted gates, badly mended holes, drains running underneath and a hundred other ways to get inside. The *Sternwood*, as a wool carrier, would be at Queen's Wharf and I knew a spot adjacent where a gate that appeared to be rusted solidly into place would open a foot or more if you knew how to push it.

A near-full moon emerged from behind clouds as I skirted around the fence to locate the gate. By its light I could see that the perimeter had had little maintenance since the days of my youth. A new post here and a strand or two of wire there, but nothing extensive. I moved cautiously, keeping to the shadows thrown by piles of timber, bond stores and other buildings inside and outside the docks. I was close now, close enough to hear the water slapping the wharves and the creaking of planks and hawsers. I could smell the salt water and that's a smell I've always rated highly, up there with good brandy, Havana cigars and French perfume.

The gate was in the same condition as when I'd last seen it. I crouched down and looked for signs of activity within. Nothing. The wool ships, unlike general cargo vessels, were safe from pilferers and if dock routine hadn't changed there would be a midnight and dawn patrol, nothing more. I went through the gate and scuttled across some railway tracks which would have been a hazard in the uncertain light had I not known exactly where they were, and gained the cover of a shed. It was a strange feeling, like being thrown back into the schoolyard. I remembered games and companions – Robert Armstrong, swarming up anchor chains like a monkey, Ben Stafford with catlike eyes, killing rats with a slingshot, Kevin Kearney falling from the wharf and coming up covered in oil, slick and black as a nigger.

I worked my way closer to the dock; there were four ships tied up opposite the long, low sheds where the wool was stored. My luck was in. The *Sternwood* was fourth in line, furthest from the dim lights that burned along the dock between the sheds and the ships. There would be a watch for'rard or aft but not both and, at this time of a quiet night, asleep or close to it. Along behind the sheds to the ship. She was a medium-sized, rather grubby looking vessel, riding high at the wharf as the tide rose but not too high, as she was fully loaded. I had an hour before the crew would turn out for the early departure.

The moon was obscured. I waited for it to shine clear again and when it did I caught a glint on metal and saw a slight movement in the stern. The watchman tipped dregs from a tin cup over the side, stretched and yawned. His head fell back into shadow. I could see an iron ladder at the bow of the ship which ran down to within a few feet of the wharf. Now was the time. I ran a strap through the handle of the valise and slung it over my back. I moved forward.

'Stay where you are!' The voice was thin and old but strong and clear. 'And put yer bloody hands in the air!'

28

The words chilled me of course; I got the cramp in my leg and other associated infirmities, but I recovered fast because I recognised the voice.

'Paddy,' I croaked, 'it's me – Dick Browning.'

'Turn around, bloody slow.'

I did so. The old man was holding a long barrelled revolver the weight of which threatened to break his skinny wrist. He looked smaller than when I'd last seen him, which must have been eight years back. More shrivelled, less hair, more smelly. Paddy Sullivan was a dock watchman, long past retiring age even when I first met him and almost self-appointed. He'd worked at Port Hunter in one capacity or another for over seventy years and the dock authority provided him with a shack and rations and let him patrol the area because they knew there would be a massive strike among the wharfies if Paddy were expelled.

'Paddy, you know me, don't you?'

I stepped closer. He tried to raise the gun but couldn't manage it. He peered at me through pebble glasses.

'Christ and the saints, I believe it is Dick Browning. Where's the girl?'

I laughed. This was a reference to my last escapade

here when I'd brought a girl down to launch a ship. We were both more than a little drunk at the time. Paddy had discovered us, helped us drink the bottle and escorted us out of the shipyard. There was nothing wrong with his memory. 'No girl, Paddy. I'm glad to see you. Still at work, eh?'

'And why not?'

He was touchy on this subject. 'No reason, no reason.' I looked anxiously to the east but the sky was still dark.

'What brings you down here, Dick boy?'

'Trouble, Paddy.'

'Your middle name. Has your father disowned you yet? Or shot your mother or burned the bloody house down?'

He knew the Brownings, you see. I put my hand out and lowered the pistol so that it was pointing to the ground. 'Nothing like that, Paddy. But I have to get away – from Australia. For a time.'

'A woman?'

I nodded. 'And the police.'

He scowled and for a second I was afraid he'd hawk and spit which would have certainly woken the watch on the ship. Women and the police were Paddy's sworn enemies; he'd do anything to spike their guns. I realised then that I should have sought him out for help in stowing away. Don't know why I didn't; I suppose I thought he'd be dead. He must have been well over eighty. Perhaps he'd given up spitting. Anyway, he just scowled and stuffed the pistol into a deep inside pocket of his pea jacket.

'Can you help me, Paddy?' I unbuttoned my coat and shirt, put my hand inside and undid one of the flaps on the money belt. My fingers slid out a couple of sovereigns. 'I can pay you.'

'For what?'

'Help me get on board the *Sternwood*. Get me safely stowed away. Two sovs.'

'Five.'

'All right.'

'You're on.'

I gave him the two coins. 'The rest when I'm aboard.'

He nodded and peered up at the ship. The moonlight flooded his glasses. 'That lazy bastard's deaf and blind. I know the ship, she's been docking here since before the war. Ah . . .'

'What?'

'The war. Christ. I wish I could've been in it.'

Another lunatic. I shuffled him forward. 'I was, you didn't miss anything, believe me.'

'Were you now! You must tell me all . . .'

'Shh, not now. Do you know a place, a safe place?'

'I know ten. It'll be easy. Come on. In the war, you say. I'd not have thought you the type . . .'

I had to practically push him across the dock to the iron ladder. He went up it, spry as a ten year old and I followed with my cramped leg and knocking knees. Paddy climbed over the rail and I had to hiss at him to stop. He was about to step out across the deck as if it was an empty dance floor. It was littered with objects I could hardly see, much less identify.

'Take it easy, Paddy. This is like a bloody minefield. Where are we headed?'

'By the hatch over there.' He pointed into the murk. 'Just stay close, I'll steer you.'

He did – across the deck, between bits of equipment and fittings to a structure about the size of a small tent. There was a funnel sticking up near it and a powerful stench of greasy cooking and cockroaches. Paddy flashed his torch once and crouched to ease open a small door.

'What's this?' I whispered.

'Sail locker. She's been diesel for years. They'll never find you here. Let's have the money, Dick.'

I gave him three more coins and added a fourth.

'For luck,' I said.

'Thank you, boyo. I always said you was never as bad as you was painted.'

'I'm relying on you, Paddy.'

'You can.' He pushed me suddenly. 'Get in there. Someone's comin'.'

I stumbled forward into darkness and heard the door click softly shut behind me. The smell of damp, ancient canvas almost made me vomit. I moved into the locker and my foot went through the stuff, packed tight but rotten. I sat down on a clump that was as cold and hard as iron. I could hear voices on the deck.

'What're you doing here, Paddy, you bloody nuisance?'

'Keep a civil tongue in yer head,' Paddy snapped. 'I thought I saw somethin' movin' up here.'

I cursed him silently – he was going to turn me in.

'You're seeing things. Clear off. I've been on watch and there's been nothing up here.'

Their feet moved away on the deck.

'Could be a stowaway,' Paddy said.

I cursed him again.

'Stowaway!' the watchman sneered. 'Who'd be stowing away from here?'

'Les Darcy did,' says Paddy.

They were well away from the locker now. I let out a strained, wheezing breath.

'Yes, he did,' I heard the watchman say, 'and look what happened to him.'[21]

APPENDIX

THE ANTECEDENTS OF RICHARD BROWNING

Research in Australian historical records has revealed that Richard Browning was the great-grandson of Henry Browning (?-1848) who was transported to New South Wales for life in 1801. Henry Browning's crime was murder; he was tried at the Middlesex assizes and escaped the hangman because evidence was given that he 'was woefully far gone in drink at the time and his victim likewise'.

For twenty years after his arrival in the colony Browning was continually in trouble with the authorities; he was twice sentenced to death for robbery with menaces and reprieved for reasons which are not clear. One reference in the *Sydney Gazette* suggests that he owed his second reprieve to the pleas of his employer, a Mrs Kilpatrick, who insisted that there was 'as yet un-tapped, much good in him'.

Browning lost the use of one arm in a shooting accident in 1821 and soon after married Ellen O'Rourke, formerly a convict and at that time an innkeeper, of Parramatta. Browning appears to have settled down as a married man. He acquired a reputation as a pistol shot and was said to be able to hit the markings on a playing card at fifty paces 'when sober'.

The union between Browning and Ellen O'Rourke produced two daughters, Sarah and Dora, and a son, Phillip. Phillip Browning (1836-93) was the antithesis of his father. A quiet, retiring man, small in stature and inclined to be dreamy, he worked as a clerk in the same shipping firm for almost fifty years. He seems to have been dominated by his wife, Mary Little, who, belying her name, was a large woman with a loud voice and a commanding manner. Mention is made of the Brownings in a police report of 1867 when their home was invaded by 'violent inebriates'. 'Mrs Browning', the report says, 'valiantly defended her infant son against the intruders and succeeded in felling one with a broom and propelling another through a window. Mr Browning took shelter behind his wife and manifested no physical courage at all.'

The infant son mentioned, the only issue of the marriage, was William Browning. Scanty records confirm Richard Browning's account of him: he evidently inherited his mother's stature and his grandfather's weakness for drink. He came to the notice of 'the Fancy' as a bare knuckle boxer when still in his teens and won several gruelling fights against older, heavier opponents. He also lost several, on one occasion because the brandy he drank between rounds 'overcame him'.

Bell's Life for 1884 quotes Browning as saying that 'glove fighting is for women; my Ma would have done well at it'. The sporting paper reported that Browning was leaving the city to work on the land, evidently the beginning of the career Richard Browning sketches.

William Browning married Colleen Kelly in 1885 and had six children – two sets of twins (girls), born in 1885 and 1887, a son, Thomas, born in 1889 and Richard Kelly Browning, born in 1895. Colleen Kelly was also of convict stock, possibly related to the family of the famous outlaw, although no direct connection has been established.

NOTES

1. James Leslie (Les) Darcy, 1897-1917, was middleweight and heavyweight boxing champion of Australia. He beat a number of imported American fighters and had a claim to the world middleweight title. Darcy, wishing to postpone military service until he had earned enough money to make his family secure, left Australia illegally in 1916. He was branded a 'slacker' (draft dodger) in the US and was unable to secure fights.

Darcy made moves towards taking out American citizenship and enlisting in the military and he was in training for his first licensed fight when he collapsed. He died of blood poisoning and heart failure in Memphis, Tennessee. His remains were shipped back to Australia to an emotional reception and a cult, based on Irish and Australian nationalism and anti-American sentiments, grew up around him.

Darcy appeared in the 1915 semi-documentary two-reeler *The Heart of a Champion*, produced and directed by J. E. Mathews. Nothing survives of a 1916 filming as recounted by Browning and it is probable that the film was not completed. See Raymond Swanwick, *Les Darcy: Australia's Golden Boy of Boxing*, Sydney, 1965; Ray Edmondson and Andrew Pike, *Australia's Lost Films*, Canberra, 1982.

2. Peter Dawson, 1882-1961, was a popular baritone who made recordings and concert appearances in Australia and overseas.

Browning does not sing on the tapes which cover this early period of his life so it is impossible to judge the quality of his voice. He may have made recordings or worked on musical films later but this will not be known until more of the cassettes are transcribed.

3. Raymond Longford, 1874-1950, was born in Sydney and followed, as Browning says, a number of occupations before directing his first film in 1911. His greatest success was *The Sentimental Bloke* in 1914. Few of Longford's 30 feature films survive. Lottie Lyell, once regarded only as an actress, is now credited with a major role in the writing and directing of Longford's films.

4. The Temperance Movement added patriotic arguments to its case against alcohol in 1916. A drunken riot by soldiers from the Casula camp near Liverpool had an effect on public opinion. A plebiscite in New South Wales on the question revealed that a majority of the voters were in favour of restricting hotel hours. As a result, regulations were passed which closed hotels at 6pm 'for the duration'.

5. Farnol would have been referring particularly to John Jeffrey Farnol, a successful romantic novelist of the period. Among Farnol's best-known works are *The Amateur Gentleman* and *Peregrine's Progress*.

6. Kathleen Behan (Kate) Leigh, 1887-1964, was a sly grog seller, brothel keeper and drug peddler notorious in Sydney for the first fifty years of this century.

7. Eugene St Clair (Hughie) Dwyer held, at different times, the lightweight, welterweight and middleweight boxing championships of Australia. After his retirement as a fighter he became a successful boxing promoter.

8. Daniel Mannix, 1864-1963, became Catholic Archbishop of Melbourne in 1917 and remained so until his death. He was an ardent spokesman for the anti-conscription case, Irish nationalism and later for a variety of conservative social and political issues.

9. The figures on the first conscription referendum must have had a strong impact on Browning for he recollects them

accurately. Serving troops also rejected the measure. A second referendum held in 1917 also failed.

10. Browning was evidently inattentive at Dudleigh Grammar; the accurate quotation is:

. . . while to my shame I see
The imminent death of twenty thousand men
That for a fantasy and trick of fame
Go to their graves like beds . . .

Hamlet, IV, v.

11. Raymond Chandler, 1888-1959, was the greatest exponent of the hard-boiled detective story. His serial character, Phillip Marlowe, much imitated, remains the most appealing hero in this genre. Chandler was educated at Dulwich College in England, hence the accent reported by Browning. He served in a Canadian army unit and later, briefly, in the RAF. Later, as a famous and successful novelist, he worked in Hollywood writing scripts for such films as *Double Indemnity* and *The Blue Dahlia*.

12. Raoul Walsh, 1887-1981, was a prolific Hollywood director who used such stars as Douglas Fairbanks Snr, Errol Flynn, Humphrey Bogart, Gary Cooper and Clark Gable in his films, among the best known of which are *The Thief of Bagdad*, *The Big Trail*, *High Sierra* and *The Revolt of Mamie Stover*.

13. A volunteer expeditionary force, which included some Australians, invaded North Russia in 1919 with the intention of uniting with local dissidents to overthrow the Bolshevik Government. Two Australians were awarded the Victoria Cross for bravery during this ill-conceived and unsuccessful action.

14. William Somerset Maugham had two plays running in London in 1919, *Caesar's Wife* and *La Princesse de Clèves*.

15. This was a sensationalist concoction by Ambrose Pratt who specialised in this form of 'literature'. The book was denounced as fraudulent by various authorities but had large sales and went through several editions.

16. Details of Browning's involvement with *Gone with the Wind*, *Casablanca*, David Selznick and Raoul Walsh (see note

12 above), will no doubt come to light when more of the cassettes are transcribed.

17. Browning's is a sketchy, but accurate, account of the shoot-out between the giant thug and gunman 'Long Harry' Slater and the big-time two-up operator, Harry Stokes. Both were wounded and left Victoria, possibly to avoid serious police charges being laid. See Alfred W. McCoy, *Drug Traffic*, Sydney, 1980, p. 108.

Leslie 'Squizzie' Taylor was a gangster, razor gang member, bank robber and police informer. He was killed in a gun fight with another hoodlum in 1927.

18. Louis Lumière is regarded by some as the 'father' of the modern cinema. His photographic innovations and advances speeded the sophistication of filming. Lumière produced and directed many films including pioneering shorts such as *L'Arivée d'un Train en Gare de la Ciotat* which startled audiences with its image of a train rushing towards the camera and *L'Arroseur Arrosé*, the first cinematic farce and fiction.

19. Browning's judgement is perhaps excessively harsh. *The Kelly Gang* drew some favourable comment but was not a great commercial success, nor were subsequent films by Southwell. In all, he made four films based on the Kelly story. In Europe he made the Biblical drama *David* and *Le Juif Polonais* which he later re-made in Australia as *The Burgomeister* (1935). See Andrew Pike and Ross Cooper, *Australian Film, 1900-1977*, Oxford, 1980, p. 131.

20. The International Workers of the World ('Wobblies'), were radical and sometimes violent agitators for improvement in working conditions. They were not a force in the Australian film industry but were present in Hollywood as Browning may later have discovered. See Kevin Brownlow, *The Parade's Gone By . . .*, London, 1968, pp. 68-9.

21. See note 1.

'Box Office' Browning is the first book in a new series. The next book, 'Beverly Hills' Browning, continues the adventures of Richard Browning with his arrival in the U.S.A. and entry into the burgeoning Hollywood film industry.

To be published soon in Viking.